X-MEN
THE LAST STAND

X-MEN™
THE LAST STAND

A novelization by
Chris Claremont

**Based on the motion picture screenplay
written by Simon Kinberg & Zak Penn**

BALLANTINE BOOKS • NEW YORK

X-Men The Last Stand is a work of fiction. Names, places, and incidents either are products of the author's imagination or are used fictitiously.

A Del Rey Mass Market Original

™ & © 2006 Twentieth Century Fox Film Corporation. All rights reserved.

Published in the United States by Del Rey Books, an imprint of The Random House Publishing Group, a division of Random House, Inc., New York.

DEL REY is a registered trademark and the Del Rey colophon is a trademark of Random House, Inc.

X-MEN Character Likenesses: ™ & © 2006 Marvel Characters, Inc. All rights reserved.

ISBN 0-345-49211-0

Printed in the United States of America

www.delreybooks.com

OPM   9   8   7   6   5   4   3   2   1

X-MEN
THE LAST STAND

Chapter One

The moment her best friend died, Jean Grey first dreamed of fire, and dancing among the stars.

Neighbors since they were born, inseparable once they could crawl, she and Annie Malcolm shared toys and sandboxes, secrets and dreams, their parents, their entire lives. They had ten years together.

They never saw the car that brought that to an end.

Blind curve, guy's in a hurry, Annie feeling competitive, totally focused on the Frisbee Jean had thrown. Reacting, not thinking, no consideration of anything but the prize, as a wayward breeze scooped the plastic disk up just beyond her reach. Tantalizing, infuriating, beyond wicked, to come so close and then fall short. For Annie, that was unacceptable.

She made a spectacular catch. Jean cheered.

Her smile was so special, a flash of pure delight that burned itself indelibly on Jean's memory.

Then she was gone, wiped away so suddenly, so completely, it was almost as though she'd never been, thrown aside like a sackcloth dummy. There was a flash of shape and color, something big and powerful moving too fast to properly register—afterwards, when Jean tried to describe the vehicle to the police, what came out was more monster than machine. It was the first time—the only time—that her perfect memory ever failed her.

Or perhaps it was just that she didn't care about the car.

She heard a squeal as the driver fought for control, stomping on his brakes too late to make a difference, then the roar of an accelerating engine rapidly fading in the distance, as shock gave way to panic and he decided to save himself instead.

Jean had eyes only for her friend, draped against the wall of piled fieldstone that formed the property line along River Road. Annie lay unmoving, all crumpled and bloody and broken.

Sobbing, face twisted with denial, Jean dropped to her knees, hands trembling as she reached out, not a sound issuing from her lips save Annie's name—although every family in the neighborhood claimed later that they heard her piercing scream of anguish and horror. She repeated the name over and over, like a mantra, as if simply by saying the word she could anchor spirit to flesh and keep her friend from slipping away.

Then, she heard Annie call *her* name.

Instinct guided her to take a hand in both of hers, and Jean cried out again, a hoarse coughing exclamation that gave voice to all the pain balled up inside her friend. There were bursts of ice and fire along one side, scrapes and busted ribs, and a burning within one arm that told Jean it too was broken, and more pain where Annie had cracked her skull against one of the stones. That was the source of a lot of the blood, painting her face and now Jean as well as she stroked Annie's brow and tried to kiss the pain away. There was a dull ache near the bottom of her back, a gaping hollowness in the center of her chest. With a start, Jean realized she'd forgotten to breathe, and with a frantic gulp of air realized to her horror that Annie couldn't.

Her back was broken.

She couldn't bear to look anymore and closed her eyes—only that didn't help. Instead, it simply took her somewhere else.

Her own heart was a trip-hammer, pounding too hard and fast for her to separate the beats, her breath coming in shallow gasps that matched its cadence, like an animal in a terror trance, standing helpless before the predator who seeks its life. That made Jean angry; she hated being afraid and refused to be a victim, even of fate itself.

She thought at first she'd blacked out, because around her all was darkness. And then, of course, she assumed hallucinations as images rolled towards her out of that darkness, blurry in the distance, resolving as they moved closer into visions of people and places. She saw herself, arms thrown straight up as though signaling a touchdown, thought (absurdly) how familiar those clothes looked, until she realized she was wearing them now and she was looking at herself only moments ago, celebrating Annie's catch.

Her mind took the connection a step further; she looked more closely at the other images floating past her and she knew that they were Annie's memories.

They seemed to be coming from a central source, like stars being spun clear of the core of a spiral galaxy. Without hesitation she plunged into the heart of that glorious radiance, face transfixed with awe and wonder at the unimaginable myriad of colors and shapes that represented all of her friend's life-experience. She couldn't help grinning at the recognition of how many of them seemed to relate to her, and how richly textured they were.

She was still thinking in purely human terms and assumed that when she reached the heart of the radiance, she'd be this incredibly tiny dust mote facing some unimaginably huge representation of Annie. Instead, she came to her as an equal—only her body appeared wholly solid, whereas Annie's was boiling away at the edges.

Aghast, Jean watched a string of memories—some birthday or other, a trip to grandma's, boring days at school—tumble off into the distance until they were gone, swallowed up in darkness. Again operating from an instinct she didn't understand, Jean reached out to try to catch them, but she might as well have been a ghost herself, grabbing at the wind. They wouldn't be snared, couldn't be held.

She heard Annie call her name.

They both knew what was happening; neither dared say it aloud.

"Don't be scared, Annie," Jean said.

"Show me how, 'kay?"

"You've got to hold on, Annie, you can't give up."

"I'm broken, Jean. There's nothing I can do."

"*Stop it!* Don't you dare talk like that, I won't let you go!"

The passion surprised them both, a fierce rage that outlined Jean, just for a moment, in a corona of fire, like a star casting forth a solar flare. The fire plunged into Annie, making her gasp with surprise as her fading radiance glowed more brightly.

"See," Jean cried triumphantly. "*See!* I *can* help! I can *save* you!"

But Annie knew better.

"It isn't making a difference, Jean, not so it matters."

"Shut up, I'm working here."

"Do you have a clue what you're doing?" Annie asked.

"Making it up as I go. What do you care, so long as you come out all right?"

"Ain't gonna happen."

"Watch me."

"No, Jean," Annie said, "watch *me*."

Jean didn't want to, but Annie was by far the more determined of the two, always had been, with a focus (stubbornness, some said) that was legendary. They were still of the same size, a pair of galaxies, islands of breathtaking light and color, all by themselves against the backdrop of infinity. Now though, while Jean remained essentially coherent, Annie had spun off so much quanta that she was translucent. Yet she was visibly the more dynamic of the two—the part of her that remained burned far more brightly than it should, because Jean was sustaining it with her own energies. The consequence was that Jean's own life-glow had dimmed considerably.

"Let me go," Annie said quietly.

"No." Jean could be just as muleheaded.

"Please."

"You're my best friend."

"Can you make me better?"

"What do you mean?"

"Can you fix the all of me that's broken? Can you find the all of me that's lost?" Annie waved a barely corporeal arm to indicate what remained of her body, the mass of imagery cascading ever faster into oblivion.

Jean's face twisted with a grief she'd never imagined, didn't think could possibly be endured.

"I. Don't. Know. *How!*" And with that terrible admission, her face went still with resolve. She would find a way, no matter what it took. She refused to accept that she couldn't.

"You can't stay," Annie told her.

"I won't leave you."

"Do you want to die, too? Look at yourself, Jean."

"I'm fine."

"I can barely see you. You've poured so much light into me, yours is almost gone. If you give me all your strength, how will you find your way home?"

"We're going home together."

"No."

With that, Annie lunged forward, catching Jean by surprise in an embrace that carried with it every bit of love and affection, every remaining aspect of their shared lives. She thrust both hands into the core of Jean's being and returned the strength Jean had given her.

Too much power, too fast! It burst outward like a star going supernova, impossibly—for that single flash of time—turning a totality of darkness into an absolute of light. Against such a display, Annie was too small to even quantify.

For Jean, this was beyond revelation. She understood none of it, on any level. The emotions were too primal for a child's mind to comprehend, and she had no resources of intellect or spirit that could give her even a hope of coping. She'd been cast into a maelstrom and knew only enough to hold fast to herself until it ran its course, praying fate was smiling on her enough to survive.

She thought the darkness would return but the light remained, as though someone had just lit the match of Creation within her, intoned those fateful first words of Genesis. Around her, it seemed as if tangible shapes began to gradually assert themselves, although in reality only the merest fraction of a second had passed. She couldn't help but be fascinated, as motes resolved themselves into electrons and protons and neutrons, as these various particles bound themselves into atoms and those atoms into molecules, growing ever larger and more wondrously complex as they evolved into increasingly intricate combinations. And then, with the blink of an inner eye, she found herself looking at a road, where a moment before had been a vast plain of scattered particles defined more by the subatomic spaces between them than the illusion of solidity they created.

There was a sour smell to the air, the scorched residue of burned rubber, and a metallic taste in her mouth she knew was blood. Not her own; this was a sense memory of Annie's, and with that realization came the bone-deep certainty that none of what she'd just experienced had been a dream. All of it had actually happened, and as if to add a stamp of authenticity to the thought, came that last, wondrous image of Annie's grin.

Jean's tears burned scalding hot against her cheeks, scoring channels that would mark her always, of that she was sure. She couldn't stop crying. In part it was because of her lost friend, lying so still in her arms, a look of peace on her face, replacing the one of shock and outraged disbelief that had been there before. But also, it was for what had happened to Jean herself, and for all that was to come.

She heard more voices, cries and calls from the surrounding houses, but paid them no attention. What mattered so much more was the richer symphony inside her head, composed of not simply what was said aloud, but also what was thought and felt.

Annie's mother, gripped by a terror that would never leave her. Jean's own mom, feeling that selfsame spike of anguish at the sight of her daughter's bloody face, giving way immediately to a sense of heartfelt relief. That had been Jean's doing, inadvertently. She'd wanted Mom to know she was all right and just like that, the message was sent, not so much as a string of words, like speech, but more a complete certainty.

Hands took hold of her, gentle as could be, and she howled with what everyone assumed was anguish over her friend's death. They couldn't be more wrong. She was discovering that windows opened aren't so easily closed, and that proximity and physical contact amplified the ambient psychic noise around her to an unbearable degree. Everywhere she turned, there was another life, in all its myriad textures, crashing down on her like a rogue wave, sucking her into a riptide undertow that refused to let her come up for air, threatening to overwhelm her own psyche—more fragile from this trauma than she could know—with all of theirs.

Her psyche did what it had to for its own survival. Yet as she collapsed into what was later described as a fugue state brought on by extreme trauma, the last image that came to her was a memory of her body in Annie's soul, wreathed in flame, turning the darkness of forever into magnificent, glorious light, and the certainty that somehow she had touched the very stars.

X

1985

Jean was reading up in her room when she heard them talking. One of her favorite authors, one of her favorite books, one of her favorite scenes: the unveiling of the Overlords from Arthur C. Clarke's classic *Childhood's End*. Aliens who'd effectively ruled the Earth in peace and prosperity for a human generation while keeping their true features hidden behind space armor, deciding at long last that humanity had matured to the point where they could look upon their friends and not be afraid. The joke being, of course, that the Overlords turned out to be the spitting image (horned heads, skeletal wings, cloven hooves and tail) of the classic cultural depiction of Satan.

Nice ride, she thought, seeing it through the mind's eye of some neighbors, pulling a memory from one of them to more properly identify it as a Mercedes-Benz Maybach saloon car, evidently some kind of classic. She didn't care much for cars. But she caught a resonance from one of the occupants that made her quirk an eyebrow in fascination, a surprisingly adult gesture for a girl of such ostensibly tender years. Given his history and the emotional memories held on a very tight leash, she wondered why he'd possess a German-made car. Spitting in the face of the past, perhaps? She considered probing further but even that cursory stroke of his thoughts had left her with a skull-splitting headache. Neither of the men, she realized, much liked psychic intruders.

They were expected. She picked that up from her parents right away, bothered a little that she hadn't noticed earlier. It was second nature to pry; minds for her had quickly become so transparent that it was like walking through a world made of glass. Almost nothing could be hidden from her, and so much of it was stuff that was so banal, so beyond boring—occasionally so disgusting—that she'd had to remind herself, then force herself, more and more often lately, to mind her own damn business.

She put the novel back on its shelf, pausing a moment to caress the spine of the one beside it, James Blish's equally classic *A Case of Conscience,* and beyond that Frank Herbert's *Dune* trilogy. She'd always enjoyed them; now, though, they had resonances that she found comforting while sending chills skittering through her heart at the same time.

She heard a voice, in her thoughts, not her ears, although the man in the car spoke aloud.

"I still don't know why we're here, Charles. Couldn't you just make them say yes?"

She didn't much like that, and stepped to her window to see for herself who'd come to meet her parents.

She saw a man, thirtysomething and prematurely bald, eminently respectable in a bespoke suit. Hawklike features, piercing eyes, a born hunter. He carried himself with the easy grace of an athlete, comfortable in his strength, confident of his abilities. There was a twist of sorrow to what little of his inner self she could divine, a sense around the edges that he had been places and done things substantially at odds with his upright demeanor. He'd been to war, she realized, when he was very young; he'd needed to prove something to himself, and it had left its mark. First impression, she liked him.

His words cemented the feeling. "Of all people," he said to his companion, "I would expect you to understand my feelings about misuse of power."

The second man emerged and the contrast couldn't have been more pronounced. Dress and manner, as well as accent, suggested a European background. The color of his suit made Jean smile. Not many men would dare to wear royal purple, but he made it work. It was like watching a pair of warrior princes take the field, and she had a sense that she was looking at two men who, in their own way, were as close as she'd been with Annie.

" 'Power corrupts,' and all that," said the taller man, the European, with the air of someone who'd had this discussion too many times. "Yes, Charles, I know. When *will* you stop lecturing me?"

"When you start listening?" Charles replied easily, using a very slight smile to take the edge off words that he meant seriously.

"We're not going to meet every one of them in person, are we?"

"No, Erik. This one is special."

Jean didn't like the sound of that either and decided to let her attention drift. Mr. Pash across the street was mowing his lawn, wrestling with a plot point of his latest novel, while next door Mr. Lee was watering his prize roses. The scene couldn't be more normal, yet Jean hugged herself the way you do when you sense a big storm building off in the mountains, suddenly fearful that afternoon peace wouldn't last.

Ghosting her perceptions over to the periphery of her parents', she caught all the appropriate introductions: the bald man was Charles Xavier; the other, his friend and colleague, Erik Lensherr. Mom ushered them into Dad's study, where she'd already set out a fully laden tea tray.

"It looks wonderful," she said, once everyone was settled, gesturing towards the pile of brochures that had arrived much earlier. "What a beautiful campus. And Salem Center's only an hour and change down the Taconic; it's not like Jean's going to the far side of the moon."

"The brochure is great," her husband agreed. He was standing behind his desk, so that their guests couldn't help seeing the wall of diplomas and awards that went with being a tenured professor at a major independent college. "But I'm concerned about Jean. What about her . . . illness?"

"Illness?" Lensherr said, so quietly that both John and Xavier got the message. The one bridled while the other raised an eyebrow in what he hoped was a subtle but unmistakable warning.

Sensing the spike in tension, Elaine hurriedly intervened: "Now, John!"

"You think your daughter is sick, Mr. Grey?" Lensherr asked in that same silken tone, choosing to ignore Xavier's caution. On cue, as if to complement his undertone, the tea tray shifted ever so slightly.

"Erik," Xavier said, speaking both aloud and with his thoughts, "please."

"Call it what you like," John Grey continued, refusing to be cowed. "What's been happening to Jean since Annie's death is not normal. No one can explain it—not medical doctors, nor psychiatrists—and *none* of them have been able to help. All we know for sure is that she's getting worse."

"Are you afraid of her?" Lensherr asked, almost as if he assumed they were.

"She's my daughter," John flared, "I want to *help* her."

"As do we," Xavier interjected, playing his usual role as peacemaker, biting back the flash of irritation he felt whenever Erik let his growing antipathy towards baseline humans get the better of him. "The whole point of our school is to help people like your daughter. Perhaps," he suggested gently, "it might be better for us to talk to her. Alone."

Clearly, John Grey had doubts. Only his obvious love and concern for his child kept him from showing his two guests the door. Elaine, equally concerned, a tad more desperate, didn't give him the chance.

"Of course." She stepped out into the hallway. "Jean," she called, "can you come down a moment, dear?"

Jean was taller than when Annie died, but still lean and rangy despite the first curves of womanhood. Her hair was a dark red, like a fire seen in the heart of the deepest forest, where the flames are mostly hidden by trees and shadow. Her beauty was self-evident; by the time she was full-grown, it would be breathtaking, with the foundation of bone structure that guaranteed it would only improve with age.

"We'll leave you, then," John Grey told them.

Jean sat on the couch opposite the two men, her demeanor as polite as it was guarded. She'd decided on the way down to let them make the first move.

Xavier obliged her.

"It's very rude, you know . . . ," he said—but his lips didn't move.

Her breath went out of her all in a huff. It never occurred to her that he could do what she did.

". . . to read my thoughts, or Mr. Lensherr's, without our permission."

He was sending her more than words; there was a vast and complex texture to their communication that told her she'd been busted from the first fleeting telepathic contact as they drove down the street. While she'd been spying on them, Xavier was taking her full measure as a psi, without her being the slightest bit aware of it.

Lensherr picked up the conversation from there—only *he* spoke aloud, suggesting to Jean that his abilities differed markedly from Xavier's. "Did you think you were the only one of your kind, girl?"

She intended to keep her response to herself, and bridled ever so slightly when Xavier "heard" it anyway. *What kind is that?* she thought.

"We are mutants, Jean," Xavier said. "We are like you."

She felt a flicker of irritation, like the striking of a match within her soul, heralding a flash of temper that was coming more and more often lately, more and more intense, no matter how hard she tried to keep it under control.

She smiled in a way that promised trouble, a warning.

"Really?" The thoughts and emotions that accompanied that single word were raw and rude. "I doubt that."

Xavier reacted first, to a volley of psychic alarms, Lensherr following his gaze to look out the study window towards the street.

Mr. Pash was running headlong down the length of his front yard, partly dragged by his lawn mower, partly chasing frantically after it, as the old machine launched itself skyward as if it were wearing blue tights and a cape and was bent on leaping tall buildings in a single bound.

At the same time, the stream of water from Mr. Lee's hose decided to rebel against the reign of gravity and see what it was like to pour *up* instead of down. From him, Xavier and Jean heard a muttered expletive, while Pash's initial frisson of startlement gave way to a bark of incredulous laughter.

Then the laughter faded as he caught sight of what else was floating. All along the street, every car in view had suddenly levitated more than ten feet into the air. Nothing else had changed; it was as though they'd been lifted on invisible platforms.

All told, better than ten tons of metal hung suspended, yet Jean wasn't even straining.

Lensherr couldn't help a smile, nor a comment. "Oh, Charles, I *like* this one."

Xavier wasn't amused. "You have more power than you can imagine, Jean."

Her thought, instinctive, defiant. *I dunno, I can imagine quite a lot.*

She met his gaze.

"The question is," he continued, refusing to rise to her unspoken challenge, "will you control that power . . ."

She lost focus, just like that, and the cars crashed at once to the street. She kept her eyes locked on his, realizing that somehow he'd slipped into her mind and blocked the connections between desire and response. She understood immediately how this had happened; with no one but herself possessing psychic powers, how would she have developed any defenses against another with those same abilities? She didn't like that, hated the thought of being vulnerable; she liked even less the peremptory way he'd acted. He could have asked; sure, she was showing off, but if he'd treated her with respect she'd have listened.

". . . or let it control you?" he finished.

She didn't give him an answer because deep down inside, where the answer really mattered, she didn't have one to offer, not that had any value. She suspected it was a question—a challenge—she'd hear often in the days ahead.

She knew she'd attend his school. She'd learn from him all that he was prepared to teach—if only to be able to stand on her own two feet, free from *anyone's* control.

X

1995

Father was at the bathroom door, knocking politely. Warren refused to listen.

"Warren?" called Worthington Jr. Top tier of the Forbes 100, one of the few American billionaires who wasn't head of a computer giant or a dot-com, one of those rarer still who'd taken the modest inheritance of his own father and built it into something of tangible and lasting value. "Son?" Pause, another knock. "Everything okay?" Another pause, another knock, voice creeping up a notch in the anxiety index. "What's going on in here?"

"Nothing, Dad," called Worthington III, railing inside at the tremor in his voice. "Be right out!"

He was twelve and had the features of an angel. Blond hair, face to die for, and a body of whipcord muscle, without a spare ounce; he was far stronger than you'd expect of a boy his age. He stood bare to the waist before the big mirror in his bathroom. In his left hand he held a boning knife, swiped from the kitchen just the other day, right after the cook had done the weekly sharpening. The blade was tungsten steel and sharper than a scalpel. There was blood on the blade, blood on the sink, blood on the floor. Warren knew he should have done this in the tub, where he could wash away all the evidence, but there was no view of the mirror from there and he had to be able to see what he was doing.

Sweat coated his face, and he had to force himself to take deep, slow breaths in a vain attempt to calm his racing heart. His metabolism had always been hyper as far back as he could remember; he ate more at meals than most sumo wrestlers and had to struggle *not* to lose weight. Reactions were the same; that's why he couldn't play baseball anymore. Every at bat was an intentional walk, for his skill at making contact with the ball, if it was even marginally near the strike zone, was uncanny. Likewise his fielding. No matter how fast the play, for Warren everything happened in slow motion. And magnificent as his reflexes were, his eyesight eclipsed them. He drove his optometrist to distraction, because there wasn't a test that could accurately measure his vision. He never told anyone of the test he'd tried on his own, slipping onto the open air observation deck of the World Trade Center and looking out towards Kennedy Airport, a dozen miles away. With the tourist binoculars, you could make out the planes taking off. Warren, with his naked eyes, could read the serial numbers on their fuselage. Looking across the East River towards the Brooklyn Heights Promenade, he could see the details of people's faces and clothing as they strolled— he could even read the banner headlines on their newspapers.

But that wasn't why he kept the visit secret. While there, he had heard a high rising screech a little below and to the side, and looked down to see a red-tailed hawk soaring effortlessly on the thermals generated by the giant HVAC fans atop the Wall Street skyscrapers, cooling the offices within while creating a perpetual heat sink a thousand feet above Manhattan's streets. It was the most wondrous sight he'd ever seen and, without thinking, his head and upper body began to move in tandem with the hawk, as though Warren could also feel the swirls and eddies of the atmosphere. He imagined what it must be like to feel the rush of air across its wings, to plunge headlong towards oblivion, only to snap the wings wide at precisely the right second to save itself and bag the prey. To Warren Worthington III that seemed like Heaven.

And Heaven was likely where he'd have ended up had a woman's strong hands not caught him by the shoulders and pulled him back from the railing.

With a start that left him speechless and trembling, he realized that he'd had one foot and both hands on the rail, and his next move would have been to climb over. Yes, it was only a modest fall to the roof below—thank God the observation platform had been set well back from the edge of the building itself—but for Warren it was the thought that counted most. Or rather, the lack of it, because he couldn't remember much except wanting more than anything to soar with that hawk.

"Are you all right?" the woman asked, quite calmly, as if this sort of thing happened to her all the time. She was taller than he was, more beautiful than any of the myriad faces that stared out from the newsstand walls of fashionista magazines, but the most striking thing about her was a mane of silver hair that fell nearly all the way down her back. She wore leather with the careless air of someone dressing for comfort, knowing that on her it would always look like couture.

"I . . . I . . ." was the best he could stammer.

"It's all right to envy them," she said, with a smile that washed over him like the sun after a spring rain, just as a cry from the access door heralded the arrival of his parents. She gave him a wink and a gentle squeeze on his arm that let him know this was their secret. "We just have to remember we don't have wings."

Her words made perfect sense—and yet, there was something to the way she said them, the way she looked out across the sky towards that spiraling bird, now joined by its mate, that told him she knew far more than she was saying. He assumed she was some sort of extreme hang glider, especially with that hair.

Except—when he and the family had reached the doorway, and he'd turned back to wave good-bye, she was gone. Quickly, he swung his eyes across the entirety of the outdoor deck, but she was nowhere to be found. As if she'd never been.

Warren winced with pain, knew there'd be more blood, the memory banished by the tears that started unbidden from his eyes. He was crying like a baby—he couldn't help himself. But he steeled himself against the tears, against the pain, against the fear. This had to be done.

He scraped the blade across his back, so intent on his purpose that he completely missed the latest round of knocks on the door and the call of his father's voice.

"Come on, Warren," his father said, close to the end of his patience, "it's been an hour. Open this door." He still wasn't angry, although that would be soon in coming. At the moment he simply seemed concerned by his only son's increasingly strange behavior.

"One second," Warren cried, trying to buy as much time as he could, unaware of how clearly his pain and tears and terror radiated through those two simple words. He moved without thinking, grabbing for his tools to stuff them into the lockbox he'd secreted in the drawer.

Too late.

The door burst open and in came Warren Worthington Jr., tall as his son would someday be, the fulfilled promise in maturity of the boy's crisp beauty, yet broadly muscular in a way that Warren would never reach. Whatever emotions the father felt going in the door vanished the moment he beheld his son, standing before the mirror where Warren could see reflected what his father saw directly—a pair of ridged protrusions, as though the boy's shoulder blades had burst upwards through the skin. Only it wasn't those ridges that had torn the boy's flesh. That culprit was the length of gleaming Solingen steel in his hand.

None of that was what made Worthington Jr. gasp, and gape, in shame and horror and disbelief, his mind suddenly flooded with rage at the hand God had dealt him, not directly but through this child he loved more than his life. The objects of those emotions were scattered on the sink and floor, and some still protruded from Warren's back, where the blade had missed them, or the boy hadn't quite been able to reach.

Worthington Jr. took a step forward. Without his glasses, the scene wasn't quite as crisp as he wanted it, the objects on the sink and floor just out of focus enough to require a closer look. Warren misinterpreted the action—small wonder given the expression of horror and disgust on his father's face—and tumbled himself into the corner, hands held up before him as though he expected to be hit. That alone was enough to break the father's heart . . .

. . . but he couldn't bring himself to touch his boy, even though his pain and misery were palpable.

Instead, he reached for the objects that had been cut from Warren's back, refusing to accept what his eyes reported until he had them in his hand.

Feathers.

"No," the father breathed, in denial.

His son was sprouting feathers.

"Please God, *no*!"

His son, God help him, was growing *wings*!

"Not you, Warren. Not . . . this."

And there were tears on Worthington's face now, to

match those on his son's. One in a corner, the other on his knees, both in desperate need of comfort, neither with any to offer.

X

2000

Five years hadn't changed the father much. He wasn't quite as rich as he'd been before, but that was because he'd divested a fairly significant portion of his holdings and personal fortune to endow a number of rather esoteric research establishments across the world. He was still handsome, he was still charming—but that day in his son's bathroom had left its mark in more ways than one. There was a haunted quality to his eyes that told of a commitment to a cause.

"You asked me to come to Bangalore, Dr. Rao. I'm here. What do you have to show me?"

In terms of size, this was a modest laboratory, a small part of an industrial estate that was accommodating India's burgeoning software industry. The reason for placing it here was mainly to have access to dependable power and state-of-the-art computing facilities, not to mention the geeks to tweak the systems. Kavita Rao was both an MD and a geneticist, rated on a par with Moira MacTaggart of Edinburgh University and considered just as likely to someday claim a Nobel for medicine. The team she'd gathered in Worthington's name was nearly on a par with her, and the clinic she'd built with his money was worthy of them all.

One wall consisted of nothing but a giant flat-screen display, which would have cost a decent fortune in and of itself but for the fact that another company in the park specialized in making them. One meeting between Kavita and their managing director, the promise of medical care for their employees, and with that quid pro quo goods and services were speedily and regularly exchanged.

What Worthington Jr. saw on the display was a succession of double helices, which he knew were representations of someone's DNA, the genetic building blocks of life. He hadn't a clue what they meant, despite voluminous reading over the past half decade.

Kavita indicated a rail-thin boy, far younger than Worthington expected, lying in an isolation room. The room had been decorated with an eye to the boy's comfort and peace of mind—it was as much a boy's space as it could be given the circumstances, with games and stuffed animals sharing the venue with monitors and IV stands. He was reading a stack of comics; sensing Dr. Rao's attention on him, he offered up a wave.

"His name is Jimmy," she told Worthington. "It will take some considerable time to explain, and even more to bring matters to fruition, but the initial tests look quite promising. If the fates are kind, all our work may not have been in vain."

"Time is of no consequence," Worthington Jr. said, pulling up a chair beside her. "Tell me everything."

Chapter Two

Now

War zone, pure and simple.

Officially, it was night, but the darkness only served as a backdrop for a fireworks display of incredible lethality. The setting had once been a fair-sized town, decent central business district, buildings of some substance, two to five stories tall, built to last, of brick and stone. Spreading outwards in a grid pattern, residential streets, single-family homes, everything from Arts and Crafts bungalows to modern "McMansions." Couple of parks, one mostly green space, the other intended for kids and recreation—playgrounds, baseball diamonds, bikeways and running tracks. Schools, of course, and churches.

All gone.

The battle lines had surged back and forth over the town, in a manner more reminiscent of the Civil War than modern warfare, but played out with weapons that made the rifles and cannons of that bloody conflict look like toys. Not a building in the town had been left whole and hardly any of the ruins that remained were still standing. The trees had been reduced to shattered stubs, trunks and branches either blown to wicked-deadly splinters or scorched beyond recognition. The earth was so pockmarked with shell holes, the streets so choked with debris, that vehicular transit was out of the question. Moving on foot was no fun either, since the piles of rubble afforded ideal hidey-holes for snipers and ambush parties, as well as for booby traps of every shape and description.

It was a rat's nest, a meat grinder that would chew up any force fool enough to take it on.

So of course, the X-Men had been tasked to do just that.

In the distance, the sky lit up with a line of tracers, curving gracefully through the night as the gunner tracked an airborne target, and a few seconds later the sound of firing followed, *bup-bup-bup-bup*. Both sight and sound were then overwhelmed by an ugly fireball as the falling bombs hit their target.

Logan's eyes narrowed to slits as he watched from the minimal shelter afforded by the intersection of a house's two stone walls. His senses were more acute than any hunting predator's, but in a scrap like this the advantage became a liability. He could see clearly in almost total darkness, yet a surprise burst of tracer rounds could strip him of that night vision in a flash. The healing factor that was his main mutant power would deal with the loss in a couple of heartbeats, but in a firefight those seconds usually made the difference between survival and disaster. Logan's sense of smell allowed him to follow trails that bloodhounds couldn't trace, but there were so many scents to choose from here that it took conscious effort to process them. Suddenly, he had to use conscious thought to direct processes that were normally backbrain second nature. Didn't matter that he still did it with a speed and accuracy that left everyone around him in the dust, whether mutant or sapien. It blunted his edge—and that was unacceptable.

He sniffed the air, to catalogue who—or what—was in his immediate vicinity, and smiled at one smell he recognized.

Somebody had been kind enough to lose their cigar.

Cuban. Vintage. Hand-rolled. He caught just the smallest residual flavor of the woman who'd made it enough to recognize her if they met, smiled as he considered the possibilities.

He cupped his lighter to shield the flame from view, aware as he did that this habit from previous battlefields wouldn't help in the least against a heat-sensitive thermal imager; on the other hand, such a device would have nailed him right from the start. No response suggested no such device, which gave him leave to indulge. He didn't get the opportunity very often these days. Too many flamin' rules, too many flamin' busybodies hellbent on enforcing them, too much flamin' aggravation.

Harsh snaps through the air off to the right caught his attention and he sank a little deeper into the building's shadows, instinctively hiding the glowing end of the cigar with the hollow of his hand as multiple pulses of laser fire burned their way overhead, clipping a nearby building and creating a shower of heat-fused masonry. Like hail, only harder. Had it hit something more significant with a more powerful pop, he would have had a spray of shrapnel to contend with.

Had nothing to do with him, though; someone *else* was the target.

Logan didn't move; there was no point. Given the lay

of the ground, the intensity of the strafing fire, they had nowhere else to go but right past him.

Bingo.

Two figures, male and female, in the black leather uniforms of the X-Men. The man was in the lead, big sucker, but moving with surprising grace despite his evident bulk, bare arms standing out from the rest of him in the glow of various explosions. The skin of those arms and of his head reflected the light in a way that told Logan he was metal—even his hair gleamed as though cast from chrome. This was one of the newbies, Piotr Nikolievitch Rasputin. Colossus.

Logan spared him only the merest glance; his focus was mainly on Rogue.

She used to flinch at loud noises; now she kept pace with her companion, bobbing and weaving with practiced grace, presenting a random and unpredictable target for the opposition—showing excellent instincts for dealing with any trouble that came her way.

"How long do we have?" the man called to her.

"Two minutes, tops," she replied, as she dove with him to cover.

Smart girl. The obvious place to hide was the shadowed corner where Logan himself stood, yet she realized that any infantryman worth the name would recognize that as well, and probably drop a brace of rounds on the location just to make sure. She'd chosen a nearby shell hole instead, part of a string of depressions that afforded a messy but relatively secure means of slipping across this open patch of ground.

The moment Rogue hit, she turned her back to the way they'd come, every one of her senses on high alert. Rasputin was a step behind, his attention still on whatever might be chasing them; he hadn't yet twigged to the possibility of a threat from anywhere else. His wasn't as artful a landing, either. Downside to all that bulk was, despite his relative ease of movement, Colossus still landed like a falling bank safe. Slid all the way to the bottom and made a deeper hole of his own.

Logan couldn't help a grin. The girl was pretty damn good. All it had taken was a whiff of his lit cigar.

Better yet, he realized she was looking right at him.

But that was when she made her mistake, standing straight up to greet him, all thoughts of the mission banished behind her smile of welcome and pure delight.

"Logan," Rogue cried.

"I'm away for a while, the whole world goes to hell."

He should have known better. They had both breached battlefield discipline, had forgotten for a fateful split second what was happening all around them. And nearly paid dearly for the lapse.

He heard footsteps, the *kling* of a grenade pin flipping free, but never saw the bomb until it blew on the far side of Rogue. No time to pull her clear, no chance to cover her body with his own. She was too far out of reach.

But Colossus wasn't. His view wasn't masked by Rogue, as Logan's was—he saw the grenade—and in the instant it took to fall, the fraction of a heartbeat before it exploded, he grabbed Rogue's bare hand in one of his.

Back in the day, when Logan first knew her, the assimilation process was gradual. It took a definable length of time, enough for Rogue to have second thoughts, for the subject to pull away, as he felt his life literally pouring out of him. This was virtually instantaneous.

From the point of contact, Rogue's skin flashed chrome as armor rolled up her arm across her body—

while Peter's reverted the other way, from organic steel back to normal flesh—so that when the spray of anti-personnel shrapnel reached her, it deflected off . . .

. . . to clip Logan instead.

It hurt like hell, both from slashing open a stretch of his side—which bled freely—and because the metal was red-hot, burning him as well. That's why he favored T-shirts and clothes older than most of the junior X-Men; the way he generally got himself torn up, they were the most easily replaceable. Made him smile inside and shake his head, to wonder at the replacement cost of the custom-constructed X-Men uniforms.

Logan pressed his hand against the wound, but no more blood was flowing; there'd been just enough for that first, glorious, indelible stain before the skin regrew. It was still tender, but in a matter of minutes there'd be only a scar, and by tomorrow nothing at all. No sign whatsoever that he'd been wounded.

If only he could dump the sense memories of those hurts as easily. One thing to be a man who's almost impossible to kill; totally another to remember pretty near every one of those quasi-death experiences.

He took another puff of his cigar. They'd been here long enough.

"You gonna stand here and get blown up, or what?"

"I didn't see you at briefing, bub," Rogue sassed him back, giving as good as she got, which cheered him. "D'*you* have the slightest idea where we're goin'?"

She had the knowledge from the briefing, but he had the experience. As a brace of searchlights speared down from some hovering platform to illuminate the scene for the enemy gunners, he gestured towards a squat and ugly structure some distance away, across what had been the town's central square.

"I'm thinkin' that bunker."

The look she gave him told Logan he'd scored, and also that if she had just absorbed Cyclops's optic blasts instead of Colossus's steel, the frustration in her eyes might have propelled him all the way over there in a single shot!

He felt a tremor through the ground, saw ripples in a pool of water pulse inward to the center.

Another pulse, establishing a steady cadence whose spacing suggested the march of something massive.

"Time to go, children," he told the others, noting that both were reverting to their original states: Rogue human, Colossus in armor. She'd *way* improved since he saw her last.

"We get to that door," Rogue announced, stress making her Mississippi accent a bit more pronounced, breathless from the double-sided transformation, "we're clear."

The two younger X-Men began moving from cover to cover, just as they'd been trained.

Logan started walking, right out in the open, as though he were out for an evening stroll—making himself a stalking horse for anyone dumb enough to take a shot. Watching him, Rogue didn't know whether to admire his courage or shake him silly for being such a damn fool! *Logan,* she hissed to herself, *don't you realize, dummy, that the price of havin' friends, people who truly* care *'bout you, is that when you're hurt, we* feel *it, too! Only we maybe don't get over it quite so quick.*

* * *

Rogue wasn't the only one thinking along those lines. On the far side of a nearby hill, Storm also watched him take his walk and confined her spoken comments to a single word: *"Logan!"*

Thinking to herself, she used terms that would have given even him pause and made any telepath with access to those thoughts sever the connection instantly. He wasn't supposed to be here, and while his presence was always welcome in a firefight, she really didn't like surprises when lives were on the line.

Storm looked again through her binoculars, this time checking the integral display. Logan was fifty meters ahead, the bunker some two hundred plus beyond.

Twisting around, she used hand signals to alert the rest of her team, under cover of their own a few dozen meters back and to the side. Kitty Pryde was already on the move, body low to the ground as she sprinted in a zigzag towards Bobby Drake. The maneuvering wasn't really necessary; of all the team, she was the closest to Wolverine in her practical invulnerability to harm. Not so much like Colossus, whose organic steel armor could actually be breached with the right weapons, but because neither bullets nor energy beams can have much effect on a girl who was essentially a ghost.

Storm could feel the tremors in the earth as well, could sense the displacement in the air that told her something massive was moving through the night, closing on them with every giant step. Time had just joined the opposition.

"You okay?" Kitty called to Bobby as she slid down to join him, misjudging her angle just enough that she arrived half sunk into the ground. He didn't say anything, but his look was eloquent: she knew the casual way she walked through walls really creeped him out.

"Yeah," he replied. "You?"

"A little dusty."

He reached out and brushed her shoulder clean. She'd invited the contact, and he'd responded, both operating on instinct. That was as far as either was prepared to take things. Now.

Still, he couldn't help giving her a smile. It was clear he liked her. Problem was, while Kitty was a free spirit, Bobby already had a girl—Rogue.

"Storm's signaling; she wants us to catch up. Your lead?"

She grinned and took off, and Bobby had to scramble to keep up. She was as dangerously arrogant as Wolverine when it came to getting hurt. She didn't believe it was possible. Kitty didn't even have to worry much about being taken by surprise, because for the most part her power was always "on." Her natural state, according to Professor Xavier, was to be phased; she stayed coherent by an act of will.

Laser pulses sought them out, and Bobby blocked them with a wall of ice that was porous enough to allow them through but filled with enough impurities— namely dirt—to diffuse the beam to the point of harm- lessness.

But those beams weren't the only threat. A brace of rockets shot in from another direction. Bobby was only aware of them after Kitty suddenly grabbed him, crush- ing her body against his in a hard embrace that allowed her to phase them both so the missiles passed through them as if they were air. His insides tingled as they did, reminding him of a joy buzzer–pen his brother had once blown his allowance for on Halloween.

Across the field, Rogue had also seen the approaching missiles—they'd passed her on the way—and in the moment before impact, when she saw Bobby so vulnerable and unaware, her heart stopped and leapt up to her throat. She was happy to see him survive unscathed, but a lot less so when she noted that it took way too many extra moments for him and Kitty to break apart.

"Keep movin', kid," Logan told her. He'd seen what she'd seen, damn him; he didn't miss anything. "And keep your eyes dead ahead."

Storm missed it all. She was focused on their objective, and the handheld display which presented her with a map of the battlefield, complete with the disposition of her team and a counter that was just passing ninety seconds.

"Time, people," she told Kitty and Bobby as they arrived, using the comset clipped to her ear to alert the others. "No more margin for error. Iceman, Shadowcat—get in position." This was to Bobby and Kitty directly, using their code names. "On my mark."

They moved forward at a jog trot, quick but careful, in a V-formation led by Storm, with her younger teammates trailing by a couple of steps, covering her flanks while she concentrated on the way ahead.

The last bit of cover was a pile of junked cars; beyond was nothing but open ground, an ideal killing field. Somebody with a mortar got their range and began bracketing them with rounds as they approached the checkpoint, inching closer with every shot, the last forcing them to pitch forward in an undignified scramble that brought them with a crash down beside the other assault team, who'd gotten there first.

Logan was leaning against one of the cars, apparently without a care in the world.

"What are you doing here?" Storm flared at him, letting a bit more of her feelings show than she'd actually intended. High above, a complement to those emotions, came a blinding flash, gone almost before it had time to register, accompanied by a basso drum roll that was instantly recognized. A bolt of lightning, a trill of thunder; the elements were echoing Storm's emotions.

That wasn't good. The fact that she had to take a moment to master herself didn't help her mood. Chances were, when this op was concluded, someone, somewhere might have to deal with some very nasty weather.

"Enjoying the scenery," he suggested, choosing the completely wrong moment for levity and then making it significantly worse by using a piece of flaming debris to relight his cigar.

For a moment, Storm seriously considered going "Zeus" on his insubordinate ass and using her next bolt of lightning to knock him flat. Perhaps a very near miss would knock some sense into his thick Canadian skull. Or at least inspire a modicum of respect.

She dismissed the inspiration even before it was fully formed, because she knew it would do no good.

And suddenly, there was no time for conscious thought at all as she sensed movement in the air—that same massive shape she'd noticed before, only much, *much* closer. *How had it crept up on them so unawares?* Realization and action came as one as she grabbed for her friend and teammate and yanked him bodily clear of the car, just as a massive armored foot the size of a semi-trailer squashed it flat.

They ended up face-to-face, tight against each other, and for that briefest of moments *that* was all that mattered.

"I got this," said Storm, as the foot moved on. Through the smoke and the shadows, the literal fog of battle, none of them was in a position to see what it was attached to. The younger X-Men weren't sure they wanted to.

"Watch my back, okay?" she told him.

"Not a problem," he replied.

It was a spectacular back, Logan thought, even masked as it was by the cloak of her uniform. To call Ororo Munroe beautiful was merely to state the obvious. There was no one—among the X-Men, in the world—who even came close. Except, the thought came to him, a memory of a wound still fresh enough to hurt: Jean Grey.

"Hey, bub," Rogue chided gently, "eyes front, right?"

He slid a look her way, which made her grin. Logan subvocalized a warning growl that set hackles rising on the backs of the necks of both the boys and Kitty, but seemed to make Rogue's grin grow even wider.

Storm, all business, brought them back to the task at hand.

"Stay in formation," she instructed. "Wait to make your move."

They knew whatever cues she was talking about, but Storm knew Logan didn't. She grabbed him as he stood to make a move of his own.

"Logan," she snapped, "we work as a team!"

He smiled tolerantly and she thought more seriously this time about that lightning bolt. "You let me know how that works out for you, darlin'," he replied, and resumed his evening stroll, complete with cigar

So obvious a target couldn't be ignored. Their adversaries opened up with everything they had.

So foolhardy a friend couldn't be abandoned. Bobby and Peter exchanged quick glances. Then Peter rose to follow.

"Peter!" Storm snapped, genuinely furious now. "Get back here!"

The raw edge of command in her voice actually got through to him, and to Bobby as well, who'd been caught halfway to his feet. Peter stopped, torn between wanting to follow the Wolverine and his responsibility to Storm as mission commander.

As Logan knew, as the others were about to learn, in battle a single moment can swing the balance. Thus far, they'd operated mainly in shadow and anonymity. Their foes had occasional glimpses of them, and a general sense of where they were, but no clearly defined fix on their position.

Right then, right there, that changed.

Bobby was the first to see the light, attracted by the commotion. He screamed a warning.

"Peter!"

Too late. Even as Colossus turned, the searchlight found him, and that contact brought all its fellows to bear. Just like that, the team's position was illuminated in a flood of light that defined the scene as bright as day.

A moment later, the bad guys opened fire. With everything they had.

"Move out," Storm yelled. "Stay *together!*"

Instead, they scattered.

Momentarily forgotten amidst the suddenly target-rich environment, Logan kept walking, the personification of calm amidst growing chaos.

With a multitude of small, fast-moving targets to choose from, however, the gunners found themselves facing a completely different challenge than when the teams had been clustered together. The X-Men couldn't share their abilities to cover one another, but at the same time, they were individually facing a smaller array of weapons. They all began making quick progress towards their final objective.

In the lead, Storm's glance kept flicking between the battlefield and the countdown clock strapped to her wrist. Time was the inflexible adversary here, not the guys with the guns. The X-Men had a deadline, and they couldn't be late.

"Storm," called Bobby, indicating the bunker, like the kid with the winning touchdown in hand, a step from the goal line, "we're almost there!"

It blew up in his face.

She wasn't sure whether it was a shell from outside or some hidden sapper charge; what mattered was the spectacular explosion that would have knocked her off her feet had she not used her own innate control of the winds to shunt the pressure wave around her. Bobby wasn't so fortunate. He not only went flying, he got clipped by debris for his trouble. Bad landing as well, that left him in a twisted, crumpled, unmoving heap.

Something passed over Colossus, moving on the bunker and Bobby. He wrenched the door off a ruined car and hurled it like a discus at the oncoming figure. Metal clanged on metal . . .

and the door, suitably crushed, thudded back to Earth at his feet.

Logan, still playing the role of nonchalant observer, was impressed.

"Good arm."

He looked the other way, saw Bobby fallen, Storm unable to reach him, the remaining two girls isolated and under considerable and growing fire. Things were out of hand.

Kitty summed it up, from her perspective: "We're screwed."

Logan had other ideas.

"Throw me," he told Colossus.

"*Shto?*" replied the young Russian. He didn't get it.

"Logan," Storm called, racing to join them. "*Wait—*"

"Y'understand baseball?" Logan demanded, popping his claws, darting quick, repeated glances over his shoulder at the source of the mighty footsteps, which could now be heard as well as felt. Colossus nodded. "Y'know, like a fastball?" Again, he nodded. "Then follow where I point and *throw me*! *Now!*"

The armored Russian scooped him up, cocked his arm and let fly.

Logan disappeared into the low cloud of smoke that provided a quasi-roof over the town roughly a hundred feet overhead.

* * *

The firing slackened, enough for the X-Men to hear the sound of rending metal, followed by an almost unendurably high-pitched *squeee!* It didn't take a rocket scientist to figure out what that meant—the Wolverine had used his claws, pure adamantium, unimaginably and perpetually sharp, wholly unbreakable, on something that didn't much like it.

Confirmation landed before them with a thud that shook the ground, momentum rolling it over two complete revolutions before it came to rest in front of the kids. It was a big, giant head, belonging to some kind of equally impressive robot.

They then heard an explosion of such force that the airborne shock wave struck them like a lesser punch, staggering them on their feet. Some seconds later, whatever the head had been attached to crashed and blew itself to bits.

That was when Logan made his entrance, before any of them had a chance to worry about his fate. He looked a bit the worse for wear but, even as he approached, his injuries were healing with every step. He appeared far more concerned about his leather jacket, which was both torn and scorched.

He popped a single claw, forefinger for once, instead of the middle claw he generally tended to favor, and made ready to carve his initials into the crown of the robot's head . . .

. . . when a klaxon sounded . . .

. . . and the head dissolved before his eyes.

Same applied to the scenery. Night vanished, replaced by the institutional illumination of a vast and sprawling concourse the size of a commercial jumbo jetliner hangar. The lay of the land was "real," as the floors re-aligned themselves to provide for a flat and featureless surface, but the town itself was not. On every side surrounding the X-Men, huge panels of photon imagers—capable of generating constructs that were not only three-dimensional but significantly tangible as well—withdrew into their housings.

Logan shook his head. Not a lot got his full attention, but the Danger Room snagged it every time.

"You find a way to market this to Hollywood and the theme parks, 'Ro," he said, speaking mainly to himself though he used Ororo's name, "your collective fortune is made!"

He twisted his back, shoulders, finally his neck, gradually working out the kinks, as he did after every scrap, then looked expectantly at the others.

"I'm starved," he announced. "Who's up for pizza?"

Bobby pushed himself up, Kitty hanging back as Rogue slipped an arm through his, visibly and intentionally reminding all of their relationship. He wasn't hurt. The Room's core programming wouldn't allow it. Death held no sway here, and the worst the room would do to anyone was stun them and then use its projectors to paint the most horrendous wounds imaginable on the body.

As they all started for the exit, Logan threw an arm companionably across Peter Rasputin's shoulder.

"Hey, Tinman," he said, making Peter roll his eyes. The Russian didn't much care for the nickname and pretty much knew what was coming after. "Gotta tell ya—you throw like a girl."

Storm stopped Logan dead in his tracks, her eyes

flashing a dangerous cerulean blue—a precursor to them going white and her turning loose the extreme weather.

"I *am* a girl," she said simply, throwing down the gauntlet as hard as she knew how before turning on her heel and beating them through the doorway.

She was waiting in the hallway beyond, with such electricity in the air surrounding her that her team beat a hasty retreat into the locker room, figuring to take their time getting changed in hopes that the "storm" would quickly pass.

Logan took a moment to look fondly at the stub that remained of his cigar, then tossed it into the disposal.

"What the hell was that?" Ororo demanded.

"Danger Room session."

Kitty had her ear partially phased through the wall, relaying the gist of the conversation to the others. She visibly blanched when she heard what was being exchanged, wondering aloud if that Canucklehead *wanted* to get turned into a crispy critter.

Surprisingly, Ororo kept a leash on her emotions.

"You know what I mean."

Logan spread his arms wide, close to a shrug. This was somewhere he didn't want to go.

" 'Ro," he began, and then after a pause and an awkward silence between them, "Storm—"

"No," she said flatly. "You can't just come and go as you please. We're trying to run a school here."

"Well, I taught 'em something."

She wasn't amused.

"They're mainly adolescents, Logan. Teenagers? Ring

a bell maybe, what that was like? At this age, especially when they have powers, they're hardwired to act like fools. I don't need you encouraging them."

Backed into a rhetorical corner, he said nothing.

"If you'd read the syllabus, you'd know this was a defensive exercise. Evasive maneuvers."

"Best defense is a good offense," he countered, but then thought better of it. "Or is it the other way 'round?"

"I'll try to remember that for my next class." Her tone was acid. This hadn't gone well.

Logan understood only too well. He just didn't have a clue how to make it right. So he took a page from his own dictum and closed the conversation by charging her barricades.

"Hey, 'Ro, I'm just the sub," he said, letting his own irritation show. "You got a beef, talk to Scott."

X

Scott Summers was cold.

It wasn't simply a physical sensation—it went far beyond that, encompassing every aspect of his body and mind and spirit. He was cold in a way that told him he'd never know warmth again, in the way he always imagined deepest space must feel, the way the Cosmos must have been in the *whatever* space of nontime there was before the Big Bang brought it into being.

He bundled in sweaters, he warmed himself in down quilts, cracked the heat, stood before roaring fires— none of it helped. The cold was in the core of him. He might alter things on the surface, but that was for only a painfully small measure of time.

It sapped his strength, it sapped his will, it made him a shadow of the man he'd been.

He'd sought refuge in the school library, reading enough on depression to treat the disease himself. Scott talked to the professor, but Xavier's telepathy didn't help, nor did any of the current regimes of drugs.

He knew he looked like hell, and he simply didn't care.

Somewhere—and this thought brought the hint of a smile to the corner of his mouth—he must have been infected with an active case of Wolverine. Too bad the disease hadn't also come with its own healing factor.

He took a deep and reflexive breath at the consideration of the other man, his rival for so many things, and his brow furrowed as he recognized the scent of pine sap and fresh-fallen snow, and suddenly the cold had a focus and an identity he'd never noticed before. The shore of Alkali Lake, in the mountains of western Canada, where—

And just like that, the cold changed again, pressing in on him from every side, filling him inside and out. He flailed on his bed, mouth agape in a frantic quest for air while his mind shrieked the utter *wrongness* of that action, because there was no air to breathe. He was underwater, he was at the bottom, he was tangled in weeds, caught in the muck amidst a mad forest of boulders big as houses and slabs of rebar-threaded masonry that were bigger still, deposited here by the monumental outflow of water that had occurred when the dam had burst.

He was screaming, which only generated a flood of bubbles, marking the final passage of his life as they cascaded up to the surface.

Then something caught his eye that drove all fear and thought from him and touched his heart with the first semblance of warmth he'd felt since—

The X-Men were fleeing for their lives. The dam had failed, a flood was coming, they had perhaps a minute before oblivion. Their *Blackbird* stratojet was literally stuck in the mud after a less than perfect landing; the vertical thrusters couldn't lift it clear.

Jean had been injured in battle earlier, her leg broken. Scott had left her in the passenger compartment, while he scrambled forward to help on the flight deck. There was so much confusion nobody noticed she'd left the plane until Professor Xavier announced it.

She was the team telekinetic, and she intended to use the power of her thoughts to hold the flood at bay until she lifted the *Blackbird* free. It was an impossible ambition. She'd never exhibited even a fraction of that kind of power, or control. One or the other would pose a supreme test of her abilities, but both—never happen, not a prayer.

Without her they were all doomed anyway. That too was part of the equation.

Scott raced after her but she closed and sealed the hatch in his face. He might have been able to blast it open with his optic blasts. Wolverine for sure could have cut through with his claws, but instead Logan held *him* back. He wouldn't try himself, and he wouldn't give Scott the chance. So what if Jean was doing this for him, because she loved him; didn't she, didn't *any* of them comprehend how hollow his life would be without her? He'd been alone his whole life, for as far back as he could remember, in the Nebraska State Home for

Foundlings; he couldn't bear the thought of the woman he loved facing her final moments without someone to at least hold her hand.

He remembered her voice coming from Xavier's lips as she spoke through him, but what mattered more was the warmth that flared within Scott, a glorious celestial chorus that—even though he knew he was experiencing but the smallest portion of the transcendence Jean herself embraced—filled him with a sense of wonder unlike anything he'd ever known.

He wept then, not for grief—that would come later, a knife through the heart—but in awe at such impossible, eternal beauty.

Then the plane rose above the flood and before they could bring her home . . .

. . . she was gone.

The fire went with her, that loss made infinitely worse by the memory of what had been.

Yet here, and now, with each beat of his broken heart came the faintest resonance of what he'd felt during those last moments of her life.

And even though a part of him knew he sat in his room at the Xavier Institute, he also fully accepted that he stood as well at the bottom of Alkali Lake.

Staring at a body.

A woman. Clothes and features all obscured, wreathed in a crown of dark red hair, the fiery auburn of leaves turning in fall.

Quick as it had come, the image was gone, as suddenly as if one of the Fates had flicked a switch.

Scott trembled, rubbing his hands, keeping his eyes shut tight as he pulled off his visor and rubbed his face, realizing as he did that he didn't feel quite so hollow anymore. Things had changed. The best part of his soul had come back to him.

He didn't stop to think, replacing the visor, unzipping his carryall and stuffing in whatever clothes came imme diately to hand. This wasn't a moment for rationality or explanations—and once more the image of a character infection passed on by Wolverine slipped through his awareness—but for action. Make the move, worry about consequences later.

The only things he knew for certain were that this had to be done, and that it was *right*.

And with that thought, he was gone.

Chapter
Three

The estate had been in Xavier's family since this part of New York—roughly an hour north of the City—had still been considered Indian Country. Considering the locale, its size was remarkable: three miles along the shore of Breakstone Lake and a mile inland, in upper Westchester County hard by the border of neighboring Putnam County and the state of Connecticut just to the east. Most of the property had never been developed, beyond the immediate vicinity of the great house itself, and still essentially remained virgin Hudson Valley forest.

The Mansion itself had been built during the so-called Gilded Age of the late nineteenth century, by an ancestor who wanted to prove himself on a par with the Vanderbilts and the Goulds and the Astors. It was an attempt to construct outside Salem Center a home that would rival, and preferably surpass, what was filling the Newport shoreline in Rhode Island.

What resulted was a monument to wealth that beggared modern conceptions of the term but also exemplified rather extraordinary good taste. No expense had been spared in the Mansion's construction, while at the same time neither owner nor builders ever lost sight of the fact that they were creating a home that was actually to be *lived* in. Something that the residents might actually *enjoy,* more than a proclamation of excess.

The main building rose a total of four stories above the knoll on which it was built (including the topmost turret, which Kitty had immediately claimed for her own), allowing for a commanding view of the surrounding countryside. There were also three full levels *below,* for staff facilities—which proved a godsend to Charles Xavier when the time came to adapt the building to the needs of both his planned school and the X-Men who would grow from it. A multitude of secret passages were left over from Prohibition by a more recent ancestor who financed the upkeep with some rather high-end bootlegging. Considering the mansion's recent history, which included a full-scale armed assault by a cadre of Black Ops paramilitarists, in addition to the everyday wear and tear from scores of energetic youngsters with superpowers, the house had held up incredibly well.

After Kitty's gossipy report on the exchange between Ororo and Logan, Rogue and Bobby came up the elevator on their own. Kitty was the resident geek, and she often seemed far more comfortable with the server array that ran the Danger Room than with the students who used it. She could invariably be found either down in the catacombs or up in her room, but rarely in between, outside of mandated classes. She hung a lot with her partner in crime, Doug Ramsey, whose mutant skill with languages made his facility for writing software code the perfect complement to her intuitive brilliance with hardware, and there were also rumors of a long-distance friendship with Peter's kid sister Illyana, back in Russia. But beyond that, Kitty pretty much kept to herself.

Bobby actually didn't mind her absence. Rogue was in a foul mood and he was determined to ferret out the cause, and then hopefully stomp it to death. He cared too much for her and hated seeing her so torn up inside. So he pushed and pushed as they rode the elevator and finally she caved, spitting the words out like bullets.

"What's wrong," she announced in that tone of hers which suggested she was annoyed to have to be stating the obvious, "is that I can't touch my boyfriend without killing him. Other than that, I'm wonderful."

Wasn't much he could say to that, considering it was mostly true. With tutelage and practice, she'd gained a measure of control over her ability to assimilate powers and psyches. She could do it much faster than before, as she'd proved with Colossus in the Danger Room, doing far less harm to her subjects in the process. But those were flash-hits, combat situations. Rogue borrowed a power for a specific reason and just as quickly gave it back again. *Or*—she'd touch a bad guy a bit longer to take him out of the fight. Her upper limit would allow her use of powers for twenty-four hours max, putting the guy she nailed out cold for the same length of time.

At the moment, though, Rogue had no need for her powers. Bobby was her guy. She didn't want to just touch him for a fleeting, stolen second, she wanted the entire romance package. The kissing, the stroking, the hugging, the sex. She wanted all of him, but knew that if she tried, it would be the end of Bobby.

Rogue heard titters from a corner. She didn't look because she knew the voices, but her eyes tightened to the dangerous, get-outta-my-way-bub glare she'd learned from Logan. Bobby looked and blushed. It was the Cuckoos, of course, blond triplets, Polo poster girls, telepaths. They dressed in white, following the style of their headmistress at the incredibly pricey Massachusetts Academy, and they loved to pry, perpetually trolling for any stray or wayward thought. Wicked sat in her usual corner, playing chess with one of her dead friends. She had a million of them, spirits at her beck and call, who would do her bidding, or could merge with her to add their raw strength to hers.

The school had grown since Rogue's arrival, to the point where even this huge old house was threatening to burst at the seams. That's why the Cuckoos were visiting. Xavier was considering an affiliation with the Massachusetts Academy, whose head, it turned out, was a fairly impressive telepath in her own right. The professor wanted to see what kind of students they recruited, and how well they played with others.

Thus far, Rogue hadn't been impressed.

Bobby moved in front of her, apparently not ready to let the conversation drop. "That's not fair," he protested. "Have I put any pressure on you?"

No, she conceded, swearing that if she heard the slightest snicker from those fashionista wannabees, there'd be blood. *You've been the perfect gentleman. It's me who's goin' crazy.*

But sadly, that wasn't what she chose to say aloud.

"You think I can't tell? You're a guy, Bobby. There's only one thing on your mind."

* * *

This time, Bobby chose not to follow as Rogue moved around him and headed off. Better, he decided, to let her cool down and hope for a more rational conversation later.

He offered a wave and a hello to Scott as the bigger man strode past him, down the grand staircase to the foyer. Bobby was completely ignored, which wasn't like Scott at all.

Bobby heard familiar voices—Logan calling "Hey, Scott!"—and snuck a peek over the gallery railing to see if anything was playing out downstairs.

As usual, Logan and Scott were about to have a testosterone throw-down. They couldn't be in a room together for any amount of time without going mega-macho in each other's face. The student body had a pool going, to see who'd eventually walk away in the end. Bobby always figured that was a waste of money, was sure the two men would one day work things out.

Listening now, though, he wasn't quite so sure.

"They were looking for you downstairs," Logan commented companionably, with just a hint of an edge in his voice to let Scott know this was serious. "You didn't show."

"What do you care?"

"I had to cover your ass, for starters!"

"I didn't ask!"

"No," Logan interrupted, calm in the face of Scott's anger, "you didn't. The *professor* did." Fractional beat, to let the fact that he used Xavier's title sink in. With Logan, it was invariably "Charley," with the occasional "Chuck" when he wanted to get Xavier's attention, not necessarily in a good way. Then: "I was just passing through."

Scott didn't bat an eye. "So? Pass through, Logan. It's what you do best."

Another beat, only a moment in real time, but it seemed to stretch like taffy to an almost unendurable length.

"Look, Scott, I know how you feel—"

This time Scott cut him off: "Don't."

"When Jean died—"

"I said, *don't*!"

Watching from above, conscious now that he had company—the gallery was crowded with kids drawn by the commotion—Bobby wondered if he had been foolish to skip that pool.

Logan stepped in close, but when he reached out to Scott it was with an open hand.

"Maybe it's time for us to move on."

Scott didn't give an inch.

"Not everybody heals as fast as you—*bub!*"

Logan watched as the great front doors of the Mansion closed behind Scott, listened to the sound of a bike engine being pushed to its limits and fading quickly into the distance, taking as much time as he needed to compose himself.

He knew he had an audience. With his eyes closed, by scent alone he could name them all. He jerked his head to indicate the show was over, and then found himself looking at Rogue, who'd rushed to the base of the stairs, probably to back him up in case he needed it.

She was only a kid the night she had crawled into his truck, in the ass-end of upper Canada, in Laughlin City, a dot of a prairie truck stop with dreams of grandeur.

That journey together had ended with their introduction to the X-Men. Now she was a full-grown woman—and Logan knew that he'd found something that hurt her far worse than his claws ever could.

As Rogue stepped forward to offer a little comfort, perhaps only company over a beer, she didn't need words to tell her that Logan still grieved for Jean.

He shook his head.

As Logan went his own way, impulse drew Rogue's gaze up to the gallery, to the only person left watching—Bobby. And she knew that they must have had the same notions skittering across their thoughts: could either of them bear to be hurt so deeply? Could either of them bear to walk away?

X

It was a modest office block by federal standards, left over from a more decorative age, like the Old Executive Office Building and the Smithsonian. But what it lacked in modern aesthetics, or the practicalities of state-of-the-art internal data networking, it more than made up for in proximity to the *one* building in town that mattered. The one with the address 1600 Pennsylvania Avenue.

The offices housed the youngest of the president's cabinet departments. But the reason both for its importance and for its being treated as a bastard stepchild could be found on the official identification plaque out front: UNITED STATES DEPARTMENT OF MUTANT AFFAIRS. As usual, despite the constant surveillance of CCTV cameras and patrols by the DC metro police and federal security, someone had still managed to tag the sign during the night, using spray paint to cover *Affairs* with the word *Abominations*.

The third-floor front suite, with a view of the White House, belonged to the secretary. Alicia Vargas—former Secret Service bodyguard to the previous president, now employed by DOMA as unofficial bodyguard and thoroughly official executive assistant to the secretary—strode down the elegant wood hallway and, with a pro forma knock, opened the door to her boss's office.

The room was exquisitely furnished; whatever else you could say about Henry McCoy, DSC, PhD, he had excellent taste. At the moment, he was also hanging upside down from the suitably reinforced chandelier, thoroughly enjoying the latest issue of the *Economist*.

Alicia was a lovely woman, the kind you'd expect to be chairing a PTA meeting, with a remarkable knack for blending into a crowd. She was as professionally turned out as her boss, although her suit, while a quality design, was off-the-rack, and his wholly bespoke Savile Row. The major difference was that hers was cut to hide the SIG Sauer automatic she still wore in a belt holster, while his suit was built around a six-foot, nearly three-hundred-pound, immensely athletic body completely covered in rich blue fur.

He had fangs, too—a mouthful. And claws that became quite evident when he neglected to keep his nails properly trimmed. He had a leonine mane of hair which was a discernibly darker hue than his body, swept elegantly back from a dramatic widow's peak, as well as sweeping side whiskers that bore an uncanny resemblance to one of the major villains of a world-famous comic book. He could bench press twice his body weight without trying, had reflexes that were almost a match for Alicia's—because *she* was a mutant too, just not quite so obvious a manifestation, thank God—and agility that could send the most madcap of monkeys back to school. He was, in fact, everything implied by the nickname he'd been given back in college—the *Beast*.

McCoy could also speak a score of languages fluently, was one of the more respected genetic anthropologists on the planet, a demon dancer, and apparently an even better lover. He enjoyed fine wines with his brother, the Jungian psychiatrist, preferred cooking to eating out because he was a better chef than most professionals, and had an unfortunate weakness for karaoke bars. His speaking voice was wonderful, but his singing tended to recall cats congregating on a backyard fence.

What endeared him most to Alicia, however, was the fact that he needed reading glasses. He wore a classic pair, perched on his rather dramatic nose.

McCoy raised an eyebrow over the spine of the magazine as she snared his jacket off the back of his chair.

"The White House called," she told him. "They've moved up the meeting. Something to do with Bolivar Trask."

"Hmnh" was Hank's only comment as he flipped through a crisp, confined somersault to land on the floor with feline grace. He frowned as he slipped on his shoes—Alicia was the only one who ever saw those reactions, the only one he truly trusted—he'd much prefer to go barefoot. His feet were designed for it, not for being strapped in. But people were spooked enough by his appearance as it was; dressing respectably was the first, big—necessary—step towards winning their tolerance, if not their acceptance.

"Your car's waiting downstairs," she told him as he donned his jacket, taking a moment for their usual exit ritual as she smoothed the suit across his shoulders and straightened his tie.

Then, twitching her own suit jacket to make sure her gun was in ready reach, she followed him out the door.

Another surprise awaited Hank and Alicia when they checked in at the White House: the meeting originally scheduled for the Oval Office had been moved downstairs to the Situation Room. It was a small and select meeting: the president, his national security advisor, the director of the FBI, a pair of uniforms, one representing the Joint Chiefs, the other the National Security Council, and the secretary of Homeland Security, Bolivar Trask.

Big as Hank was, Trask matched him in every dimension, tall and broad and radiating the impression that he remained as powerful and dangerous now as he was in his youth. He'd come out of Detroit, served a career in Army Special Ops before confounding everyone when he turned in his papers and built a new life for himself in disaster management. Trask had barely made it out of high school, yet over the course of his two careers he had amassed more practical knowledge than a roomful of certified academics, possessing an eclectic mix of street smarts and on-the-job training. He was a brilliant manager, as gifted in the military and defense aspects of his department as the civil, and seemed soundly determined to protect the country both from natural disasters and terrorist threats.

"Sorry I'm late, Mr. President," Hank apologized, as he strode into the darkened room. Display screens were already active, filling the wall at the far end of the room, where everyone at the table could easily see them.

President David Cockrum indicated the open chair to his left. "Have a seat, Henry. Sorry for catching you short, but things have been happening."

Trask sat opposite McCoy, at the president's right hand. From everyone's body language, McCoy knew this was Bolivar's briefing.

"Homeland Security was tracking Magneto . . ."

With that cue, surveillance images appeared on the display wall, showing a tall and handsome man of naturally aristocratic bearing. Sometime in the recent past, he must have grown a beard, neatly trimmed of course, which gave him the air of a Shakespearean warrior king in exile. *A lion in winter,* McCoy thought, with a pang of regret at the promise of brighter, younger days, and all that might have been.

Trask was speaking, using a laser pointer to highlight his bullet points with the appropriate image: "Homeland Security has been coordinating with all the relevant alphabet agencies—CIA, NSA, DIA—plus their counterparts overseas. As you can see, we got hits on him in Lisbon, Geneva, Montreal. NavSat lost him crossing the border. But we did get a consolation prize . . ."

Different screen now, the biggest in the array, with a crawl at the bottom to inform everyone that they were watching real-time streaming video. The setting was obviously an interrogation room of some sort, with a double-door security airlock and double-paned observation glass, suggesting something more appropriate to a biohazard containment facility than a standard lockup. There were two figures in view, interrogator and prisoner. No guards—that could be seen..

The object of all this attention lounged in a chair as though she owned the place, and hadn't a care in the world. She was naked and flaunted a perfect body as proudly as any other woman would a new designer gown. Her skin was as blue as McCoy's fur, her hair the color of blood, swept straight back from her forehead and face to end in an impossibly precise blunt cut at the base of her neck. Her body was decorated with ridges, down the arms, the breasts and belly and groin, with a scattering along her legs. Hank had always been curious whether they were decorative or had some functional value, and the scientist in his soul wondered, *How hard would it be to get a cell sample?* Her eyes were a gleaming chrome yellow, the same vibrant hue that van Gogh tried to capture in his paintings around the town of Arles: the flower called rape. They glowed in the dark, Hank knew, when the rest of her became effectively invisible. The way they flicked from camera to camera, the way she allowed herself the smallest of smiles, told Hank that the woman knew she was being broadcast, and probably who was watching.

She called herself Mystique. She'd been by Magneto's side for almost as long as he had been in active opposition to Charles Xavier. No one had ever been able to fathom the precise nature of their relationship, beyond the obvious fact that she was utterly devoted to him and to his cause, and that Magneto cared for her as he did for few others in his life, past or present.

She was a metamorph, a shape-changer able to transform herself with a thought into any other human form she pleased. What they were viewing now was supposedly her default form; it was certainly the skin she was most comfortable wearing, the one she always returned to.

The main screen was complemented by an array of lesser display windows, showing different perspectives on the scene. Looking at the one aimed at her eyes, McCoy couldn't shake the sense that she was looking right back at him through the lens. That she could actually *see* him.

With an inner wrench, he turned his attention back to Trask, who was still speaking.

"We picked her up breaking into the FDA, of all places."

"Do you know who she was imitating?" the president asked in an aside to Hank. "Secretary Trask."

That must have been a sight to behold, Hank thought, and almost as if he'd heard the comment aloud, Trask cued an archival shot of the scene in question, showing Mystique before, and then right after, the takedown. Hank looked from the man himself to the screen and back again—as did everyone else present. The match was flawless.

"Yes, sir," Hank told the president. "She can do that."

"Not anymore, she can't," Trask said with pardonable satisfaction. Smart as she may have been—and that reputation was as well-deserved as it was formidable— he had found a way to nail her: "We got her."

"You think your walls can hold her, Bolivar?"

"We have some new walls, Henry," came the reply, with the hint of an edge. Trask's tone indicated that he thought Hank's question was utterly foolish. What was the point of taking the woman if you didn't have a means to keep her? "We'll be a step ahead this time."

Hank was about to press him on that point when Trask gestured with his remote and added sound to the streaming video from the interrogation room.

"Raven," the agent with her said softly, and was ignored.

"Raven," he repeated, "I'm talking to you."

She flicked her eyes dismissively. "I don't answer to my slave name."

"It's on your birth certificate, Raven Darkhölme. Or has he convinced you that you don't have a family anymore?"

No one needed to be told which "he" was being referred to, but the question did provoke a response. Mystique swung around in her chair to face the agent. Her look promised mayhem. The interrogator took it in stride.

"My family tried to kill me, you pathetic meat-sack."

"So now *he's* your family?"

She sniffed, haughty as a queen, and half turned away, striking a glamour pose that flaunted her body to him and to the cameras.

McCoy heard a mutter from down the table: "My God, it's like watching cable!"

The interrogator's tone hardened.

"Are you playing games with me?"

She gave the agent a smile as overtly sexy as her pose, and then morphed into a mirror image of him.

"What makes you say that?"

"Is it worth it, all this, to protect him?"

"You *really* want to know where he is?" He didn't need to reply. He didn't have to, the answer went without saying. "All right then, I'll tell you . . ."

She leaned forward. Inviting the interrogator to meet her halfway.

Hank's eyes flicked a warning to Trask. Both men were on the same wavelength. This was too soon, too easy, *way* too good to be true. Trask already had a phone in hand, a direct line to the holding cell, but he never got the chance to warn him.

Even as Hank heard the ringing phone through the main display, Mystique struck, grabbing the interrogator by the ears and delivering a vicious head-butt that would have him in the hospital for the better part of a week with a wicked concussion.

Now the previously unseen guards made their entrance, hard and fast and in no mood to play. Their adversary was faster than they were, stronger as well, likely more skilled in the martial arts. She'd slipped herself free of every restraint, making her hands momentarily boneless so that they'd slid loose from her cuffs. But the room was too small and suddenly filled wall-to-wall with muscle. She had no room to maneuver, and when she tried morphing into one of them Hank saw that they'd been biotagged. External surveillance systems told the team outside who was who so that they always knew who to hit.

It was a gallant, desperate struggle that reminded Hank too much of a wild animal being caged. It was doomed from the start and quickly over.

Trask shut off the feed.

"One down," he said quietly, "one to go."

Hank stared at him. "You know her capture will only provoke Magneto."

"So? Do we forgo the capture of terrorist lieutenants because we're scared of their boss? If that's our policy, why don't we just hand over the country to him and be done with it?"

Trask gestured to the screen.

"Henry, be real here. You *see* what we're dealing with."

"All the more reason to be diplomatic."

"You expect me to negotiate with these people?" asked the president pointedly.

Hank's first reaction was a thankfully unspoken thought: *And* what *people precisely would you be referring to, sir? The "terrorist" mutants or mutants in general?*

Aloud, he chose to follow his own advice and speak diplomatically: "All due respect, sir, I thought that's why you appointed me."

Hank shook his head, realizing from the look on the president's face and the way the other man's eyes shifted ever so slightly that the venue for this meeting hadn't been any last-minute change, nor had its earlier start.

"This isn't why you called me here, is it, sir?"

The president shook his head. "No," he said, his tone conveying what was surely meant to sound like a sincere and heartfelt apology. He slid a file towards McCoy.

"This is what she was after."

Hank used a ritual with his glasses to regain his inner composure: he removed the bifocals, puffed on the lenses, wiping them clear on the thick and luxurious fur protruding from his cuffs.

When he was done reading, when the axis of the

Earth had finished shifting beneath him, he didn't know whether he felt rage or terror, but assumed it was a decent measure of both. He pressed his hands together, resting his face against them, like a man assuming an attitude of prayer, determined not to allow them to tremble and hoping his voice wouldn't betray him when he spoke.

"Is it viable?" he asked.

"We believe it is, yes."

"Do you have any idea of the level of impact this will have on the mutant community?"

The president nodded, choosing his words very carefully.

"Yes, I do. That's precisely why we need some of your 'diplomacy' now."

Hank closed his eyes, his inner child hoping against hope that this was merely some wild flight of fancy, and that when he opened them again he'd be back in his old room at Xavier's, young and carefree, with no thoughts for the day ahead other than charming the daylights out of Jean and teaching Ororo how to slow dance.

And then came a darker image, of a movie he'd watched far too often, one to complement the books and files he'd committed to memory while researching his first doctoral thesis, which hadn't been on medicine of any kind, but history. In 1942, there'd been a conference in Wannsee Villa, a resort outside Berlin, chaired by Reinhard Heydrich, who'd go down in history as "Hangman Heydrich" (his fellow Nazis called him "the Blond Butcher"). He was then Deputy Reichsführer, a handsome, powerfully commanding presence who everyone assumed would claim the leadership of the

Third Reich if and when Hitler passed from the scene. He'd gathered the top bureaucrats in the Reich, from all the key departments of state, and in a meeting that lasted ninety minutes, they'd resolved the "Jewish question" in Europe. In terms both barbaric in their racial virulence and damnably chilling in their institutional banality, these men signed the death warrant of millions.

One or two among them weren't comfortable with the idea, one may have vaguely considered opposing it, but in the end the vote was unanimous. The choice was stark and terrible: consign the Jews to their fate, or share it.

A part of Hank knew there was no comparison between that room and this. None of the men and women around this table considered themselves bigots, or monsters—if anything, far too many people still considered the likes of *Hank* the true monsters—but neither then did the men at Wannsee. They were simply trying to deal once and for all with a perceived threat to the survival of their country, their culture, their race.

And for the first time in his adult life, he found himself facing what had previously been utterly unthinkable, alien to everything he'd been taught and believed—that Magneto, who'd been a victim of the decision made that day at Wannsee, who'd grown to manhood in the most terrible of those death camps, Auschwitz, might actually be right.

X

"Power corrupts," Charles Xavier told his ethics class, "and absolute power corrupts absolutely. This is a lesson every one of us must learn and live. Why? Because we are mutants.

"Will it be for the greater good," he continued, "or personal, destructive, and tyrannical? This is a question we must all ask ourselves. Why? Because we are mutants."

Kitty answered him with a sigh and briefly considered relaxing her hold on her power, just for a heartbeat, her phased form remaining at rest while the Earth continued merrily spinning on its axis. Just that little burst would put her outside the building. If she held her breath for a couple of minutes, she could be miles away.

It was tempting, but it would be wrong. Like it or not, responsibility had become her second nature. She had Xavier to thank for that.

"Riiight," she agreed. "Power corrupts and absolute power corrupts absolutely."

Xavier shook his head. He didn't like it when she was intellectually lazy.

"Kitty, that's not an argument, it's a cliché and a generalization. And like all generalizations, it's only partly true. Unfortunately, students"—he expanded the colloquy to embrace the entire class—"there are no absolutes when it comes to questions of ethics. For psychics, such as myself . . ." As he said this, Kitty felt his thoughts jump into her mind: *and as well for those who can walk through walls.* She got the message, sitting straight up while her cheeks flushed tomato scarlet, pursing her lips in embarrassment at being busted. Xavier continued, ". . . this presents a particular problem. When is it acceptable to use our powers and when do we cross that invisible line that turns us into tyrants over our fellow men?"

"Professor," Kitty countered, seizing the opening with a question that was actually pertinent, yet also just that faintest bit naughty, "if the line is invisible, how do we know when we've crossed it?"

Some of the others grinned, and even Xavier permitted himself an itsy-bitsy quirk of the lips that might be interpreted as a smile. His game of choice had always been chess, but Kitty's was tennis, and she served to win.

Behind the professor, a flat-screen display revealed a hospital room, together with a legend that identified the source as the Muir Isle Research Facility, Scotland. It was an isolation cubicle, marked with the international biohazard trefoil and an *M* stamped in the middle to indicate mutant biohazard. A man lay on the single bed, clearly not in the best of health. Beside him stood a woman, Dr. Moira MacTaggart, old friend of Xavier's, a former lover, and partner in many of his current researches.

"This case was forwarded to me by a colleague, Dr. MacTaggart."

Everyone took notes. Kitty couldn't help sneaking an envious peek over at Weezie, who was merely running a pair of fingertips along each line of her notebook page. In their wake, every word Xavier spoke was transcribed automatically from her ear to the page. Although it seemed to be going smoothly now, it wasn't always as easy as that; when she got distracted, Weezie's transcription power tapped into her thoughts and her notes became a stream-of-consciousness exercise that put Joyce's *Finnegans Wake* to shame. Then, of course, it was all hands to the rescue among her best friends at school, Kitty included, to try to separate out what was *supposed* to be there. This morning, though, she looked totally on track.

Dr. MacTaggart was speaking, the screen obligingly providing subtitles for those who found her Highland accent a bit hard to fathom.

"The man you see here," she said, indicating her patient, "was born with no higher-level brain functions. His organs and nervous system function normally, but he has no consciousness to speak of. That has been confirmed both by the most comprehensive medical scans available to us, and telepathic examination as well."

Xavier paused the transmission.

"What if," he asked the class, "we could transfer the consciousness of one person, say a father of four with terminal cancer, into the body of this man?"

Kitty couldn't help muttering, "Sounds like someone wants to play God."

Weezie giggled.

Xavier ignored them both.

"How are we to . . ."

He paused, looking off to the side for just a moment, then tried to move on.

"How are we to decide what is within the range of ethical behavior and what is . . ."

His voice trailed off and this time he wasn't the only person to look out the window. When class began it had been a bright, sunny afternoon; now it was completely overcast, dark with clouds that were growing thicker and angrier by the moment.

"We'll continue tomorrow," Xavier announced suddenly, to the surprise of very few. You didn't have to be a student at Xavier's very long to figure out what moments like this were all about. "Class is dismissed."

Charles tried reaching her telepathically as he rolled his wheelchair through the halls, but as was usually the case when her powers were this active, there was so much charged electrical energy coursing through her system that it coated her mind with a sleet storm of psychic static. Even the fleeting contact necessary to determine her location threatened a nasty headache.

By the time he left the shelter of the doorway, wind was whipping enthusiastically across the Great Lawn and the scattered figures of students were racing for cover. He could taste the ozone in the air; it made his skin crawl.

The cause of the sudden weather change stood alone, staring off over the trees, so lost in thought she had no idea what was happening around her.

"Ororo," Xavier called quietly, when he'd approached close enough for her to hear him and not be startled. Taking Storm by surprise at moments like this, he risked a close encounter with one of her lightning bolts. Not a happy experience. "The forecast was for *sunny* skies."

She blinked, pulling back to herself, reintegrating both halves of her mind. Storm glanced upwards, her shoulders twitching with the sudden realization of what she'd unwittingly done.

"Oh," she said, and then, underneath her breath, *"Shit."* And finally, "I'm sorry."

She turned to face him, a courtesy, acknowledgment that movement wasn't easy for him. Her eyes had turned as silver as her hair, no sign of iris or pupil, indicating that her power was under her active control.

As smoothly as it had arrived, but far more quickly, the supercell above the mansion went away, restoring the lovely day that had been before.

"I needn't be a psychic to see that something's bothering you," he said.

There was a stone bench nearby, and she sat down so they could converse more as equals.

"In the village where I grew up," she said, referring to the wilds of northern Kenya, among the Masai, although Ororo herself was no part of that tribe, "when droughts were at their worst, I brought the rain. My powers were seen as a gift."

"As I remember, they were worshipped."

There was much left unsaid between them, although Charles knew the story. Ororo'd had no one to teach her, and she'd learned the use and extent—and the price—of her abilities the hard way, with the toll exacted on the very people she sought to help. She'd had to learn through experience that when she generated rain in one place, she ran the risk of taking it from somewhere else; a drought easily ended might as a consequence *trigger* one elsewhere, and ultimately do far more harm than good. Such a harsh lesson for such a young child!

"Yes, they were." Unspoken: *and so was* I. "And yet, here, Charles, in what calls itself the most advanced and enlightened society on the planet, 'home of the brave, land of the *free*' "—she'd clearly reversed the order deliberately—"we keep our gifts a secret."

"Why don't we go inside?" Xavier suggested.

She nodded, stood and followed, and both of them noticed—far off in the distance—the faintest ripple of thunder across a clear and cloudless sky.

"Magneto's a fugitive," she said as they crossed the threshold into the main foyer. "We have a mutant in the cabinet, a president who campaigned on mutant under-standing and tolerance—so why are we still hiding?"

"We are *not* hiding."

"Professor," Ororo objected, "we live behind stone walls, we keep our true identities a secret!"

"As a precaution, Ororo. I have to protect my students." Unspoken, reflexive, came another thought from Ororo: *"Protect them" from what? Why must we be so afraid?* "You know that."

She looked at a couple of passing students, then back at her mentor and friend.

"Charles," she said, "we can't be students forever." *We have to learn—we have to be* trusted—*to protect ourselves.*

"Ororo, I haven't thought of you as my 'student' for years. In fact . . ."

They reached his office.

". . . I've been considering that you might take my place someday."

Storm wondered if she had heard him correctly.

"But I thought Scott . . ."

Xavier shook his head. "Scott has taken Jean's death so hard." His thoughts now came through to Ororo as plain as if he were speaking aloud: *Some are tempered by adversity, others are broken, no matter how much we may wish otherwise. Time has not healed this wound.*

Despite all our efforts, it's as though Scott himself had died with her.

"As for Logan"—and they both smiled, simpatico in both their affection for the man and their mutual awareness of his shortcomings—"well, Logan is a loner. He has neither interest nor real aptitude, not for this."

Having nothing to say, Ororo kept silent.

"Things *are* better out there, Ororo—and certainly much better by far in America than in other parts of the globe. But you of all people should know how fast the weather changes." He offered a playful grin and surprised her with his next comment. "What's that Mel Brooks line, from *The Twelve Chairs*? 'Hope for the best, expect the worst.' "

She'd shared popcorn and wine with him and Hank McCoy and Scott and Jean, watching those classic comedies, and had damn near split her sides with laughter. She completed the couplet: " 'You may be Tolstoy, or Fanny Hurst.' "

Then, more seriously, responding to the undertone beneath the banter, "Charles, you know something you're not telling."

He opened the door and she found the answer rising from one of the big, comfy chairs in front of the desk.

"Hank," she said in greeting, following Xavier into the room.

"Ororo," McCoy replied.

The hug she gave him matched her strength to his and was filled with very real affection from them both. It was like snuggling with a lion, and she grinned wide, wondering if he knew how many girls at the school wove their fantasies around his silken coat and romantic hero manner. Not for nothing were DVDs of *Beauty and the Beast* among the most popular in the library.

She gave his side whiskers a tug: "I just *love* what you've done with your hair."

He gave hers a flick. "You too—what there is of it." What once had fallen most of the way down her back now barely touched her shoulders, and she was considering cutting it back farther still. Seasons change, so could she.

Hank and Xavier shook hands, and Ororo's eyes were drawn to one of the photos on the wall, of the original class of students. She couldn't help noticing the sight of herself sitting so stiff and formal beside a girl whose hair looked like it had been dipped in blood-hued flame. Jean in her Goth phase, which had lasted barely a semester before she got bored; *she got bored so easily back then,* Ororo remembered. She was so desperately hungry to learn—they all were. *Know the world as the key to knowing thyself.* Had they ever truly been that young? And what could have possessed them to wear those dreadful costumes in public? Thing was, and this she had to admit to herself, back then they considered them the height of cool. New millennium, new attitudes, something else that had changed.

"Thank you for seeing me on such short notice, Charles," McCoy told his mentor.

"You're always welcome here, Henry. You're a part of this place, as much as anyone."

"I have some news." This wasn't a social call.

"Erik?" Xavier asked, obviously fearing the worst.

It was the right impulse, just in the wrong direction. And again, Ororo thought: *Everything changes.*

"No"—McCoy shook his great, shaggy head—"although we're making progress on that front. Actually, Mystique was apprehended last week."

"They caught her?" He sounded so certain, but Ororo had her doubts.

Xavier took him at his word: "The question is, how will they keep her?"

"For the moment, that's Bolivar Trask's problem, thank God," Hank said. "I—"

"Who's the furball?" challenged a new arrival, from the doorway.

McCoy bristled. Storm knew he hadn't been fond of the nickname when he was a student here. But he'd also learned manners. "Henry McCoy. Secretary of Mutant Affairs."

"Right," Logan acknowledged, "the secretary." The way he said Hank's title, it wasn't a compliment. "Nice suit."

Hank held out his hand. Logan ignored it. Xavier sighed, mainly to himself. Not a great beginning.

Xavier said: "Hank, Logan is—"

"The Wolverine," Hank acknowledged. "I read the file." To Logan directly, "I hear you're quite the animal."

Logan sniffed. "Look who's talking."

Ororo was done watching this display of testosterone. She addressed Xavier: "Magneto's not going to be happy about Mystique."

"Hope your prison has plastic screws," offered Logan.

"Magneto isn't the problem," Hank told them. "At least, not our most pressing one."

He had their attention.

"A major pharmaceutical company has developed a . . . mutant antibody. A way to suppress the X-gene."

" 'Suppress'?" asked Logan after a very awkward silence.

Hank looked at him. "Permanently." Another, longer, silence while they digested the news. "They're calling it a 'cure.' "

Logan snorted in disgust, which took care of his opinion.

Ororo spoke up: "This is crazy. You can't cure being a mutant."

"Well, scientifically speaking—" Hank began, but she allowed him to get no further.

"Since when are we a disease? I've been called many things in my life, Henry, but a *disease*?" Raw rage and contempt laced her words.

"Ororo," Xavier said quietly, and then, when she didn't respond, "Storm!"

She looked at him.

"It's being announced right now."

X

"They've been called saints and sinners," announced Warren Worthington Jr. to the assembled crush of media. "They've committed atrocities and been the victims of atrocities themselves."

He stood hatless against the stiff breeze blowing into San Francisco Bay through the Golden Gate, in the shadow of the long-decommissioned prison of Alcatraz, with Kavita Rao, bundled far more snugly, standing a bit behind him on the dais.

"They've been labeled monsters, and not without reason," Worthington Jr. went on. "But these so-called monsters are people just like us. They are our fathers and mothers, our brothers and sisters—they are," and here, just for the briefest instant that only Kavita noticed, his voice caught, "our children. Their affliction is nothing more than a disease. A corruption of healthy cellular activity. Finally, there is hope. A way to eradicate their suffering and the suffering of those who love them."

He held up a slide of a DNA helix in one hand. And in the other, a photo of Kavita's long-time patient, young Jimmy.

"A few years ago, we found a mutant with the most extraordinary ability—to repress, and even *reverse,* the powers of those other mutants who came close to him. Now, after much research and experimentation, we've found the means for *all* mutants to get 'close' to him."

He set down the photos and held up a vial. He paused while the crowd before him erupted in flashbulbs. He didn't need his media advisor screaming through his ear-bug to know that with those words, every news channel on the spectrum had just gone live to this press conference. He wasn't just a sound bite on the evening news any longer, he was speaking to the whole world.

Among them, President Cockrum, watching with Bolivar Trask and others of his key staff in the Oval Office.

"This site," Worthington was saying, "which was once the world's most famous prison, will now be the source of *freedom* for mutants everywhere."

* * *

Among them, the students of the Xavier Institute, gathered in common rooms throughout the great mansion.

"Ladies and gentlemen," Worthington concluded, "I proudly present the answer to mutation. Finally, we have a *cure*!"

Rogue let out her breath, unaware that she'd been holding it all this while, trolling her gaze over the assemblage of students, noting how folks were sitting, what they were wearing. She was covered head to toe, a fact of life for a girl who could steal memories and lives with the slightest *accidental* touch. She licked her lips, remembering a moment like it had just happened, the taste of Bobby Drake when she'd kissed him, the delight she'd found when her breath puffed cold just like his. That taste hadn't been enough, and they'd tried again— he promising it would be all right, assuring her he wasn't scared, she wanting to believe, certain it would end badly. She was the one proven right.

Her eyes went to the TV, which had cut to a talking head recapping the announcement while they rustled up learned commentators, promising an in-depth interiew and analysis with author Laurie Garrett. Then, Rogue looked down at her hands, gloved as always. She made a face, glanced towards Soraya, sitting demurely by the window in her burqa. At least the Afghani girl covered herself up by choice, as an article of her faith. Rogue was stuck like this, she'd thought for forever.

But now—and her eyes rose once more to the screen—but *now* . . .

X

Storm looked ready to hit something, radiating a violent fury that seemed to impress even Logan, and Hank thought it was probably because it reminded the Wolverine of himself.

"Who would *want* this cure? I mean, what kind of coward would take it, just to fit in?"

Hank bristled ever so slightly.

"I understand your concerns, Ororo. For God's sake, that's why I'm here! But not all of us have such an easy time as others 'fitting in.' "

She looked at him, and the pain that showed in his eyes wholly belied the joking words that followed.

"*You* don't shed on the furniture."

"I'm sorry," she said. "I didn't mean it that way—"

"Don't apologize," Logan told her, sounding one small step removed from a snarl. "For all we know, the government helped cook this up. I mean, let's be rational for a second and consider the *civil liberties* side of things. Do parents have the right to impose this cure on their kids? Employers on their employees? Suppose someone decides mutants are a public safety issue and society's better off without 'em? Or better yet, let's turn the tables—if you can make a drug to erase the gene, how 'bout one to *create* it? You thought nukes were scary, folks, howzabout *us*? Why bomb an army when Storm can drown it? And what then, the feds decide—for our own 'protection'—maybe we belong on a reservation, where we're available if needed but can be kept isolated from the general population? Pandora's box has *nothing* on this."

"I can assure you," Hank said stiffly, defensively, because Logan's impassioned argument walked the same path as too many recent, increasingly heated, conversations between himself and Alicia Vargas, himself and his own soul, "the government has nothing to do with this."

Logan looked at him pityingly: "I've heard that before, bub."

"My boy," Hank snapped, provoked past caring about propriety, "I've been fighting for mutant rights since before you had claws!"

Logan looked to Ororo. "Did he just call me 'boy'?"

"*Enough.*" Hank apparently wasn't the only one short of patience. Xavier's voice was harder and flatter than he'd ever heard before. "All of you."

"Is it true?" Rogue suddenly asked from the doorway. "Can they . . . *cure* us?"

All of them exchanged looks, but Ororo was the first to answer. "No," she said flatly. She stepped towards Rogue, holding out her hands, offering all her strength and courage, sick with fury at the realization that it wouldn't be enough. "They can't 'cure' us. D'you want to know why, Marie? Because there's nothing to cure. You might as well cure Mozart of writing music, or daVinci of the ability to make machines, or Edison, or Archimedes, or Shakespeare."

She tried to take Rogue's hands, but the young girl pulled them away, flinching.

"Marie," Ororo said, in a tone that would not be denied. "*Nothing* is wrong with you. Or *any* of us, for that matter. You understand?"

She nodded, but Ororo knew that her words had fallen on rock. Rogue heard, but would not listen.

Ororo turned to Xavier, and this time the thunder outside wasn't shy. It came in a burst that shook the house like the end of the world, and the sunny day gave way to rain that fell in torrents.

She held his gaze and said, softly, "Guess you were right about the weather."

Chapter Four

The meeting started badly and then it went to hell.

Jack Stover held the mike and tried to keep at least a semblance of order. He looked like your classic Harley-riding outlaw biker: long-haired, bushy-bearded; massive in the body with a belly that was, surprisingly, mostly muscle spilling over his Levi's; a black singlet that showed off a torso and arms crowded with magnificent body art. Those who'd seen him at the beach knew every inch of him was covered, except for his face and hands and feet, making him Valle Soleada's very own "Illustrated Man." What was even more delightful was that the images always changed, because they were constantly being refreshed and played with by his wife, also a mutant, whose talent was painting on flesh.

Folks had gathered at the old Sea Breeze, on the boardwalk, and emotions were running hot.

". . . listen to me," Jack bellowed into his mike, making folks wince as he generated a wicked pulse of feedback. "*Listen* to me." He'd have better luck yelling at a typhoon, but he somehow persevered regardless. "This is about getting organized, bringing our complaints to the right people! The DMA won't take us seriously if—"

One of the razor-boys from up on the Heights cut in, "The DMA is bullshit!"

Jack ignored him. "We need to put together a committee and talk to the government!"

Someone else yelled, "Goddamn it, Jack, they want to *exterminate* us!"

Jack tried again. "The cure is *voluntary,* Louis. Nobody's talking about extermination."

"No one *ever* talks about it."

The rich and resonant voice filled the theater, making those six words sound like a call to arms.

"By all means," Magneto continued as he strode into view onstage, followed by a young man who took a position where he could watch the much older man's back, and who then proceeded to start flicking the lid of a Zippo lighter open and shut, open and shut, like he was channeling a pulp fiction bad guy. "Go about your lives. Ignore the signs all around you. And then, one day, when the air is still and the long night has finally fallen, they will come for you. And it is only then—"

Jack knew who he was, and what he could do, probably with less thought than anyone else would take to squash a bug. But this was his town, his family, and he was prepared to stand up for them, to the feds if he had to, and certainly to the world's most wanted mutant terrorist.

"Excuse me," he said, "this is supposed to be—"

Magneto cut Jack off with a warning smile, and addressed the hall as if *he* was the one who'd summoned them.

"It is only *then,*" he repeated, with emphasis, "you realize that while you were talking about organizing and committees, the extermination had already begun."

Jack was about to try again to reclaim the floor, when a flick of the igniter wheel sparked a flame from his lighter, and a gesture from Pyro intensified it to a white-hot flame.

Jack got the message and allowed his wife to draw him into the shadows as Magneto went on.

"Make no mistake, my brothers, *they* will draw first blood, *they* will force this cure upon us. *They* will steal away our future! The only question you must answer is this: What side are you on? Who will you stand with? The *humans*"—from him, that sounded like the dirtiest of words—"or with us?"

"You talk pretty tough for a guy in a cape."

Although Jack dressed the part of an outlaw, Callisto was the real deal, utterly hard-core, an urban legend from the catacombs of Manhattan to the Cali backcountry. She lived in her leathers, and her skin—like that of the gang who followed her—was painted with art and accented with piercings that would make any gangbanger worthy of the name appear modest by comparison. Rumor had it she'd almost been affiliated with Xavier back in the day, that she'd even been responsible for the loss of the use of his legs, but that was a place nobody went, to her face. Not more than once, anyway. She kept her past a private thing, and at present she placed herself on the cutting edge of mutant rights. If anyone did harm to a mutant, they maybe had to answer to her. After all, the X-Men couldn't be everywhere.

Except, unlike the X-Men, there was no mercy in her.

The only mark all of her gang had in common was the Greek letter omega on their necks, signifying the end of things. In the case of her Marauders, that applied to anyone who actively did a mutant harm—in other words, it would be the end of them.

"You're so proud of being a mutant, old man, where's your mark?"

She wasn't a bit afraid of him. Pyro, not knowing any better, started forward, only to be held back by a signal from Magneto.

"I have been marked once, my dear, and let me assure you . . ."

He wrenched up his sleeve, with a convulsive violence that spoke volumes to the crowd about the depth of his wounds and the hatred that sprang from them, revealing the number etched along his forearm.

". . . Proclaim your loyalties as you will, no needle will ever touch my skin again."

Callisto shrugged, not so easily impressed as others present.

"Hey," called Pyro, "you know who you're talking to?"

The withering glare that she answered him with made clear that whatever she might think of Magneto, his companion didn't rate any higher than a bug on her windscreen.

"I know that you can control fire and he controls metal. And I know by my count there's a hundred sixty-five mutants in the room, and not a one of 'em above Class Three. Other than you two." And, unspoken but plain, herself.

"So you have talents." Magneto sounded intrigued.

"That, and more."

Magneto pressed on. "You can sense other mutants, and their powers?" Callisto nodded. He was delighted, in his restrained, magisterial manner, like he'd just found a much-desired surprise beneath the Christmas tree. "A living cerebro, bless my soul," he muttered, mainly to himself. "How utterly foolish of you, Charles, to let *this* one slip through your fingers." And then, so that she could hear, "Could you *locate* one for me?"

"If I wanted to," she answered.

"Trust me," Magneto assured her, "you want to."

He turned to leave. He didn't ask for recruits. The only ones who mattered were the ones who followed without being asked.

X

Scott travelled as far as he could by bike, and went the rest of the way on foot. He couldn't remember when he'd last had a decent meal, but he knew he hadn't slept an unhaunted night since Jean died.

Alkali Lake hadn't changed. Scott had assumed—as subsequent rainfall and snowmelt ate away at what remained of the dam—that the lake would be well on its way back to its original state of being, a wild and untamed river. But Fate wasn't done joking. Turned out there was a sharp bend about a mile downstream from the dam that formed a natural choke point, preventing the water from draining completely. The level had dropped by more than half since the breach, but had finally reached a kind of equilibrium that still left the industrial complex beneath the dam's face significantly underwater. Worse, the clearing where the *Blackbird* took off, where Jean had died, remained likewise buried.

He looked haggard, his lean features gaunt, as he stood at the water's edge, staring at nothing.

Once more, he heard her call.

"Stop," he pleaded. "Stop it."

But she wouldn't.

"Scott," he heard, in the voice she once used to call him to bed, "please. Help me!"

That was the last straw.

With a cry torn from the deepest part of him—*"Jean!"*—Scott tore off his visor and opened his eyes wide.

Scarlet glory erupted through the air, as though someone had opened a window to the surface of the sun, and raw concussive energy gouged a momentary trench directly to the bottom of the lake, parting the waters like the hands of God through the Red Sea. Unchecked for once, wholly unrestrained, the bolt hammered at the rock along the opposite shore, following Scott's line of sight so that when his gaze flicked towards one of the remaining towers of the dam, the entire structure shuddered with the initial impact, as though struck by a celestial battering ram. Then, with breathtaking suddenness, it shattered, not into rocks and boulders but powder, allowing the implacable beam to strike the mountainsides beyond.

And then, just like that, the beam was gone, and the only sign marking its passage through the lake was the crash of water filling space, coupled with the rise of vapor.

Scott collapsed to his knees, although even then—spent and exhausted as he was, in spirit and mind and body—he still reflexively groped for his glasses and snugged them back into place.

He was done. He couldn't even cry, not tears anyway. Wherever the optic blasts came from inside his head, they annihilated his tears the moment they were formed. He could feel the ache of sobbing, he could give voice to his grief, he just couldn't physically cry.

Then the water was stirring, almost boiling as he rose to his feet for a better look.

As the display built to a crescendo, water shot skyward in a magnificent fountain easily a hundred meters across, rising three or four times that into the air, better than a thousand feet, generating a shock wave that bent the lodgepole pines around Scott almost double and knocked him off his feet.

He picked himself up, stunned, senses kicking into proper gear, reacting now from his training and experience as Cyclops. And he found himself facing a radiance as welcome and comforting as the morning sun.

"Jean?" He didn't believe it as he spoke, certain that somewhere along the way he'd stumbled headlong into madness, and he was beholding what he yearned for rather than what was.

Her laughter convinced him otherwise.

He could feel her in his heart, the special rapport that had always joined them, casting its warmth throughout his soul, spring arriving to a realm too long beset by the cruelest of winters.

She was fire.

She was life incarnate, in all its glory.

She was his love.

And the smile she gave him when she heard that thought proved it beyond all doubt.

"Scott," Jean called, laughing with delight at the sight of him, yet still skittish to somehow find herself alive once more. Those last moments were still vivid in her thoughts. The wall of water had struck like it was made of steel, shattering her on contact; she didn't even have a chance to drown. Everything was over in an instant.

Or so she'd thought.

"How?" he asked, reaching out in surprise to her hair, which now fell in glossy waves to the small of her back.

"Dunno," she told him truthfully.

And for a long while there were no more words, nothing at all save for two lovers holding each other close, savoring the joy that comes with finding your heart's desire. Neither had ever been more happy, or at peace.

Jean pulled back, just a little.

"I want to see your eyes," she told him, reaching for his glasses. "Take these off."

"Jean—don't!"

She shook her head. "It'll be all right."

"You've seen what my optic blasts can do. You know these glasses and my visor are the only things that can control them!"

"Trust me," she said. "*I* can control them."

She laid a palm against his cheek, and he couldn't help leaning into it. Smiling in that special way that was for him alone, Jean slipped her hand along the line of his jaw, her forehead creasing with concern at how harshly the last few years had dealt with him, stroking the curve of his ear in a way that made him tremble.

She thought her own heart would crack when he brushed his lips against hers, and wanted to cry to the Heavens that he didn't have to worry, that there was nothing he could do to hurt her. Instead, she returned the kiss, both of them eager for more.

"No more glasses, Scott," she said, as she gently

plucked them from his face, "no more fear. I want to see your eyes."

They were tightly closed.

"Open them. Please. You can't hurt me."

He did, because she asked, because she knew at bedrock that he would always trust her, without hesitation or question, because she held dominion over the best part of him.

Nothing happened.

She'd put a telekinetic film over his eye sockets, configured by her thoughts to the same resonance frequency as the ruby quartz crystal of his lenses, holding in check the power within more easily than the glasses ever did.

"They say," she told him, "the eyes are the windows to the soul."

He couldn't hide a bit of bitterness: "Imagine what that says about me?"

Jean would have none of it: "Yours, like your soul, my love, are beautiful."

Looking into Jean's eyes reminded Scott of staring up at the stars, back before his power manifested, when he was a kid, with a kid's dreams, when he could see the world through normal eyes. In that moment, he knew he beheld forever, as rich with endless possibilities as it was with mysteries. And, unbidden, jarring, a warning: *Danger.*

One kiss begat another, each caress built on the one before, stoking a passion more intense than either had ever known. They surfed the crest of a tsunami, a wave that would engulf the world, where one misstep would mean oblivion, and neither cared.

They were happy, and they wanted it to last forever.

Then, the light in Jean's eyes turned to fire.

They opened wide, her lips turning from the latest kiss to an O of alarm, shared in that perfect moment by Scott. Something basic had changed, and neither knew what would come next, nor how to cope.

Scott started to shiver, his skin like the corona of a star boiling off excess plasma.

He looked into the eyes of the woman he loved and saw something that had never been before, that had never even been suspected, and he knew what was coming, both now and in the days ahead.

And because it was his turn, because he knew what it would mean to her, he gave her a smile, the one that came to him when he realized this was the woman he loved and that, now and forever, she would love him. He gave her trust, he gave her strength, he gave her courage.

Not forgiveness, though—because for him, there was nothing to forgive.

Then the world went white.

X

Two thousand miles away, Charles Xavier screamed.

For Logan, it was a spike through the skull, a lance of pain not even his healing factor could mitigate.

He threw himself out into the hallway, staggering because his head was so screwed up he couldn't walk straight. He heard cries and whimpers, and more than a few sobs, from every direction. Making his way through the rapidly crowding halls, he passed students by the score, some holding their heads with pain, a few nauseous to the point of vomiting. All were scared, demanding answers he didn't have or comfort he was ill-equipped to offer.

Ororo caught up to him at the base of the Grand Staircase. She had farther to come, from her attic loft, but she could always move faster.

"What happened?" she demanded.

"No clue," he replied, and bulled his way into Xavier's study.

"Professor," Ororo called, while simultaneously from Logan, "You okay?"

He was sitting at his desk, pale as the sheet of paper held in trembling hands.

"I'm fine," he assured them, although neither believed it. Logan could smell blood, and a quick glance at the trash can revealed a badly stained handkerchief that Xavier had used to wipe clean his bloody nose. Forebrain hemorrhages, Logan knew, because he made it his business to catalogue the strengths and weaknesses of people who mattered, and of those he may one day have to fight. A major sign of trouble in a telepath.

"You need to get to Alkali Lake," Xavier ordered, in a tone he rarely ever used with the two of them. It mandated absolute, immediate obedience, no back talk, no bullshit. *"Now!"*

They went.

X

They got the *Blackbird* prepped and airborne in record time. Ororo took the plane suborbital, shooting almost straight up once they cleared the launch bay, arcing north by west as they cleared the atmosphere along a track and at a speed that would bring them to their destination in barely a quarter hour.

Neither said a word during the ascent. Ororo was busy piloting, while Logan struggled not to lose what remained of last night's dinner. The intensity behind Xavier's command had been such that there'd been no time for uniforms. They'd departed wearing the clothes on their backs.

"Shit," Logan grumped as he dropped into the copilot's seat.

"You don't want to go back to Alkali Lake," Ororo noted.

He said nothing at first, but instead rubbed his fingers over the space between the knuckles where his claws were housed. So much of his life was bound up in that place: It was there Logan had become the Wolverine. It was there he'd found a place and purpose greater than himself. And there he'd found the woman who made it all worthwhile, who had owned him from the moment their eyes met, only to lose her, knowing that she loved another man more.

He figured his answer was too obvious to be spoken aloud. Instead, as Ororo canted the nose downward for reentry, he asked: "Do you?"

"No," she said plainly. "I don't."

The hull heated with atmospheric friction and bucked like a mule as the Blackbird started the transition to the deeper atmosphere. Logan busied himself with his harness, growing less thrilled with every incident of turbulence.

"You know," Storm said, "if you ever want to talk . . ."

"Oh yeah," he retorted, "absolutely. That's what I want."

The look she tossed his way spoke volumes.

Damn, he thought, *she's a lot less of a princess than when I first rolled in the door. Still a long way from "just plain folks," but she's got possibilities.*

"Look," he said, the best he would offer in explanation, "talk is not what I do."

Her sigh was even more devastating then the look.

"Right," she said, her tone assuring him that this conversation was most definitely not finished. "Same old Logan."

He wasn't, really, any more than she was the "same old Storm." But the oldest habits are the hardest to kick.

One of the glass panels on the flight control console generated a schematic map of the valley and the lake. As they continued their descent, and their scanning array got down to business, a dot of light began pulsing. Logan didn't need coordinates to pinpoint the location. It was within spitting distance of where Jean had died.

" 'Ro?" he began to say, intending to make amends. But she didn't give him the chance, throwing the *Blackbird* into a tight descending spiral that pinned him to his chair and made him suddenly wonder if she was going to land the damn aircraft right on its pointy nose.

"Hold on," she told him, after the fact, which was just about as unnecessary a command as he'd ever been given.

She flattened out at a hundred meters, shifting to vertical flight mode and skimming the treeline like they were flying a helicopter. Logan had taken his turn in the simulator; if the need ever arose, he could take the controls. But with Storm it was different; she handled the plane as if it were part of her. She could dance it through maneuvers the others wouldn't dream of trying—except maybe Scott. He was as much a natural flier as she was and the only one to ever match her skill in the air.

Unfortunately, there was no sign of the ground. Below thirty meters everything was shrouded in fog, for as far as the eye could see, from one end of the valley to the other.

"We got nowhere to land," Logan commented.

Without a word, Ororo's eyes went momentarily white and, just like that, the fogbank melted obligingly away, revealing that they were right where they wanted to be.

Eyes normal again, she cocked an eyebrow at him.

"Thanks," he said.

"Anytime." Smooth as could be, without even a bump, she eased the ebony aircraft down from the sky. "In preparation for landing, please restore your seats to their upright and locked position, store all carry-on items and tray tables, and make sure your seat belts are securely fastened."

He gave her a look; she gave him back a smile.

The moment passed. They got ready for business.

With his first step off the ramp, Logan knew it was bad. Every sense screamed alarm—the air smelled wrong, the ground felt wrong. There were no natural sounds, nothing to indicate the passing of a breeze between the trees, or water lapping against the shore. Not the slightest hint of animals of any kind. Logan wasn't surprised at the last; the part of him that was most like them was shrieking to flee this haunted, accursed place. And Ororo, whose sensitivity to the world around her was just as acute, seemed spooked as well.

Even the crunch of boots on snow was strangely muted, reminding Logan of an anechoic chamber that deadened every sound.

Something caught his attention, right at the edge of his peripheral vision, tumbling end-over-end as though possessing a personal exemption from the laws of gravity—and of motion as well, Logan realized, as the object accelerated past him, not the slightest bit affected by the resistance of the air it passed through.

He moved ahead with a silence and a fluid grace that belied his personality, gliding through the forest without making the slightest noise, or leaving any sign.

With a hand gesture, he motioned for Ororo to halt while he took a closer look at some leaves on a low-hanging branch. They were thick with moisture from the fog, but that wasn't what caught his attention. His lips tightened, while Ororo's formed a small O of aston-ishment as she joined him; the water was dripping *up* the leaf and falling towards the *sky*.

Logan held a hand over the leaf. It felt perfectly normal—except that when the droplets splashed against his palm, they flowed up and around his hand and then plopped free to continue on their way.

Ororo moved on ahead, while Logan homed in on another object, spinning lazily in midair, like a gyro-scope that hadn't quite wound all the way down. He hunkered down to watch, unsure if he wanted to break the spell by reaching out to touch the object. No damage that he could see, nor any sign of violence. Nothing at all out of the ordinary—except its presence, and what it was doing.

With an almost convulsive grab, he gathered Scott Summer's ruby quartz glasses into his hand.

He was about to call out to Ororo when she beat him to it.

"Logan!"

Despite the flatness of the air, the urgency of her tone was plain. Shock, disbelief, fear, those reactions came through plainly and pulled him to her at a run.

He found Ororo down on the beach, kneeling over a body.

She looked up at him, stricken, but he wasn't looking at her, he couldn't bear to, not yet. He'd known at once who was lying there, without altogether knowing why, so he stalled by sweeping the vicinity for signs of anyone else.

Waste of effort. There was nothing to be seen.

He made a wider, more thorough sweep before they left, searching the ground while Ororo paced him over-head aboard the *Blackbird,* using its sensors. He already suspected they'd find nothing—you should expect so much only from a miracle—but they had to be sure.

"She's alive," Ororo said, as she turned the aircraft for home. There was a faint catch to her voice; she was both glad and scared, just like him.

He looked down at the glasses in his hand, at the still water of Alkali Lake, taking in a succession of slow, deep, calming breaths, unwilling to trust himself to speak, or take the smallest of actions, until he'd mastered control of himself. He understood instinctively about balance, without being able to articulate the why or wherefore; he had an equally instinctive comprehension of what had likely happened to Cyclops. And with it, a fury at whatever deity or fate or whoever had al-lowed it to happen. At bedrock, Logan was a far more honorable man than he'd ever admit; for him, there were some things that were fundamentally right, as there were others equally *wrong*. He'd always known that Creation wasn't fair, his own life was proof of that, but that never stopped him from believing that it *should* be.

Wanting your heart's desire was one thing. Having it—like this!

Thoughts for another time, perhaps. He shoved the glasses in his pocket and dropped to one knee, reaching out with unaccustomed tenderness to sweep a fall of dark auburn hair aside, and once more looked upon the face of Jean Grey.

X

"Jean Grey was the only Class Five mutant I've ever encountered," Xavier told them a day later, back in the mansion's infirmary. "Her potential was practically limitless."

She lay on the examining table. Her body was dotted all over with direct sensors, surrounded by the information panels of their remote scanning counterparts. They provided a constant and comprehensive stream of data to the Institute mainframe for analysis, right down to the firing of her individual neural synapses, with the most current readings being projected on a phalanx of nearby flat-panel displays.

Her vitals were totally nominal, and had been since they found her, wholly consistent with her last physical, not long before her death.

"Her mutation was seated in her limbic system," Xavier continued, taking refuge from his own deep feelings by adopting his most professorial tone, "the unconscious part of her mind. And therein lay the danger."

Logan snorted, gaining him a sharp look from both Xavier, seated in his wheelchair at Jean's head, and Ororo, flanking him opposite Logan.

Logan didn't bother explaining aloud; it wasn't his way. He was still trying to figure things out himself. He'd never been one for movies, yet he found his inner self wandering through the fantastic vista of a planet called Altair IV, to behold the final, fatal argument between the hero, the woman he loved, and that woman's father—a brilliant and loving, but ultimately misguided, scientist—on the nature of "monsters from the id." *The nightmares that come from our deepest, most primal and passionate subconscious, that go bump in the night.*

Out loud, he said: "I thought you were treating her," and got another warning glare from Ororo about his tone. He didn't much care.

"I tried . . ."

Another image came, equally unbidden, that Logan couldn't banish, mixing moments from the mission that led to Jean's death—Magneto's quiet, constant jibes about Xavier's failure to treat the mutant son of William Stryker, Xavier's own very real regret, and worst of all, the very real consequences that arose from that failure. Jason had been made by his father into a weapon; their attempt to stop the use of that weapon had led to Jean's death.

If Xavier sensed Logan's thoughts this time, he gave no sign as he laid his hands gently on Jean's head and closed his eyes. The monitors flickered, charting his progress as he resumed treating her.

Logan paid him no attention. His concentration was locked on Jean's face, as if his own senses could tell him what Xavier's telepathy and devices could not.

"I created a series of psychic barriers," Xavier said, "to separate her powers from her conscious mind, until such time as she could integrate the two properly and safely. However, in doing so, she developed a split personality . . ."

This was news to Logan and, by the look on her face, to Ororo, too. Neither took it well.

Logan spoke for them both. "What?" he demanded.

"The conscious Jean, whose powers were always under control, and that dormant side, a personality that, in our sessions, came to call itself *The Phoenix*. A purely instinctual creature, all desire, and joy and . . . rage."

He checked the monitors, made some notes.

Logan had grown ominously still and quiet, in a way that would clear even the most roughhouse saloons the world over.

Then, "Jean knew about this?"

Ororo watched Xavier shake his head, so engrossed in his work that he missed the cues and warnings Logan was radiating. She shifted her stance just a little, but knew her options were limited. The infirmary was no place for lightning, and Logan was so quick that she'd likely have no time to stop him with her powers if things went south. Ororo knew that Logan was a creature of primal passions who fought to keep them in check with his own rigorous code of honor. Now, with Jean, both elements were in play—his feelings for Jean combining with growing outrage at Xavier's revelations. It was a deadly mix, more volatile than matches and gasoline.

"It's unclear precisely how much she remembered," Charles told them. "The more pressing issue is that I'm not sure whether the woman we see in front of us is the Jean Grey we know, or the Phoenix, violently struggling to be free."

Logan took a step closer, and Ororo tensed.

"She looks pretty peaceful to me, Chuck."

"That's because I'm keeping her that way," Xavier replied, not rising to the bait. For all the attention he paid them, despite their ongoing conversation, it was as if Logan and Ororo weren't even there. "I'm trying to restore those psychic blocks, and reenergize them, and cage the beast again."

Logan's nostrils flared, and this time Xavier seemed to react to the subvocalized growl that issued from deep in the other man's throat.

"What did you just say?" Logan demanded.

"Logan, try to understand—"

"We're talking about a person's *mind* here, Charles, about Jean! We could be talking about her goddamn *soul*! How could you do this to her?"

"She has to be controlled. She isn't safe."

" 'Controlled,' Professor, or cured? Because sometimes, when you 'cage the beast,' the beast gets angry."

"You have no idea what she's capable of."

"No, *Professor,*" Logan spat with finality, and he made Xavier's title sound like the most profane of epithets. "I had no idea what *you* were capable of."

After this last comment, Logan knew that, had Xavier still possessed the use of his legs, the professor would be right up in his face, probably challenging him to do his worst. Logan never denied the man had balls, but this was the first he'd ever considered that Charles

Xavier might be lacking something essential in the way of a heart.

"Damn it, Logan," Xavier flared, "I want her back as much as you do!"

Logan shook his head: "Not even close."

Xavier couldn't stand Logan's glare for more than a few seconds. It wasn't that he lacked the strength, but—being a more intensely private man than even Logan—Charles couldn't bear to reveal to them the depths of his own pain. Or the concern that walked with it hand in hand, growing with each and every step into a very real and present fear.

He turned his back on Ororo and Logan and motored his chair towards the door, pausing at last to tell them, "I had a terrible choice to make, Logan. Hobson's choice. I chose the lesser of two evils."

Logan wouldn't—couldn't, Charles knew—let him go. "Sounds to me like Jean had no choice at all."

Logan looked away from the departing form of Xavier, briefly to Ororo, and then once more rested his eyes on Jean. He had a hunter's patience. He'd wait as long as he had to.

And after that . . .

. . . after that . . .

He met Ororo's gaze, then flicked his eyes towards the door, now closed, Xavier long gone, then back to Jean.

More gently than Xavier's touch, more gently than Ororo's lightest breeze, he stroked his rough palm from the crown of Jean's head back across her hair, and breathed in the scent of her. Not a lot of great things happened in his life, but he knew with certainty, this woman was one of them. Likely the best of them.

He repeated to himself what he'd sworn the moment they met, what he'd failed to do at Alkali Lake.

I'll save you, Jeannie, he promised silently. Whatever the case.

I'll save you!

Chapter Five

When McCoy saw the room, the first thing he did was look for black curtains, finding none, of course, since there were no windows. But from then on, at the most irksome and inconvenient moments, he found he couldn't get the lyrics to Cream's classic "White Room" out of his head. Telling Ororo that would make her laugh, he knew.

Hank didn't believe Kavita Rao had that much of a sense of humor. He doubted she had any sense of humor at all. He was wholly the opposite, but so anarchic in temperament that he'd long ago learned to keep his acerbic wit on the tightest of leashes, lest disaster result. But what else could one expect, he supposed, from a guy who'd been big and blue and furry since college?

He faced a modified Level Four extreme biohazard containment module, four meters by six, and three high. Every surface—walls, floor and ceiling—was painted white. One of the long walls was dominated by a mirror, constructed of transparent plastic that was stronger than steel in every respect. This was Hank's vantage point, allowing him an unrestricted view of the room. As per protocol, the environment was kept at negative pressure—lower than the ambient pressure outside—so that in case of any breach, air would naturally flow *into* the room, thereby containing any stray bugs and preventing contamination of the installation outside.

A door at the rear of the room led to the bathroom, where the walls were opaque, giving the illusion of privacy. But there were a score of minicams here, too, and the mirror was two-way glass. Every surface was sterile. There wasn't a spec of wayward dust to be seen. On the outer door was etched the *M* trefoil, for mutant biohazard.

It could have been a lab. It could have been a hospital room. It was a little bit of both.

Most of all, though, it belonged to a child.

Pretty much a normal boy, too, as far as Hank could tell, if the toys and the mess were any indication. Shelves had been provided, and bins for storage, but the kid used the floor instead. Books were strewn haphazardly about the place. No computer, just a desk with a keyboard and a screen, both connected to I/O ports in the wall. He was linked into the project network, so Dr. Rao could see what interested him and, if necessary, how the behavior modification was progressing and whether she needed to tweak it.

The flat-screen monitor was big enough to double as the room's TV. Jimmy was using it for video games, perched cross-legged on the end of the bed. He was working his thumbs to distraction as he blew the living daylights out of cars, trucks, pedestrians and just about an entire Cali city. He stole a muscle car and headed for the border—where, unknown to him, monsters awaited.

As Kavita described the action, and Hank followed

along on a convenient monitor outside, he couldn't help wondering if the boy had any awareness of how close he was to *real* monsters.

"You know, Dr. McCoy," Kavita began, as they watched the play, "I wrote my thesis on your theory of genetic recombination." Behind them a nurse in a modified biohazard suit entered the airlock.

Jimmy was on the cusp of adolescence, but had not one hair on his head. He wore a white Houston Astros jersey and a pair of white boarder shorts, and white sneakers.

Hank indicated Jimmy. "I never had a subject quite like this. . . ." He paused, thoughtful. "What's the lasting effect of the boy's power?" Hank asked.

Kavita shook her head. "None." She pursed her lips, "He can only suppress the mutant gene within a limited range."

"I've heard some of the staff refer to him by a nickname," Hank noted, straightening to his full, imposing height. Kavita clearly wasn't happy about this observation.

"I've made my feelings clear, but occasionally these things take on a life of their own. I suppose it must have been much the same concerning your own soubriquet."

"That's why I brought it up." He'd never liked being called "Beast," even by friends meaning it as a complement.

"The staff are firmly instructed to never call him 'Leech' to his face, or where he can hear."

Hank looked Kavita directly in the eyes. "And you really think he'll never know?"

She looked at her watch. "I should head into the city,

Dr. McCoy. If we're quite finished here, I have many appointments."

Hank nodded. "I'm done here."

As he turned to go, it seemed as though his movement attracted Jimmy's attention, which of course should have been impossible, since there was no way for the boy to know he was there. Jimmy grinned, and Hank allowed a small smile in return, even though the boy couldn't see it. His mind was racing with possibilities, both good and bad, and he half wished the boy would wander over, and bring Hank within the activation threshold of his power. The scientist in him was fascinated to discover how the gene-neutralizing process would work on him. The man in him wondered what he would look like now, without the effects of his mutation. Was he handsome, was he aging under the blue fur? Would he like the boy he was when the mutation took effect? He couldn't remember what it had been like to appear "normal." He didn't even look at old photos anymore.

But Jimmy could bring that boy in Hank back to life.

For as long as they stayed close.

Worthington's "cure" would make the reversion permanent. Now, that was an interesting development.

X

"Is Secretary McCoy going to be a problem?" asked Worthington Jr. a few hours later, in his office atop the San Francisco lab facility. A few stories below, a line of mutants stretched around the block. The street was cordoned off, with a group of SFPD squad cars forming a barrier right down the middle. Across the road, almost as many mutants gathered, as vehemently opposed to what Worthington had to offer as the others were desperate to partake.

Kavita Rao shrugged. "Hard to say. His political views seem somewhat at odds with his . . . personal issues."

"I imagine we'll be seeing more of that."

"Quite."

He leaned forward until his forehead touched the glass, trying to direct his line of sight as close to the base of the building as possible.

"I never really imagined there'd be so . . . *many,*" he said at last.

"Does it matter?"

"It makes one . . . think. It's one thing to consider the mutator gene an aberrant quirk in the human genome—but to see it in such a broad spectrum of the general populace. . . ."

"There is no consistency to the manifestations, either in terms of who possesses the gene or the power they manifest. If this were indicative of some species-wide evolution, we would see a common element."

"The only-pizza scenario."

"I beg your pardon?"

"Basically, you throw pizzas at the ceiling, to see which one sticks."

"Which would tell you what, pray tell?"

"Metaphor for the creative process, pizzas as ideas, that sort of thing."

"I stand with Einstein, thank you. God does not play dice with the Universe, nor does he throw pizzas."

Worthington certainly hoped so, but he also had to confess that the notion appealed to him. He used to think of God as having a sense of whimsy.

Until he saw how his son was changing. Then he'd decided he'd be better off without a God at all.

"Mr. Worthington, sir," announced a technician. "He's arrived."

Train of thought almost prompted Worthington Jr. to ask if the technician was referencing the Almighty. But he shunted the notion aside and said instead, "Good. Bring him in."

Rao touched his arm. "Are you sure you want to start with him?"

"I think it's important, yes."

She pulled on surgical gloves and selected an appropriate vial and syringe from the tray.

Two orderlies brought in Worthington's only child, his son—his heir.

Warren had wholly fulfilled the promise of his youth, with a face and form that belonged on a movie poster— a leading man capable of breaking every heart alive, and jump-starting a few that weren't. Tall and lean as ever, with hair a burnished gold swept messily back from his face, he was more handsome than a young Brad Pitt. He wore an overcoat, and there was a strange hump between his shoulders that made the coat ride up tremendously. To call the hump a deformity wasn't right, because he carried himself far too easily, so Worthington could only hope that people assumed his son was wearing some kind of backpack underneath.

It was clear he didn't want to be there. He wasn't fighting the orderlies, but he wasn't cooperating either, and they had to gently but firmly pull him forward to face his father.

"Hello, Warren," Kavita said brightly. She was ignored; if that bothered her, she gave no sign.

"You okay, son?" Worthington asked, like a man biting a bullet, or a boy slugging down medicine. He got a shallow nod in return, from a son that seemed unsure how to answer. "Did you sleep all right?"

"Yeah, I guess."

"You know I'm proud of you, for doing this."

Warren took off his overcoat, revealing an open shirt, and underneath, a complex leather harness reminiscent of a straightjacket, only the young man's arms were completely unrestrained.

"The transformation can be a little jarring," Kavita cautioned. Sweat popped on Warren's brow, suggesting that wasn't an altogether helpful thing to say.

"Dad," Warren asked pleadingly, the sheer desperation in his tone catching his father's heartstrings, taking him back to the nights he'd sat with his boy after lights-out, staying with him until he fell asleep to protect him from the monsters under the bed. "Dad," Warren repeated with more intensity, displaying more overt fright. "Can we . . . can we . . . talk about this a second?"

Worthington took his son's hand. "We talked about it, son. We agreed. It will all be over soon."

But Warren wouldn't stop squirming. Things got worse as he tried to wriggle his way loose from the orderlies, from his father.

"Wait," he demanded. "Just *wait* a minute!"

Worthington Jr. tried his "dad" voice: "Warren, calm down!"

"I . . . no . . . I can't do this!"

"Just relax, son," Worthington Jr. tried in a more placating tone. The orderlies were having an increasingly harder time holding on.

The young man's struggles had loosened the harness to the point where Warren could actively strain against it. The orderlies were built for the job—they looked a match for pro linemen, twice Warren's size and change in every which way.

But he shrugged them off as if they weighed nothing, and they smacked against the walls of the spacious office.

He showed no interest in the guards as he tore at his shirt, yanking it open to the sound of popping buttons. He flexed his chest with a great outcry . . .

. . . and the industrial-grade belting leather shredded like tissue paper, reminding Worthington Jr. of an article he'd read when he was younger about the wings of large birds. The wings of a goose propel that great bird through the sky for thousands of miles. A swan's wing, that thing of poetic beauty, can break a man's arm.

How much more powerful then, those of a man, capable of lifting him from the ground and hurling him through the air? How strong were the muscles required to sustain that flight?

Beholding his son, Worthington Jr. couldn't help but think of the flights of angels he'd seen depicted in catechism class, and of all the representations of doomed Icarus.

The fantasy paled in comparison to the reality.

Warren's wings stretched twice his height and more, tip-to-tip across a back that suddenly seemed much broader and indecently muscled than his father remembered. They were a pristine white that was almost radiant. The orderlies were so dumbstruck with the incandescent beauty of the man and the moment that they almost forgot their purpose.

"Warren," the father tried when words came back to him, "it's a better life we offer. It's what we all want!"

Looking down at his father, Warren replied with a harsh and unforgiving scream: *"No!"*

The orderlies had withdrawn to the doorway once Warren's wings had opened, and they'd summoned reinforcements. There was no escape that way.

"It's what *you* want!" Warren yelled. Seeing guards in a phalanx at the door, he ducked towards the windows.

"Warren, *don't*," cried his father. *"No!"*

And just like that, with a resounding crash, he was gone.

On the street below, warning cries rose from the crowd as they scrambled for protection, covering their heads as the broken glass came raining down. Some instinctively used their powers—telekinesis for deflection, and invulnerability of all shapes and sizes to cover themselves and those around them.

Only a few actually saw what happened, and most of them didn't believe it. Afterward, they would certainly be reluctant to tell. Just because they were mutants, too—and a few resembled the next best thing to a gila monster crossed with a Mack truck—didn't make them all that eager to boast that they'd seen a bona fide *angel* soaring over San Francisco.

Warren noticed none of this, and if he had it wouldn't

have mattered. All he was aware of was the metronomic beat of his wings as they grabbed great gouts of air and thrust out behind him, and the feeling of climbing ever higher, rushing ever faster, through the afternoon sky. The wind rushed across his face, flushed with the unaccustomed exertion and the terrific demands he was placing on his system. He'd have to eat soon and rest. Wouldn't do to black out from hunger at this altitude.

He was flying.

His heart pounded in his chest, pushing blood through his body like rivers of molten flame, searing him from crown to toes to the tips of fingers. He believed he was burning up, yet knew as well, with that same irrational certainty, that he'd be all right. This was where he belonged.

He was flying!

That deserved a cheer, and he gave one he hoped was loud enough for all the Bay Area to hear.

He didn't know where he was going, and he had no clothes, no cash, no ID—but it didn't matter. All he could say for sure was that he probably wasn't ever going home again.

The rest, he prayed, would take care of itself.

He was flying!

He passed the Worthington Research Facility, so high and so quickly that he was barely seen—save by one.

Jimmy's attention had been caught by the strange new shape up in the sky, and he watched without consideration of what it might be or what this might mean. He'd never seen anything so beautiful, *ever,* and was content to pass the time, however fleeting, simply enjoying it.

X

"Let me *out* of here," bellowed President Cockrum, shackled at wrists and ankles and waist, and fastened to a bar that extended the length of the cell, allowing minimal freedom of movement—basically a traverse from cot to toilet to table. "God*damn* it, do you know who I am?"

He stood in the last of a line of cells, each holding its own single prisoner bound by a complex and formidable array of restraints. A hall ran the length of the single-tiered cellblock, with a fully enclosed guard station at front and rear. The entire enclosure rocked and trembled as though on moveable springs, and the air was filled with a faint and pervasive hum. It was night, and after lights-out, so the cells were mainly defined by shadow.

The guard flicked on the light for the last cell, and keyed in the feed for the master security station, plus the satellite uplink. He didn't deviate from protocol, no matter how annoying or trivial the provocation. He was a trained professional, ex-military. This installation was operated jointly by the departments of Homeland Security and Mutant Affairs, with some help from the United States Marshals Service. The Bureau of Prisons had learned, to its sorrow, the ultimate and tragic cost of incarcerating prisoners like Magneto, after the destruction of the Mount Haven complex during his escape, and the execution of its entire complement of guards and staff. This was intended as an interim solution until a more secure facility was constructed. Now, however, with the introduction of the Worthington serum—and pending the usual avalanche of injunctions, appeals and court-room motions—places like this, specialized prisons to hold mutant inmates, could well end up like Alcatraz Island, once the most fearsome penal institution in the land, now obsolete, good for nothing but a local tourist attraction and the occasional movie set.

Twisting his mouth in irritation at a sudden, inexplicable smear of static across his display screens, which messed up his view of the cell, the guard finished his reports and took a stroll along the catwalk for a closer look.

The president was in fine form: "I'm the president of the United States."

Tough luck, asshole, thought the guard, enjoying the moment. *I sure as shit didn't vote for you.*

"I demand that you release me!"

"Mr. President, sir," he replied with unexpected good humor, "shut the hell up."

He was finished here, but as he started back along the catwalk, his hand stayed light and ready on the butt of the weapon holstered at his side. He was rated Expert with a pistol, and before reporting to this new station had spent a couple weeks of refresher training with the FBI. He could draw and fire with a speed that would have left Billy the Kid stunned, and shoot with more precision than that legendary pistolero ever possessed.

"Please," came a new cry from the same cell, but a little girl this time. "Please, I haven't done anything, it's all a big mistake, I'm not supposed to be here—please let me go."

He glanced back in, and saw a kid who looked like she'd been snatched from her First Communion, as innocent as could be. She'd somehow taken the place of the president.

It was late, near the end of a double shift, and he was tired. The guard spoke from the heart, without thinking of the consequences.

"Keep it up, Mystique, I'm gonna spray you in the face, bitch!" For emphasis, he brandished a can of pepper spray—while his gun hand never strayed far from the pistol on his belt.

The girl responded with a smile that was way too wicked for someone her age, and with an equally unlikely come-hither look, whispered, "When I get out of here, I'm going to kill you myself."

"That'll be the damn day," he muttered, although he was tempted to draw his weapon and take a shot, just to see what would happen.

The guard followed proper procedure and walked away, while behind him in the cell, the little girl shifted position, her body elongating, maturing, losing its clothes, turning a deep cobalt blue. For Mystique, nothing ventured, nothing gained. This ploy had worked before, so it was certainly worth the try. It had also told her something important: this guard was smarter than most, more careful than most, and surprisingly, more considerate than most. The threat had merely been an expression of frustration. He'd likely been dozing when her bellowing called him back to duty. Most guards she'd known would have sprayed her just for spite; he'd simply made the threat.

On the whole, a pretty decent guy.

But she'd kill him just the same.

* * *

Inside the cellblock, clocks and lighting conspired to convince the inmates that it was the middle of the night. In fact, it was quite the opposite.

They were incarcerated in a supersemi, a double-length tractor trailer, cruising the back roads of heartland America.

In the beginning, and for as long as it worked, it had been an inspired idea. With the destruction of Mount Haven, the federal government had nowhere to hold superpowered prisoners. Every attempt to establish a replacement led to an acute attack of NIMBY—*Not in my backyard, goddamn it!*—on the part of all the governors approached, as they proceeded to wrap themselves in the mantle of states' rights. Given what happened last time, it was hard to argue the point, especially when it came to someone as personally and professionally valuable to Magneto as Mystique. That's when the idea was pitched for a *mobile* prison.

There were a helluva lot of roads in the contiguous Forty-Eight, and a *helluva* lot of trucks. This wasn't searching for a needle in a haystack, it was searching for precisely the right needle. One that was constantly on the move, and thoroughly shielded against Magneto's magnetic scans. He could be standing right beside the truck and never sense Mystique's biosignature. The number crunchers ran the probabilities of discovery and came up with a number in the billions.

How were they to know Magneto would cheat?

The first anyone was aware of it was when every vehicle in the convoy started shaking itself apart at the seams, and every electronic instrument started bugging out big-time.

The duty officer slapped the panic button, never realizing that his signal was degraded the moment it left the antenna.

That's when Magneto stepped out into the middle of the road.

The escort drivers floored their accelerators, hoping for a chance at running him down. With a casual flick of the wrist, he sent both armored Suburbans tumbling end-over-end off the road. Same applied to the afterguard.

The supersemi driver stomped on his brakes in a futile effort to save himself as the cab was torn from the trailer and pitched through the air, soaring the length of a football field before crashing to the road in a ball of fire and torn metal.

Momentum kept the trailers coming, although the front end, deprived of the cab's support, crashed down to the pavement and started sending up an impressive rooster-tail of sparks.

Magneto stood his ground, as casual as if this was merely a Sunday stroll through the park. As the lead trailer approached, he simply crushed it, letting the screams of tortured steel absorb those of the living inside.

By the time it stopped at his feet, he'd reduced a twenty-meter container to the size of a shoe box, while the second trailer, the longer one containing the prisoners, was altogether intact.

The moment the alarm sounded, the guard ran for his station, but the sudden disengagement of the cab and the destruction of the lead trailer left his partner sprawled on the monitor console, shocked unconscious by a massive series of short circuits as Magneto overloaded the internal security systems and the comnet. The guard himself was tossed to the catwalk right at the rear, by Mystique's cell.

Knowing things would only get worse and that his chances of making it out of this alive were almost nonexistent, he grabbed for his sidearm regardless. He was a trained professional and he had a responsibility. The guard had sworn an oath.

That oath was his epitaph. Mystique snaked her legs through a ridiculously tiny breach in the wall of her cell, twisting her malleable form through some impossible gyrations, making herself as boneless as an anaconda so her feet could find and embrace the guard's neck.

He felt her touch, heard her laugh . . .

. . . and she broke his neck.

"Told you so," she said, extending her toes to the length of a chopstick, and using them to hook the keys from his belt and bring them back to her.

Magneto made his way to the back of the prison truck, where he was joined by Pyro and Callisto, who'd dealt with the last of the escort. Beneath the façade of what appeared to be ordinary truck doors was a second level that would have done a bank vault proud, secured by a series of massive, high-tech locks. The entire body of the vehicle was composed of nonferrous ceramic composites, both lighter and significantly stronger than any metal this side of pure adamantium. Magneto cocked an eyebrow at the inventiveness of the design, reminded of a piece of information gleaned by Mystique some while back, that there was a mutant inventor working for DARPA, the Defense Department's Advanced Research and Planning Agency, known only by the code name Forge. If this was Forge's work, that made him—or her—a force to be reckoned with, on a par with Xavier himself.

He brought his thoughts back to the business. He couldn't affect the fabric of the truck directly, and suspected that the armored shell would withstand any modification he might make to the escort vehicles— which *were* made of steel—to use them to breach the walls. He permitted himself a smile. Did they truly think him such a simpleton? Did they think that in the decades his powers had been active he hadn't devoted a substantial portion of his life to researching all there was to know about the nature and properties of magnetism, one of the four fundamental forces of Creation itself?

He attacked the truck directly, but on a subatomic level, refining his perceptions to the point where the world was no longer composed of tangible, readily identifiable objects, but instead flash points of energy, lines of force. It wasn't easy, and here he cursed the ravages of time, wishing he'd had such a level of insight at an age when he'd been hale enough to utilize it properly. A slight reshuffle of the alignment of atoms within a molecule, molecules within a lattice, and *presto*!

What had been unbreachable was now as brittle as rice paper.

With a confident smile, he restored his perceptions to normal, then reached up to the nearest lock, giving a hearty tug—and the whole door popped off its hinges.

Callisto caught it as it fell, and tossed it aside with an ease and power that revealed an impressive physical strength. Magneto filed this information away for future reference.

Mystique was standing in the doorway, and at the sight of him she struck one of her more delicious poses, radiating irresistible temptation and intolerable insolence, all in the same sultry look.

"About time," she chided.

He answered with a thin smile, "I've been busy, my dear." She ignored the veiled reprimand because she was clearly happy to see him, telling him so with a smile. Which he didn't answer.

"Did you find what we were looking for?"

She nodded, and the smile went away.

"The source of the cure is a mutant, code-named Leech. A child at the Worthington Labs in Berkeley. Without him, they have nothing."

Magneto took a moment to consider what she'd told him, and then decided to acknowledge the tumult coming from the other cells.

"And who do we have here," he mused aloud, eyeing a clipboard on the catwalk and using a minor burst of power to toss it into Pyro's grasp.

"Read off the guest list, if you please."

As they made their away along the catwalk, John Allerdyce flipped to the appropriate page.

"James Madrox," he announced, at the cell next to Mystique's.

"This one robbed seven banks," she told them. "At the same time."

"His mutant name is . . ." Pyro began.

"Multiple Man," finished the voice within the cell.

Magneto popped the lock and a normal-looking young man—dark hair, average height, athletic build—rose to his feet.

"I could use a man of your talents," Magneto told him.

As Madrox approached, he stepped momentarily through a pool of deep shadow, and just that quickly, between one step and the next, he was leading a column of identical duplicates, all of whom responded to Magneto with a different expression or greeting, establishing their innate individuality. They were all cut from the same cloth, so to speak, but they could apparently operate independently.

"What they know, I know," Madrox boasted. "What they learn, I remember."

With a glance at her nails, Mystique asked innocently, "And if they're hurt, do you feel it? If you're knocked out, do they stick around?"

The multitude of sour expressions was all the answer they needed. Magneto understood the limitations, but repeated his invitation regardless.

"I'm in," Madrox told them, in a chorus of eager voices.

"Splendid," Magneto acknowledged. "Welcome to the Brotherhood."

The next cage was massively reinforced, with huge locks for emphasis. Magneto peeked through the small access port.

"Careful with this one," Mystique cautioned.

Shackled to a chair, complete with head restraint, was the largest figure Magneto had ever seen, more impressive than Sabretooth, far more so than the X-Man Colossus in his armored form. A veritable mutant behemoth.

"Cain Marko," Mystique announced, prompting a

wry sidewards glance of bemusement from Magneto. She shrugged back as if to say, *not her fault, she* certainly hadn't christened him.

"Solitary confinement," Pyro told them, reading from the file. "Zero contact. Check this out." His voice rose in excitement, reminding Magneto that he was still a lot younger than he liked people to think. " 'Prisoner must remain inert at all times. If he builds up any momentum, he becomes virtually unstoppable.' "

"How fascinating," said Magneto, and proceeded to open the cell.

"What do they call you?" he asked, once inside.

"Juggernaut," was the reply.

"I can't imagine why."

The huge truck creaked ominously as Juggernaut propelled himself from his chair. As he reached down for his helmet, Pyro couldn't resist a jibe.

"Nice helmet."

Juggernaut looked at the boy as if he were a bug about to be squashed. "Keeps my face pretty."

Pyro had sense enough to leave things at that.

The remaining cells were empty.

As they exited the truck, no one noticed a stir on the monitor console. Hermán Molina knew the safe play, the smart play, was to stay right where he was and do nothing. But he'd earned his six stripes in the Marine Corps, and the Navy Cross, as the hardest of hard chargers. Being assigned as security for this run wasn't a dead-end job for losers who couldn't cut it elsewhere— they had recruited the best of the best, and drummed into them from the get-go how vital their responsibility was, how dangerous their charges were.

Now the three prisoners were not only loose, but they were walking out with Magneto. Something had to be done, and after taking a glance around, it was plain that he'd drawn the short straw.

He was a first-tier sniper, as deadly accurate with a pistol as a rifle. But the range was too great; he had to get closer.

Mystique caught the green dot of a laser sight out of the corner of her eye, centered on Magneto's back. They were too far apart to push him clear and there was no time to yell a warning as she registered the faint *thip* of a weapon discharging.

She dove forward, and felt a sting between her breasts as the dart struck home.

Magneto whirled about, saw the guard tracking to take a second shot, and instantly manipulated magnetic fields around him, popping the plastic weapon from his grasp as though it were a wet and slippery bar of soap. He brought it carefully to rest, making sure the barrel was pointed well away from everyone present. A second later there was an awful shriek from inside the truck, mercifully cut short, accompanied by a rush of heat and smoke from a fireball so instantly powerful it managed to stagger him. Pyro's doing.

The young man pulled the flames back into himself, leaving only the charred and stinking remnants of the guard. Magneto turned in frantic concern to Mystique.

Mystique wasn't interested in what was happening around her. She had problems of her own. It was as though she'd been stabbed by a spear of ice, and a cold more intense than anything she ever imagined radiated outwards from the point of contact, behind a wave front of such agony that she found herself hammered to hands and knees on the ground. Without any conscious direction, her body curled in on itself, impossibly tight, returning instinctively to the fetal position as—in a very real sense—she was being remade and reborn.

Gradually, her vision cleared and she blinked many times, trying to center herself. The impossible cold she'd felt had passed, not even leaving a memory, yet she didn't feel quite right. She felt chilled in a way that was new to her. She shivered, something she'd never done before.

The others were staring. She was used to that, it was the price to pay for walking around in her skin. Their expressions didn't register—or perhaps, she simply chose to ignore them.

She plucked the dart from where it had landed, brow furrowing as she felt a small trickle of blood. Her morphing ability allowed her to cope with injuries as instantly and comprehensively as the Wolverine's healing factor; usually it took the near-mortal wounds to draw blood.

Then she saw her hand.

It wasn't blue, it was pale.

She rose to her knees, with the same balletic grace as always, and stared aghast at her body. No more scales and ridges—she was truly, completely naked and nothing she could do would change that.

"Erik?" she called, lost and aching, as she raised a hand towards him.

The look he returned matched her grief.

"I'm sorry, my dear," he said gently, as to one dead, but who hadn't yet realized it. "You're not one of us anymore."

Her mouth opened to register her shock, her eyes brimmed with unbidden tears. After all they'd shared, after her sacrifice to save him, the finality of his rejection was too terrible to accept.

He ran his hand along her cheek in a farewell caress.

"Such a shame," he mused in a kind of eulogy. "You were so beautiful . . ."

He rose with a snap of his cloak and signaled the others to follow. Mystique stayed on her knees, watching like one who'd just been turned to stone. Pyro, at least, had the decency to appear torn, switching looks between her and Magneto. But then, with a final, farewell shake of the head, he scurried after the Master of Magnetism.

Through her head ran memories of the times she'd sneered at the X-Men, and thought them fools for following Xavier instead of Erik. And especially, the realization that, if she had stood with them, powers or no, they'd have stood by her to the very end.

Chapter
Six

Logan hadn't left the infirmary since they'd brought Jean home. He watched her with his senses as intently as the machines did with theirs, and probably came away with as accurate an assessment of her condition. When Xavier came in to perform his own examination, plus whatever else he did to her in the way of his personal psychic voodoo, Logan stepped aside, staying close enough to intervene if needed but otherwise deferring to the professor. He also took each opportunity to keep tabs on Xavier as attentively as he did on Jean. The couple of times Ororo visited, she was actually as concerned for Logan as her best friend. Logan wasn't used to that, wasn't sure how to deal with it.

Occasionally, he'd talk to Jean as though they were sitting in some saloon or bar, having a normal conversation, telling her of all that had transpired with the school and the world since she'd been gone. Mostly, he just sat, with the infinite patience that was one of his hallmarks. He watched, and he listened. When she needed him, he'd be there, he'd be ready.

He saw that some wires were tangled, so he reached over to smooth them out . . .

. . . and she grabbed him by the hand.

She looked up at him with that same long, lazy smile that he remembered and yet, with something new, something . . . more. He couldn't help returning the smile in kind.

"We've got to stop meeting like this," she noted, making him chuckle. "It seems so familiar, doesn't it? Except I was in your place and you were in mine."

He couldn't help thinking, *you're wearin' a lot more clothes than I was, darlin'*, which made her blush and grin the wider. So there was nothing wrong with her telepathy, he observed, although she was keeping her own thoughts to herself. He half-expected to hear from the professor, who Logan assumed was monitoring his thoughts or Jean's, waiting for just this very moment. Thus far, though, they had complete privacy.

She swallowed, mouth dry, and he held out a glass of water for her to sip from its straw.

"How long was I . . . ?" she tried again.

"Too flamin' long," he told her, more gruffly than he'd intended, not from anger, but because seeing her awake and all right made him suddenly admit to himself just how much he'd missed her.

"You feeling okay, Jeannie?"

She sat up with surprising ease and grace for someone who'd been (a) dead and (b) flat on her back in the hospital. Jean was still smiling, radiating more happiness than he'd ever seen from her. But then, he realized, he'd hardly ever seen her truly happy—save for a couple of instances when he'd caught her by surprise, just off guard enough that he got that special smile of hers, the one that came without any of the filters of duty and responsibility that Xavier had layered on her.

He wondered if things had been any better with Cyclops.

Logan had never felt this way; his heart was full to bursting with the brightest and best of emotions and yet, at the same time, on the verge of breaking. How could any moment seem so wonderful and potentially terrible, all at once?

"Yes," she told him. "I'm more than okay. I'm alive. For the first time in my life, I feel alive."

He glanced at the monitors, which were having major fits, but he didn't have a clue whether that was good or bad.

Jean began pulling off the sensor leads. Logan thought to suggest she wait but she gave him a look that said, *Trust me.* I'm *the doctor here, bub, I know what I'm doing.*

She was the most beautiful thing he'd ever seen, even more stunning than before. He couldn't help staring.

"Logan, you're making me blush." Logan liked that, and all it implied, and she seemed to as well.

"You're reading my thoughts?"

"Can't help it."

She took his face in her hands and pulled him close.

"There's nothing wrong with what you want, Logan. It's what I've always wanted too."

Her lips brushed his, a laughing invitation that didn't just send tingles through his body, it unleashed a lightning bolt that rocked him from his head to the tips of his toes. It was as though *he'd* been plugged into an emotional supercharger, every sense kicked into overdrive, all of them centered on Jean. The sight of her eyes, so close to his, the impossibly smooth touch of her skin, the scent of her hair, the sound of her voice, the very taste of her—all combined to fan his desire to white-hot incandescence.

The last time they'd kissed—a stolen interlude beneath the fuselage of the *Blackbird*—he'd been the aggressor, trying to stake his claim to her heart before it was too late. But she'd made her commitment to Scott, much as either of them might wish differently. And he'd respected that.

Now, by contrast, there was no holding back. She didn't merely kiss him, she forged a connection between her mind and his. He was hard, she was soft; he was soft, she was hard—the lines of demarcation blurred and re-formed so that he lost track of what was real and what was imagined. Time stretched, expanded, turned back upon itself, enabling them to live a lifetime in an instant, and then go back and try it again. They grew old together, they walked hand in hand to the end of forever; they watched Creation end and used their passion to make something new.

He couldn't breathe, didn't have to; couldn't stop, didn't want to. He beheld the world through her eyes and gasped to acknowledge a great and aching hollowness within, a sense of being incomplete, of possessing the illusion of sight while being tormented by the realization that you were actually, truly, blind. At the same time, she walked a lifetime in *his* boots, tears starting from her eyes at the discovery of truths and memories he was glad remained hidden. She saw the blood in his past and what it had cost him, the creature he had been and the man who'd grown to take his place.

Before this moment, Logan had never known the true

meaning and nature of love. He still wasn't sure he had the answer. But what he found here—what he and Jean were sharing—was just as fundamental. It had changed his life by showing him possibilities he'd never dared imagine. It was intimacy.

Unseen by Logan, just for a flash, Jean's eyes flickered, and burned with a heat that had nothing to do with the wholly human passions that claimed their otherwise full attention.

Logan sensed heat radiating through Jean's body and into his, but chose not to notice, not to care as her telekinesis tore open his belt.

Anyone walking in on them now . . .

And he remembered what had spun past him through the air at Alkali, another belt buckle, forged in the shape of an X. The one Scott wore.

"Jean," he said, pulling away a little and finding it among the hardest things he'd ever done. "Wait!"

"Why?" She wasn't interested, acting more like him than he was. It would be so easy to give in, and he remembered the story of Lancelot and the Grail, the not-quite-perfect knight doomed to behold the sacred prize but never to claim it. Was Jean his Grail *and* his Guinevere?

"Jeannie," he protested, "this isn't *you*!"

"It is me."

He held her by the shoulders, finally able to put some distance between them, but caught in a fit of trembling as she stroked with telekinesis the parts of him he wouldn't let her reach with her hands.

"Stop it," he warned.

"Make me," she challenged playfully.

"Please."

She gave him a lopsided grin that was better than any caress, and he couldn't help thinking, *I should've found you first,* and the wish had nothing to do with her relationship with Scott. The smile faded. She'd heard him, and understood.

"You've been through hell," he told her gently, "maybe you ought to take things easy." He had another thought—*she hadn't yet said a word about Cyclops.* "Charley said you might be different."

Her look darkened, and he no longer had to hold her back. The mood was broken.

"He would know, wouldn't he?" she said, and didn't bother hiding her bitterness. "You think he's not inside your head, too?" she challenged. "Look at you, Logan, he's *tamed* you!"

The words struck home, because he'd thought them himself from time to time. But he didn't react.

"Jean," he asked instead, "where's Scott?"

She didn't answer.

"We traced the beacon on his bike to Alkali Lake. I found his glasses there." He chose not to mention the belt buckle, or the weird physical manifestations they'd encountered, and considered that she might pluck them from his thoughts regardless.

Still no response, so he called her name again, "Jean!"

She looked towards him, eyes lost and filled with a mix of confusion and pain.

He set Scott's glasses down on the bed between them, and her gaze followed his down to look at them.

"Where is he, darlin'?"

"I . . ." she blinked, sniffed, shook her head, blinked again, as though waking from the deepest of sleeps, not comprehending why her eyes were filling with tears. "I'm sorry, Logan." Her expression twisted with the realization that she had perhaps lost something supremely precious, but didn't yet quite know precisely *what*. "Where am I?" she asked suddenly, catching him by surprise. She really meant it. She had no idea where she was.

"You're in the Mansion infirmary, Jean." He took her by the hand, willing his strength into her slim frame, hoping that by taking it she'd be able to use him as an anchor against the chaos swirling inside her mind. Whatever else was going on in her world, she had to accept that he loved her. That had to be the absolute, the one constant she could depend on. Why that was so important, he hadn't a clue, but he'd learned early to trust his instincts.

"Listen to me, darlin'," he went on gently, as though to a spooked filly. "You need to tell me what happened at Alkali Lake. To Scott."

She touched the glasses with the tips of thumb and forefinger.

"Oh, God," she moaned, and right then he knew for certain what had until now been just a suspicion. He'd never see Scott Summers again.

He spared a quick glance away from her face as objects began to rattle around the periphery of the room.

"Oh God, *Logan*!" This last was an outcry of desperation and terror, and he knew she had found herself facing a memory and a grief that she could not bear.

The side effects on the room worsened accordingly. Screws spun from their holes and shot through the air, the fluid in the IV bags began to drip upwards, and Logan's skin began to tingle the way it did on the eve of a wicked electrical storm. The smell of ozone filled the air.

Once more, he took her by the shoulders.

"Talk to me, Jean. *Focus!*"

She was whispering, so softly he couldn't make out the words. He read her lips as they moved, and didn't want to.

"Jean!" he cried again.

"Kill me, Logan," she said again, making sure he could hear, telling him with her voice and with her thoughts.

He shook his head in absolute refusal.

Only now, she took *him* by the shoulders, with a strength that matched his own, her voice building in power and resonance with every word, "*Kill me*—before I kill someone else! Please, Logan, I'm begging. You're the only one who can. *Kill me!*"

He looked into her eyes and saw the end, just as when they'd kissed. The end, the beginning, all that came between, as great and as terrible as imagination could make them. He beheld Creation in all its wonder and glory. He knew she was right—and found himself flawed enough, stubborn enough, *human* enough, to think he could deny it and find a way to win.

"No," he said, setting himself before her, in the flesh and in her thoughts, as that anchor. "Look at me, Jean. You're inside my head, deeper than I can go, likely deeper than Charley." He took the risk of mentioning Xavier's name, but tempered it with the suggestion that she could do far more than he. "You can see where I've been. I've lost it, too, darlin'. But you can climb out of that abyss. We can help you, Jeannie!"

The room began to calm.

"You truly believe the professor can help, Logan?" she asked in a voice that held all the sadness that ever was. "That he can fix it, make things like they were?"

"We can try."

She looked him square in the face. "I don't want to fix it."

She hit him with her telekinesis, a shot to the chest containing the full force of a Category Five hurricane. Anyone else would have been pulped on contact, but Logan merely made a body-sized dent in the wall.

"I can't go back to the way I was. I won't. I'm *free* now."

Jean looked at Logan sprawled unconscious on the floor, her face showing both longing and loss.

Very softly, she left him some last words, using telepathy as well as speech because she wanted him to remember. "I thought you more than anyone would understand that, and love me enough to let me go." The image that went with the thought was that of his claws.

With a wave of the hand, she blew open the door and was gone without a backwards glance.

X

Hank McCoy had a big, bold signature, a match in its way for that of John Hancock on the Declaration of Independence. The letter it closed was brief and to the point. Everything that needed to be said had been—face-to-face.

The president stood behind his desk in the Oval Office. Hank stood opposite. It was an awkward moment. Neither had wanted to come to this juncture, yet now that they had arrived, there was a certain inexorable momentum.

"I'm not happy about this, Hank."

"Neither am I, sir."

"You think resigning is going to make a difference?" A wave of the letter for emphasis. "That's no way to influence policy."

"Due respect, sir, policy is being made without me. Mr. President, the decision to turn the Worthington-Rao cure into a weapon was made *without* me!"

The president actually looked surprised as Hank tossed a file on the desk, previously restrained anger taking him to the precipice of disrespect. The file contained photos of what was left of the convoy, including some of Mystique.

"I know precisely what happened on that convoy. I do have some friends in the Pentagon."

"Hank, that was an isolated incident. You've got to understand, those mutants were a real threat."

"So you say. But who decides what constitutes a threat?"

"For God's sake, McCoy, they were convicted criminals!"

"Jamie Madrox was a bank robber. Juggernaut's crimes were all against property. Are these capital crimes? Are we at the point, sir, where—like in olden days—we cut off the hands of thieves and burn out others' eyes? The 8th Amendment of the Constitution prohibits 'cruel and unusual punishment.' I submit, sir, that stripping a mutant—*permanently*—of his or her abilities falls wholly under that definition. And that's just for starters.

"Altering a person's genetic code without their consent is the ultimate illegal search and seizure, not to mention a violation of fundamental privacy."

"We do much the same with sexual predators, in terms of drug therapy and incarceration."

"We don't castrate them, sir. Nothing is permanent. This process *is*. My God, David, have you even *begun* to consider the slippery slope you're on?"

The president nodded, his eyes gone hard.

"I have, Henry. Long and hard. And I also worry how democracy—that very Constitution and the Republic I swore in my oath of office to defend, 'so help me God'— survives when one lone man can move cities with his mind."

"Honorable and well-meaning as you are, sir, what about the next man? Suppose he uses your rationale to strip mutants of more rights?"

"That's why I ask you to reconsider your resignation. I need you by my side, Hank, to be that voice of reason. Your country needs you."

Hank drew himself up to his full height. "Sir, I serve at the pleasure of the president. It has been an honor and a privilege. But I serve my conscience more."

The president poured them both a measure of scotch from the drinks tray on a sideboard. Single malt, very old, very rare, and worth every drop.

"You know, my friend, it's only going to get worse."

They clinked glasses in farewell, and Hank nodded.

"All the more reason why I need to be where I belong," McCoy said.

They finished and set the glasses aside. "I try to do the right thing, Henry. It's not always easy."

"It's not supposed to be, sir."

X

Xavier pushed the chair to its limit, forcing Ororo into a quickstep that was almost a run in order to keep pace down the long, gleaming hall that led to the infirmary.

"Professor," she demanded, irked as always that there wasn't a sufficient volume of air down here for her to fly, "*talk* to me. What is it?"

"Something's happened." He paused, then more quietly, "As I feared . . ."

"What? What aren't you telling me?"

She stopped as they reached the wide-open doors and beheld the mess inside.

"Why didn't the alarms—" Ororo started to ask.

"For the same reason," Xavier broke in before she finished, "none of us were the slightest bit aware that anything was amiss until it was far too late."

Logan was awake, seated on the floor, back to the wall beneath a major dent that he'd clearly made with his body, knees drawn up to his chest as he idly examined one set of his extended claws as though surprised to find them in view. His clothes were in rags and from the gingerly way he moved as he pushed himself to his feet, Ororo realized that he was still in the midst of a major healing.

Ororo rushed at once to his side, immediately taking in the fact that he was alone in the room. The monitors had been reduced to less than junk, components strewn across the floor like a high-tech carpet. If they did try to access the data they'd recorded, Ororo knew they'd find it irretrievably corrupted as well.

Fearing the answer, she had to ask anyway, "Logan, who did this?"

"Jean," he said.

Logan hesitated before explaining things further. "She's . . . she's not herself." It took an effort to say this, because he still hurt more than ever, but also because each word seemed like a betrayal of Jean. "I think . . . she . . ." But the truth had to be faced, and his honor required him to face it. So, when he spoke at last, there were no doubts. He told them what he believed to be the case. "She killed Scott."

Ororo refused to believe. "No, that can't be!"

Xavier was grimly calm.

"Don't look so surprised," Logan said to him.

"I warned you about her," Xavier replied, and his own sadness was palpable. "I told you what she was capable of."

"What does that mean?" Ororo asked.

Logan tossed a thumb in Xavier's direction. "Ask *him*."

Xavier's thoughts, however, were obviously elsewhere. His eyes were closed, and he was concentrating.

"She's left the Mansion," he reported. "She's blocking my thoughts." He kept trying to reach her, clearly a struggle. "She is very strong. I hope we're not too late."

"What about Cerebro?" Logan suggested.

Xavier shook his head tersely, as if it was all the effort he could spare. "She's keyed into it, just as I am. Given her current state, she could easily wrest control of it remotely and use it to amplify her own abilities beyond comprehension. Believe me, that is a scenario you do *not* wish to behold. I'm afraid . . . I must do this . . . on my own."

He redoubled his efforts, and for the first time Logan could remember, he actually saw sweat building on the professor's forehead.

X

Magneto held the guard's plastic pistol in his hand. He'd yanked it clear the instant Pyro had torched the wretched creature and had spent much of the time since examining it. Now he was explaining his discoveries to his troops. Quite a simple device, really. It took a magazine like any ordinary automatic pistol and used compressed air to propel the darts at an equivalent range—which in the hands of a superior marksman, as they'd seen themselves, could be considerable. Worst of all, one hit was evidently all the drug needed to take effect. Whether a direct hit was required or even a scratch would do, he did not care much to find out.

"I told you they would draw first blood," Magneto reminded them, brandishing the weapon.

He stood surrounded by a half dozen of his new Brotherhood, in a bunker of his own construction, built entirely of metal, with a metal staircase leading up to a trapdoor in the ceiling. Not the most elegant or comfortable of surroundings, but for their present needs it would serve.

Pyro gestured at the gun: "What do we do with that? Hand it over to the walking wrecking ball?" By that, he was referring to Juggernaut, who undoubtedly didn't take to his sense of humor as tolerantly as any X-Men used to.

Magneto shook his head: "This weapon . . . will become *our* weapon, my friends. A lightning rod that will bring countless more to our cause."

He faced his troops. "Come," he told them, calling them to arms. "It's time to gather our forces."

The trapdoor overhead swung open, allowing light to fan across the room below.

Callisto closed the door behind her, hopping lithely down the stairs and over to Magneto's side. As the only one present who remembered the way things used to be, Pyro noticed how naturally she assumed Mystique's role and relationship, as well as how easily Magneto accepted her. Another difference between the Brotherhood and Xavier's, and even though he told himself that he didn't care, deep down inside it bothered him. If Magneto could so instantly abandon someone like Mystique, where did the rest of them stand? And when the shit truly hit the fan—because that was what they were planning, right?—*who* could a fella truly count on here?

"I picked up something," she informed their leader. "An electromagnetic anomaly. Massive."

Magneto obviously wasn't interested, but she wouldn't let him push past, speaking hurriedly while she had the chance.

"I thought it was a power grid, a surge in the system. But it's *not*—it's a mutant!"

She had him now, Pyro saw.

"Class Five," she said triumphantly. "More powerful than anything I've ever scanned. More powerful than *you*!"

"Where is she?" he asked, and Callisto looked at him in surprise. He actually *knew* this mutant?

X

Xavier's first thought was how little the neighborhood had changed in better than twenty years. How calm and peaceful everything looked. He wondered if he'd be able to say the same an hour from now.

Storm parked the Mercedes in front of the Grey house, and Logan helped Xavier into his wheelchair, grousing just a little under his breath about the impracticality of certain European touring sedans for folks in Xavier's condition. On one level, Charles had to agree— a minivan with a ramp would probably make more sense. But he loved the Maybach, and rationalized its use by telling himself that the X-Men had their toys. This was his.

"Wait for me here," he instructed. "I need to see Jean. Alone."

But there was already someone waiting for him. Magneto sat on the garden bench beneath the arbor outside the front door.

"You were right, Charles," he said charmingly, as if they were picking up right where they'd left off after that first meeting with Jean, as though the intervening years of conflict were no more than a dream. "This one *is* special."

"What the hell are you doing here?" Logan demanded with a quality to his voice that suggested all of them— Xavier included—take notice, and perhaps even a wary step back. The look Logan gave Magneto made it eloquently plain who his primary target would be, and that nothing whatsoever would stop him from trying. There was no threat or bluster to the man, Charles saw, just a calm and fundamental certainty, and like knowing the sun will rise, he knew that if the need arose Logan would kill.

If Magneto was bothered by any of this, he gave no outward sign. Instead, he responded as blithely as though they'd all come for afternoon tea: "The same as the professor, dear boy. Visiting an old friend."

Charles noted that Logan's eyes briefly slipped sideways, the Wolverine's sole reaction to the presence of Juggernaut, Callisto and another of the Brotherhood who called himself Kid Omega.

Xavier, however, had eyes and thoughts only for the civilians around them: kids on foot and bikes, some bound for playdates or already well under way, others doing homework, a couple holding hands, some gossiping, playing catch, griping about the day's events, anticipating tomorrow's, parents taking care of life and family, tending to gardens, grousing about cluttered rooms or bills, or stressed because of an approaching birthday, eager for an evening on the town.

"I don't want any trouble here, Erik."

"Nor do I, Charles." The awful truth was that while Xavier knew Magneto meant it, that at heart considered himself an ethical being, he also held with equal certainty that so-called humans didn't count. To Magneto, *mutants* were the sentient species; all others on the planet were merely placeholders, to be disposed of as casually as one would throw away a spent tissue.

It was a revelation he'd never actually, truly, allowed himself to face, and it struck Xavier like a spear through the heart, that his friend—whom for so long, in so many ways, he'd considered his other half, the passion to his intellect—had taken his own seat at the conference table at Wannsee. The wheel had turned full circle and brought Erik Lensherr, without him realizing, to the place where *he* had begun, except that now and quite likely forever he stood among those he hated. He had become at last the very thing that had nearly destroyed him.

"Charles?" repeated Magneto, sensing that something was percolating in his old friend's brain but unsure what—which was strange because generally Magneto found Xavier quite predictable. "Shall we go inside?"

"I came to bring her home, Erik. Don't interfere."

"Just like old times, eh?"

"You must trust me, just this once, when I tell you that Jean is more dangerous than either of us ever imagined."

"Well, then," Magneto responded, in a tone of complete assurance, accompanied by a smile of infinite confidence, "it's lucky I'm here to protect you."

As they passed the three members of the Brotherhood, Magneto spoke quietly to Juggernaut: "Nobody gets inside."

Xavier entered first, with Magneto following.

The house was utterly still, and Xavier recognized the same eerie and unnatural quiet, the deadening of all sound he'd seen while reviewing Ororo's memories of Alkali Lake.

They passed the archway that opened onto the living room and saw curtains stir as if in a breeze, although Charles didn't feel the slightest movement of air. Chairs moved across the floor, as though being rearranged by an unseen hand that was impossible to satisfy. Xavier had psi-scanned the house on the drive over and found it substantially blocked to him, gleaning instead from the neighbors' recollections that Jean's parents were away for the week, visiting her older sister, Sara, and the grandchildren, in Boston. This knowledge had been a monumental burden lifted from his shoulders.

In the kitchen, water hung reversed in a cooler, floating up at the top, air bubbles going down. More chairs were shifting, along with the lights. Nothing was at rest. Everything quivered just a little, reminding Xavier of the preshocks before a great earthquake, or the faint rumble that tells you the train is coming right before it hits.

She was waiting in her father's study, surrounded by all the photos and records of accomplishment: diplomas and citations, prom pictures, wedding pictures, baby pictures, all the tangible substance of her life floating in the air along with every piece of furniture in the room. Jean herself was sitting on nothing at all, using telekinesis to create an invisible chair that held her as easily as she did all the rest.

The moment they entered, the furniture crashed to the floor with a tremendous racket. Only her own personal items floated gently to the floor.

Jean sat mainly in a shadow of her own making, very much like a queen upon a throne, surveying them through hooded and wary eyes.

"I knew you'd come," she said, the tension in her voice establishing that this wasn't a ferociously good idea.

Magneto was perfectly content to allow his friend to play Daniel, and let him walk first into the lion's den.

"I've come to take you home," Xavier said, gently as any father.

"I have no home."

"Yes, you do. You have a home and a family who loves you."

She clearly didn't want to listen.

"You know," Magneto interjected, ignoring the sharp glare and warning thoughts hurled by Xavier; indeed, he reveled in them. "Charles thinks your power is too great for you to control."

"Erik!"

Magneto stepped fully into the room, relating to Jean as one monarch to another, manner alone dismissing Xavier as some kind of uppity peasant. "I don't think your mind games are going to work anymore, old friend."

Jean's eyes fixed on Xavier.

"So you want to control me?"

"Yes," Magneto answered for him. "He does."

"No," Xavier said forcefully at the same time, "I want to *help* you!"

"Help me?" Jean wondered aloud, as if considering something she found utterly distasteful. "What's wrong with me?"

"Absolutely nothing," Magneto assured her, daring Xavier to say different—and thereby, given Jean's evident state of mind, strike match to gunpowder.

"Erik," Xavier warned again, with a thought that expressed both desire and exasperation, *for God's sake, stop!*"

"No, Charles, not this time. You've always held her back!"

Xavier spoke to Jean, with a measure of desperation, "For your own good!"

A silver-coated softball, her sister's, shot away from where it had dropped to the floor and shattered a mirror across the room with such force that Xavier had to shield himself from the shards of flying glass.

"Get out," she said, in a tone that brooked no argument. "*Both* of you."

" 'Ro," Logan said to catch her attention, as the Greys' mailbox began to shudder.

"I'm going in," he told Storm, but she grabbed him by the arm.

"The professor said he'd handle this." Her subtext was plain: *She's my friend, too, for longer than you've known her; don't you dare screw this up!*

Juggernaut, obviously sensing a challenge, looking for a fight, strode forward to confront them.

Logan extended his claws. One hand only, three blades, ramming into view with their characteristic *SNIKT!*

"I heard those claws, they can cut through anything," Juggernaut announced. "Wanna take a shot?"

"Don't tempt me, bub," Logan cautioned, but to Storm's great relief, even though she knew how close to the edge he was, he retracted the blades. For assholes like this there'd always be another time. What mattered now, *all* that mattered now, was Jean.

Xavier, of course, didn't take Jean's hint.

"Look at me, Jean."

"No," she snapped. "Stay out of my head!"

Lightbulbs exploded in a cascade that started in the kitchen and made its way through every room. Xavier's wheelchair began to slide backwards, despite the application of its brakes. The walls began to tremble.

"Perhaps you should listen to her, Charles," Magneto suggested, not unkindly.

Xavier was beyond hearing him. "Jean," he said, speaking with his voice while at the same time opening wide the access to his mind so she would see that he was speaking the truth. It was the most calculated of risks, because he was also leaving himself dangerously vulnerable to attack.

"You must trust me when I tell you, you're a danger to yourself and others. . . ."

He forced himself forward, stubbornly determined to overcome her resistance, even though the walls advanced from trembling to outright shaking.

"But we can help you."

Magneto had a flash of inspiration, but it was dreadfully, fatally wrong. "You want to give her the *cure*?"

He of all people should have known that was anathema to everything Xavier held dear, but perhaps in the final analysis he didn't really know his friend as well as he thought he did.

Regardless, Xavier barely heard him. He had eyes only for the fire flickering in Jean's. He refused to be cowed, and held her gaze while the walls shook like they were being pounded on by trolls.

"Look what happened to Scott," Xavier told her. "You killed the man you loved because you couldn't control your power. You damn near did the same to Logan." His thoughts were racing far beyond his voice, trying just as hard to reach her. *The potential within you is glorious, my child, but it must be embraced by the maturity to know how to properly wield it. The reward that awaits is beyond belief, but you must travel the entire path to reach it. There can be no shortcuts.*

She was a grown woman, a kind and generous soul, yet on the levels she was reaching, in the terms Xavier was applying to her, she was still mainly the child he'd met so many years before. And the willful flash of temper displayed then burst forth in his face now as a full-fledged tantrum.

"No!" she cried.

The walls bulged outwards and the stone facing of the house cracked from foundation to roof. The fieldstone hearth behind her shattered, the chimney collapsed. Xavier was bounced back in his wheelchair, smashing into the wall behind him, while Magneto was shot through a set of glass doors to the kitchen.

Magneto tried to rise but the weight of the planet seemed to have settled on him, a weight that no application of muscle or mutant might was able to dislodge.

Logan, with his enhanced senses, heard more than the others.

"That's it," he said, pausing as Ororo called his name.

"Logan, wait for me!"

With that, Juggernaut lowered his helmeted head and charged.

Echoing the tactics they'd used in the Danger Room, Logan and Storm split apart at once.

With a quick glance backwards to ensure the coast was clear, Logan met the onrushing man-mountain head on . . .

. . . and just as quickly found himself at the bottom of a shallow trench gouged all the way across the street, through the sidewalk, and partially into the neighbor's front yard.

Figuring the second hit would be even more fun than the first, Juggernaut kept on coming, faster than before.

Storm, by contrast, went airborne, spinning herself out of the reach of the others left guarding the door. She held herself still in the heart of her vortex, while intensifying the surrounding winds to the point where she generated a localized but formidable tornado. Among mutants left outside, Kid Omega and Radian apparently didn't know which way to turn as the funnel descended on them, striking faster and more accurately than a cobra. Callisto was far quicker off the mark, ducking inside the house the moment Storm went airborne.

The winds slammed the two boys into each other like they were tackle dummies, keeping them so disoriented that they never noticed Ororo dropping down to finish the job with a succession of powerful, accurate blows.

Logan isn't the only X-Man who knows how to fight, she thought.

Unfortunately, she didn't have much time to contemplate this, as Callisto met Storm with a fist to the head as the X-Man followed her inside.

At the rear of the house, Xavier never slackened in his determination to reach his first and most beloved pupil, even as Jean pummeled him mercilessly.

"Jean," he demanded, putting his heart and soul into the struggle, "let—*me—in!*"

She stood over him, refusing to yield, and he knew then that things had gone too far. Neither of them would surrender. There could only be defeat.

* * *

Juggernaut hit Logan again, punching him into the neighbor's house, then through the house, pretty much demolishing it in the process. He hammered Logan up through the ceiling . . .

. . . only Logan didn't come right back down again. Not where Juggernaut expected him to, anyway.

Instead, Logan clawed himself a different hole *behind* his adversary, slashing at some vital joists as he did, to drop as much of the structure as was left on Juggernaut's head. That wouldn't hold the big guy long, he knew. In fact, he was counting on it. He was also counting on making Juggernaut *really* mad. Logan figured he had maybe five seconds, tops, before Juggernaut exploded out of there, and he used them to take off back the way he came, towards the Grey house, to be in a position to meet him.

Jean's eyes glowed with fire. Her hair stirred languidly, as though she were underwater, moved by currents of energy drawn from places Xavier couldn't imagine, but wished with his whole heart that Jean would share. He knew the alarms had sounded back at the Mansion. A mutant manifestation of this magnitude was one of the things he'd designed Cerebro to detect, but without him there to guide the system, all it would do was monitor the event. He assumed Kitty would take charge of the analysis, although back in the day that would have been Hank McCoy's job. Jean was clearly shredding the boundaries between states of reality and possibly even dimensions, and Kitty's phasing power gave her exceptional insight into what happened on a quantum level under such circumstances. Whatever occurred, he knew they would learn from this encounter.

* * *

This time, in the moment before impact, Logan leapt straight up in a stunt Nightcrawler had taught him, way more circus than martial arts, trusting to speed and agility—which he had in far more measure than most folks gave him credit for—to compensate for Juggernaut's unmatchable power. He used the big guy's helmet as a pivot, twisting in midair so that he landed right behind his adversary. Then, while Juggernaut was still a prisoner of his own forward momentum, Logan delivered a kick in the ass that sent him through the front wall of the Grey house like an accelerating Mack truck.

He came in right behind, claws bared, ready for the empirical test to see if Juggernaut's armor, and his power, was any defense against six blades of unbreakable adamantium, taking a moment to register Storm and Callisto messing it up pretty good as 'Ro used a succession of thunder microbursts like punches to bust up the face and body of the other woman.

He landed on Juggernaut's back, poised to strike the killing blow.

Xavier and Jean had long since passed the point of manipulating tangible objects. There were no more walls to see for these two. There was no point in hurling books when the raw energies being unleashed between them slashed across the molecular bonds that gave objects their shape and definition, reducing them in a twinkling to their component elements.

He understood why the advantage was hers. She was fueled by passion, he by intellect. Swept away by the titanic rush of these newly manifested abilities, Jean cared nothing for the consequences, whereas for Xavier those consequences mattered significantly. He didn't want to die, of course, although by now he'd come to acknowledge the very real possibility—but even more, he wanted to find a way to save her. He was a teacher and a healer, and to take any lesser path was an abomination.

He'd tried reaching her with her memories, applying to her consciousness the many talks they'd had on ethics and responsibility, reminding her as strongly as he was able that this dream was as much hers as his. That he may be the mind behind the X-Men, but she was very much their heart. Suddenly it came to him, out of nowhere really—one of those unlikely connections that land as a complete surprise yet seem perfectly obvious once they're in place—that the soul of the team, its moral anchor, was none other than Logan.

He might as well have been trying to stop King Kong with spitballs.

Jean in turn savaged the vaults of his mind for all his failures and regrets. She replayed for him the final breakup with Moira that had sent him off to war. He relived those many, many arguments with Erik Lensherr as their dreams diverged and turned them into strangers. He saw once more Jason Stryker as a boy and then faced him as a man, letting rage take him just for that moment—he couldn't save him either time.

But standing beside each of those images meant to debilitate him, to tear him down and weaken his resolve, were the faces and figures of his successes. A memory of Jean and Hank playing one-on-one basketball, where his awesome dexterity more than made up for her nascent telekinesis. Of Ororo, who'd lived and fought and prospered in the slums of Cairo and Nairobi, and survived the wild lands in between. Two women who couldn't have been more different in heritage and temperament, yet who quickly became inseparable, closer than sisters. Of Scott, who'd come to Xavier lost and alone, but had found the woman he loved.

Xavier's skin rippled then, much as Scott's had. This, he had always known, would be the ultimate danger in confronting Jean. Fighting a telepath was a battle of the mind, simply a matter of overcoming the other psi's defenses. Battling a pure telekinetic was much like any other head-blind adversary; for all their formidable *physical* prowess, switch off the brain and the fight was over. Jean, though, could come at an opponent from *both* directions, a mental attack *and* a physical.

With telekinesis she drew Xavier from his chair . . .

. . . and with him, dragged the entire building from its foundations.

Energy stampeded through the house, and all the combatants in the living room—Logan, Juggernaut, Storm and Callisto—found themselves pinned to the ceiling as inescapably as Magneto was to the kitchen floor.

By this time, however, Logan was as irrational as the woman he loved, fully in the grips of a berserker rage that would not be denied. He didn't try to pluck himself free, but went sideways instead, twisting so that he lay mostly on his belly and then using his claws like climbing spikes to drag his body along.

Xavier sensed Logan's presence and smiled. It was no accident that he alone was free to move.

Jean was now composed entirely of light, a star made

of flesh, so far beyond human and earthly terms of beauty that Charles had no words to describe her. Not even concepts. She simply . . . *was*. And through her, he beheld the window to all that was and is, and the best of all that might be. He saw in her a reflection of himself, an embodiment of all hope and dreams.

And yet . . .

And yet . . .

The very humanity that made all these things possible held in its other hand the darker demons of human nature. Heights were defined by the depths over which they towered; the greater the summit, the more terrible the fall.

Xavier bared his teeth, thankful for the aspect of his power that allowed him to mute his perceptions of pain. The outer sheath of his skin was being flayed on a molecular level and he didn't want to discover how much that hurt.

He caught a sense of Magneto in the kitchen, staring with equal parts horror and fascination. His old friend was completely entranced. He would take from this only what was useful, ignoring the rest, and that would likely be his undoing. Xavier spared a prayer that Erik wouldn't also take the world with him.

He didn't resist anymore. Charles felt an eerie, almost welcome, calm, and knew that he was shining with light too, by this point—although nowhere near as brilliant as Jean. He also knew that as energy, he could neither be created nor destroyed—although his state might well have changed beyond all recognition.

Death would not be pleased with him, this day. He meant to spit in the Reaper's eye.

Because Life—Life would find in him a champion worthy of the name. He was beaten, yes, that was looking altogether likely. But he'd never surrender. And out of that determination and defiance would come the chance, the hope, of ultimate victory. He smiled.

Then he heard Logan's hoarse cry, from very close. He'd done better than Xavier had expected.

Jean ignored Logan. She had eyes only for her teacher.

And he met that glare, continuing to smile, daring her to do her worst.

She took the challenge, as he knew she would.

Xavier had time to voice a single prayer: "Don't let it . . . control . . . you."

And with those words, he cast forth into the heart of her the very best of himself, only a fraction of an unmeasurable pulse of time before she struck what remained of his body with such force that it instantly shattered into less than its component atoms.

A shock wave erupted from the study with cataclysmic effect. In the kitchen, horrified, Magneto threw up his hands to shield his face, coating himself in such an array of magnetic force that he warped compasses for a thousand miles, aware as he did so that if Jean chose to focus on him as she had on Xavier, there'd be just as little he could do to save himself.

The walls of the study bulged and unraveled, molecules of wood unzipping as smoothly as carpet fiber. A solid battering ram of air struck the other four mutants and cast them each in different directions, dumping them throughout the neighborhood, to the astonishment of some of the neighbors, who—because events had happened so unimaginably fast—were only now coming to realize that the area was being torn apart.

The remainder of the Grey house hung suspended for the better part of a minute, and then crashed down, collapsing in upon itself, until all that remained was a pile of rubble and a single, slim, exhausted young woman with haunted eyes and hair the color of fresh-spilled blood.

Of Charles Xavier, there was nothing left but memories.

Out of the chaos rose Magneto, released at last from where he'd been trapped in the kitchen. He spared a small glance at the twisted ruin of Xavier's wheelchair, and saw that it was the focus of Jean's gaze too. She must have known what she'd just done, but was in too much shock for the events to have any true meaning. It was as if it hadn't really happened to *her,* it was just something she'd watched on the news.

He'd felt much the same, that first day at the Auschwitz crematoria, still more boy than man, but strong enough to be assigned as a *Sonderkommando,* to cart the bodies from the gas chambers to the furnaces, to search them for valuables along the way and chip out their gold teeth, and then search the ashes afterwards, just to make sure. If he'd acknowledged the horror of what he'd done, he'd have plunged himself into the flames rather than face another day. He had watched another boy do precisely that, and another still hurl himself on the guards so he could be beaten to death. He'd found a way to survive.

Now he would try to help Jean do the same. And together, they would banish all the nightmares from their past, the demons of memory who stalked them still, and build a future for their people of peace and prosperity.

That was something Charles had never given him credit for—that *he* had dreams too. Perhaps, by achieving them, they could do honor to his friend, and to *all* those who had died before.

"Jean," he said, laying a gentle arm around her shoulder. She was trembling, unable to speak, likely not even fully aware of who he was.

"Come with me."

And he led her out the back . . .

. . . just as Logan bulled his way into the rubble standing out front, with Storm right behind, all thoughts of the mutants they'd been fighting cast aside, their sole concern for their mentor and their friend.

Logan was able to make it to what remained of the study on sheer adrenaline. The minute he crossed the threshold, his body called it quits and he collapsed to his knees. Until he recovered, and he knew that would be a while, he wasn't going any farther. He tagged Jean's scent mixed with Magneto's and told Ororo so, but there was no point in following. Not after his eyes found the wheelchair. The scent combined with the flashes of memory of the things he'd seen while dragging himself across the ceiling confirmed what had happened here.

Charles Xavier was dead.

Logan threw back his head and roared, a cry that echoed out across the nearby houses and raised the hackles on the necks of all who heard it—even Magneto, ushering Jean into his vehicle. Jean blinked a couple of times, as though trying to find her way back to herself, her mouth starting to form the shape of his name, so that her next exhaled breath might say it aloud and re-store some order to her world.

But she caught her breath instead, and sagged into the remains of the furniture behind her.

Charles Xavier was dead and a terror walked the world.

Chapter
Seven

It was a glorious day, with only a bare scattering of clouds to gentle the sun with occasional moments of shade.

One and all, though, the students thought it should be raining. Something torrential, biblical even, would be far more appropriate to how they felt.

This was the private ceremony for what Charles Xavier considered his true family, the students he had gathered and mentored over the decades, all of whom— regardless of age—were feeling more than a little bereft, like ships that had lost their moorings.

There'd been the equivalent of a town meeting. Xavier had left some instructions in his will, but the faculty felt it would be best to give the students their own voice on how to proceed. Charles had wanted to rest on the grounds, among those he loved the best. The only question that had remained was where.

The decision was made to establish a memorial in the garden, because that was always where he taught the hardest cases who came to him. He would take the offending parties and set them to work doing what was difficult for him—caring for his roses. And because he was never one to let pass such an opportunity, those sessions turned into seminars of extraordinary variety and depth. A course of instruction on how to properly transfer a plant evolved quite naturally into a discussion on the nature of structure and balance, and how natural selection was affected by human engineering, which in turn led to philosophy and a measure of history. And since he'd never let anyone get away with just spouting a position—oh no, they'd had to buttress it with citations going back, invariably, to the dawn of writing— that would often lead to a course in Latin or Greek or who knows what else. The deeper into this seemingly makeshift curriculum one went, the harder one wanted to work. A lesson learned, a life saved, roots put down— and not just for the rose.

He had an infectious love of learning, and a respect for knowledge that inspired the same in those around him.

Losing that, for these people, was like stealing the sun from their sky.

There were two stones, the greater cenotaph as tall as Xavier himself, emblazoned with a bas-relief of his face in profile, along with his name and the words FATHER * MENTOR * TEACHER. Beside it was a second pillar, slightly smaller, bearing Scott's name.

The air was very still—Ororo had seen to that—yet the temperature was quite comfortable. Each breath brought them the rich and varied fragrances of the garden, and their ears were touched from time to time by the buzz of honeybees and the occasional trill of birdsong from the surrounding trees. Farther off in the distance could be heard the keen of a hawk, calling for its mate.

Only two were painfully conspicuous in their absence:

Jean Grey and Logan. Neither he nor Ororo had spoken of the events at the Grey household beyond the fact that the professor had been lost during a confrontation with Magneto, and at the moment they were content to let the blame fall entirely on him. But Jean's manifestation of power had sent ripples through the aether that were felt by every student in the school with even a smidgen of psychic awareness. Ororo had to admit, when talking about it alone with Hank, that Jean's actions had likely been sensed by damn near every psi on the *planet*! In a school full of active, inquiring minds, encouraged to think outside the box, it wasn't long before the kids began putting together the pieces and drawing disturbingly accurate conclusions. So, now, they weren't just shaken by the loss of the man who'd recruited every one of them, who'd been their guiding light as they'd explored this strange new world of their powers; they also had to deal with the inescapable fact that one of their own—perhaps the most powerful of them, as well as the member of the staff who was second only to Xavier himself as a nurturing parental figure—had gone rogue.

Nobody had to ask where Wolverine had gone. The only questions were what he'd do when he found her, and whether or not *he'd* come back.

Ororo strode to a space on the grass just in front of Xavier's stone, and took a moment to compose herself—and in that moment she inadvertently allowed all present to see and understand why during her youth in Africa she'd been considered a goddess.

"We live in an age of darkness," she began. "A world of fear and anger, hatred and intolerance."

* * *

Messages of sympathy had come, not only from President Cockrum but from his predecessor, who'd laid the groundwork for all the advances in mutant-sapien relations since. A discreet video feed had been established that allowed these proceedings to be viewed from the Oval Office.

David Cockrum sat at his desk, his wife of many years at his side. He was idly sketching—which is what he did when he was stressed, to center his thoughts and ease his mind—a rough drawing of Xavier as he knew him best, from younger, happier days. No staff were present, as this was a private moment; and presidents never liked anyone outside of closest family to see them cry.

"For most of us," Ororo said, "this is the way things are and always will be. Some maintain it is hardwired into so-called human nature. But in every age there are those who fight against it."

The news had been a body blow. None of the students had needed to be told that the professor was gone. They'd felt his passing the moment it happened—in class, in dorm rooms; everywhere on the great, sprawling campus—as shocking and undeniable as a blow to the gut. And yet—though the initial reaction of many was tears—discussion after the fact revealed that the predominant emotion, what they'd actually *felt* from Xavier, wasn't pain or anger or sadness. Quite the opposite: they'd been aware of a fierce hunger to see what lay over the next horizon, an eagerness to embark on this wonderful new adventure. They felt a sense of grace and peace—and, strangest of all, they felt joy.

* * *

"*Moses, who led his people out of slavery but never reached the Promised Land himself. Abraham Lincoln, who saved the Union and freed the slaves, but never lived to see his country at peace. Franklin Roosevelt, who led America through the Great Depression and the Second World War, yet died before the final victory. John Kennedy and Robert Kennedy, struck down cruelly before their time, their promise unfulfilled.*"

"*Martin Luther King Jr. who fought for equal rights but was struck down by an assassin's bullet.*"

Logan stood just inside the treeline, downwind so he couldn't be scented. He didn't have a great view, he didn't really want one, but he heard every word of what Ororo had to say.

"*It wasn't something they asked to do. They were chosen. And he was chosen, too.*"

She looked up, and her eyes found his at once, as though she'd known precisely where to look for him. The pain in her eyes mirrored his, only more so—and Logan knew she mourned not only the friends she had lost, but feared as well for those about to follow.

He understood, completely, but turned away regardless.

"*Charles Xavier was born into a world divided. A world he tried to heal. It was a mission he never saw accomplished.*"

* * *

Rogue sat at the end of the front row, Bobby beside her, Kitty beside him. None were shy about their tears. Seeking comfort, Rogue reached for Bobby's hand, her eyes closing ever so slightly in frustration and greater sadness at the necessity of being able to touch him only through a glove. Some instinct, perhaps a minimal shift in the way he sat on his chair, prompted a sideways glance and she caught her lower lip between her teeth at the realization that he and Kitty were holding hands as well. Only, the other girl's hands were bare. None of them noticed Peter Rasputin, sitting behind Bobby, with eyes only for Kitty. They'd been an item, once, and after they'd broken up, she'd spent a sabbatical year abroad getting over it. Problem was, he hadn't.

"But Xavier's teachings live on with us, his students. Wherever we may go, we must carry on his vision. The vision of a world united."

That was it. One by one, led by Rogue—whose idea this was—each of them walked to the cenotaph for a moment alone, to say their own farewells, and leave a long-stemmed rose at its base.

X

That night, some of them still found it impossible to sleep. Bobby Drake tossed and turned and fretted for what seemed like forever—but turned out to be less than an hour on the clock—before deciding to raid the kitchen for some soda and ice cream.

Padding down the silent halls, he was caught by a low cooing from Kitty's room, a note of such poignant beauty it stopped him in his tracks. He knew at once what it was, being one of the few who'd actually been introduced to Kitty's dragon. He eased open the door after a warning knock. Bobby had no interest in Lockheed, perched watchfully up in the ceiling shadows, only in the slim, brown-haired, brown-eyed figure slumped cross-legged on the bed.

She waved her hands helplessly when she saw him, her eyes sunken and red from crying. She'd given up on tissues after the second box—they were discared in piles all over the bed and carpet—and now had a bath towel draped across her lap.

Kitty muttered something incredibly rude, indicating her eyes and calling them "waterworks." Bobby knew that she didn't like being blindsided by feelings; taking her cue from her favorite teachers, Ororo and Logan, she much preferred control.

She wiped away her tears with her fingers, then the heel of her hand, then the towel. Didn't do much good— they just kept coming. He'd never seen her look helpless before and briefly considered making a joke, but then thought better of it. Instead, he tried to offer comfort.

"It's okay, Kitty," he told her. "It's okay."

She muttered something even *more* incredibly rude.

Then, a touch more calmly, she responded, "Xavier came to my house. He was the one who convinced me to come to this school."

"Me, too." He sat beside her, gave her a guy-hug across the shoulder. She slumped bonelessly against him and for a frantic instant made him think she'd actually phased into his body. When it had passed, he said, "We're all feeling the same."

She turned to him, her voice soft as she shook her head.

"No, Bobby, we're not. You have Rogue. I have . . ."

She trailed off into silence. He wanted to see her face but she was looking toward the window.

"I just . . . I miss home," she said. She was from a small town outside Chicago, called Deerfield. "First snow, long winters, even the wind off Lake Michigan."

"Hey," Bobby said a little defensively, "we get snow around here."

She gave him a wry look, as though to suggest he made it all himself—which he sometimes did, in fact, when they wanted to go sledding down Suicide Leap.

"It's not exactly the same," she noted. He actually thought it was better, but kept the sentiment to himself.

"What's so different?" he asked, meaning about home.

She shrugged, her voice tired. "Well, for starters, no Mansion, no cool uniforms, no supersonic jet."

"Yeah, I guess there's that."

"Don't you miss it, sometimes? Normal life?"

"What do you mean by 'normal,' Kit-Kat?"

That got him a sour look. She wasn't thrilled with the nickname, which is why he used it now and then to bust her chops. Usually worked great for knocking her out of a funk.

She gave his question due and proper consideration, then said, "I wish I knew."

Suddenly, he found himself acutely conscious of how good she looked, still very much a work in progress but showing all the signs of growing into a major and lasting beauty once she emerged from adolescence. Her lips were very close, open just enough, her eyes half-lidded, to suggest that any advance would not be summarily rejected.

He decided on discretion and indicated her skates, still in the corner where she'd dropped them, many months ago.

"C'mon, girl. Up you get, on your feet, you're with me!"

"It's after curfew, Bright Eyes. Storm told everyone to stay in their rooms."

He gave her a look, saying with his eyes and a twist of his mouth, *What, you* never *broke a rule?*

Aloud, he assured her, "Don't worry, we won't get caught." Then, with a soft and charming smile, "You *can* walk through walls, you know."

Walk through walls *and,* it turned out, on air itself, which unnerved Bobby a tad as she led him down an invisible ramp from her upper-floor room to the ground. Properly phased, her body had no coherent mass, but she could generate motion—very much like swimming. Suspending herself within a greater volume clearly worked the same whether applied to a solid, a liquid, or a gas.

Grateful to be back on terra firma, he led her to the ornamental pond out back. The swimming pool was too obvious for their purposes—too much chance of being caught. Here, hidden amidst the hedges, they were more secure. Both of them felt a measure of comfort to be under the watchful gaze of Xavier, even if it was only a representation of him in profile upon a pillar of stone.

"This place can be home, too," Bobby told her, his words reminding Kitty that he hadn't been back to Boston since the Stryker incident. No letters or calls from his folks, and everything he sent to them was returned unopened.

He touched the water, and just like that it began to crystallize.

Bobby held up her skates and in the second or so it took for her to pluck them from his grasp, the pond was solid ice, the air chill enough to prompt a cloud with every breath.

"I'm not very good," she warned, taking to the ice. In fact, she considered herself a major klutz.

Bobby didn't say a word. He didn't have to—she'd seen him skate. He was beyond gold in skill, he was platinum.

Tonight, though, he showed none of that grace and flamboyance. Instead he made plain that tonight was all about her, and she loved him for it. They skated around the little pond, which actually didn't leave much room to be fancy, and they talked. As time gradually passed, the sorrow began to give way just a little. They weren't up for laughter yet, but the ache inside wasn't quite as bad.

She whooped in alarm as he twirled behind her, hands clasping her waist—it was all she could do to keep from phasing, her reflexive response to any such surprise—pulling her up and around in a spin. She knew what was supposed to come next. The moment her blades made contact, she would allow momentum to pull her through a twist of her own and then grasp his outstretched hand, while still spinning, so that she'd end up with her arm fully extended. It was a maneuver pulled from ballroom dancing, and if she were wearing shoes she could manage it quite nicely.

But she didn't even make it through the first rotation.

She snagged her toe on his, thrust out a leg clumsily to keep from pitching flat on her face, felt her balance go all to hell, and crashed against Bobby, sensing him start to go too—but neither fell.

He caught her strongly and just like that she was cradled in his arms, their bodies tangled tightly together. He was grinning, and she smiled back. It felt good.

"Thank you, Bobby," she said, realizing their eyes had been locked a half-beat too long.

As he nodded agreement, she craned her head up to kiss him on the cheek. Kitty liked the way he smelled and let the contact linger longer than it should have, same as with their eyes. She didn't want the moment to pass.

Upstairs, another student who couldn't sleep saw their heads move together. From Rogue's angle, it looked like Bobby and Kitty were kissing on the lips. What was for them a brief but welcome interlude of peace and reprieve from the misery of recent days, was for her a spike through the heart, in its own way far worse than Xavier's passing.

Bobby was the one who pulled back, but Kitty didn't press. They were both conflicted.

"I'm sorry," Kitty began.

"No, no, no," Bobby interrupted, "I just . . ."

Both voices trailed off.

"Yeah, I know. Me, too."

She butted his shoulder very slightly with hers, a "buddy" thing. "C'mon, popsicle, we should get back inside."

* * *

Logan paused a beat by the window of his room, taking a breath to catalogue the comings and goings outside. His room was usually a mess, the floor strewn almost to overflowing with empty beer cans. It would have been odd that Xavier had never mentioned it, except Logan figured he'd known the reason why. In the dark, it was virtually impossible to find your way across the floor without disturbing them, and even the slightest noise was all the alarm Wolverine needed. Better by far than the flocks of geese that guarded ancient Rome. Today, though, he'd swept it clean, and taken care to polish the floor until it glowed.

Because this time, he really didn't believe he'd be coming back.

"Where are you going?" Ororo demanded from the doorway. He made a face. So much for his clean getaway.

"Where do you think?" he replied, slipping on his jacket.

"She's gone, Logan. She's not coming back." And he knew she wasn't talking about Jean's physical departure with Magneto.

He shook his head. "You don't know that."

He slung his backpack over a shoulder but she blocked the doorway. "No," she told him, making it an order. He quirked an eyebrow, suggesting that she not take this any further. Her eyes had adopted a blue cast that told him she was already drawing on her power; if it came to a tussle between them, it could get ugly.

"Charles was like a father to her," she said. "And she killed him." He could tell it was difficult for her to believe it, even as she said the words, but at the same time it was impossible for her to forgive.

"That wasn't Jean," Logan maintained stubbornly, without a shred of rational evidence to back it up. "The Jean I . . ." briefest of pauses, to find a stand-in for the word he wanted to say, *love,* ". . . know is still in there. I mean to reach her, to find a way to bring her home."

"You truly believe that?"

He nodded tersely. "I have to."

He advanced a step, but she stood her ground. The air around them grew charged enough to raise the hackles on his neck.

"Why?" Ororo cried out, and then, with even more intensity, "*Why?* Why can't you accept the truth?"

"Not my truth, 'Ro."

"Damn it, Logan, why can't you let her go?"

"Because . . ." he said, and found himself completely at a loss for words. "Because . . ."

Her shoulders slumped and the air between them grew calm. She looked at him with more sorrow and sympathy than he'd ever seen in another's eyes—at least directed at him.

"Because you love her."

He nodded.

"Logan," Ororo told him, "Jean made her choice." He started to protest but she stopped him by laying her fingertips across his lips, a gesture that seemed to him very much a caress. It came to him in that instant that *he* wasn't the only one held by the grip of primal emotions. "It's time to make ours," she said. "If you're with us, then make sure you're *with us.*"

She shifted her grip, sliding her hand down from his lips to cup his jaw in a way both tender and achingly intimate, revealing far more of herself with these few small movements than she'd done in all the time he'd known her.

"I've now lost two of my oldest friends, and the only father I've ever really known. I don't want to lose you, too."

With that, she left him.

X

Magneto found Jean standing on the edge of forever. An escarpment rose behind the clearing where the mutants he'd been gathering had made their camp, beneath a cliff as tall as a skyscraper. It looked as if nature had formed this little valley just like a quarry, cleaving the rocks in disconcertingly straight lines.

Jean was balanced right on the edge, staring out across the sky in a way that made him think she was looking straight through the atmosphere at the very stars themselves. And then the thought came to him that she might actually *see* those stars in ways unavailable to the finest telescopes on Earth. He also saw as he approached that she was standing as much on open air as on the rock itself, and he couldn't help but be impressed.

The more he saw and learned about her, the less he truly knew.

"Do you remember," he began, and she sent the ghostly projection of her reply skittering across the surface of his thoughts before he even completed the sentence: *Everything.*

". . . When we first met? Do you know what I saw when I looked at you?"

"A scared little girl," she replied aloud, out of courtesy.

"I saw the next step in evolution." Again, she permitted him a sense of her thoughts, which this time consisted of a round of quiet laughter, as she responded to a joke he didn't get. "What Charles and I dreamt of finding."

Words came this time—a warning: *Be careful what you wish for.*

He ignored her thoughts, and focused on the woman: "And I thought to myself, why would Charles want to turn this god into a mortal?"

"I *am* mortal."

He raised a piece of metal, shaking his head. "I can manipulate the metal in this scrap of iron. But you can do *anything*!"

She faced him at last, intrigued by what he held.

"Anything you can think of," he said.

The fragment of iron popped from Magneto's fingers and began to glow as Jean's telekinesis quickly excited its molecules. His own power gave him insight into what she was doing, and he couldn't help but be amazed as she played with the core molecular structure of the metal, altering its density, its shape, its state, its very physical nature. She made it a glob of primordial ylem, and then formed a tiny statuette. She excited it to a gaseous state, compressed it to the verge of transitioning into a microsingularity. She altered it from iron to wood and then infused that wood with a spark of life, so that if planted in fertile soil, it might very well grow into a proper tree.

Her eyes narrowed as she worked, her mouth wide with a smile of delight, like a child embracing her latest Christmas toys. She had a child's attention span, too, and very quickly she became bored.

The iron fragment flared beyond incandescent, lighting their corner of the shaded forest brighter than any conceivable sun, as bright as Creation must have been during those first moments when the universe was born.

The shock wave staggered Magneto, shook the trees around him, and generated a Fourth of July light show. Below, in the campsite, there were cries of alarm and outrage as the wave coursed through them, playing with their skin as a sudden, fierce squall might the surface of a pond. Jean didn't notice.

"Jean," Magneto commanded, "enough."

That got her full attention. Perhaps not such a great idea.

She was smiling, a little ruefully. He liked that even less.

"You sound like him."

"He wanted to hold you back."

"And what do *you* want?" Jean asked.

"I want you to be *what you are*. As nature intended . . ."

He took her by the shoulder, speaking with his full passion.

"This 'cure' they speak of is meant for *all* of us, whether we want it or not. If we want our freedom as a species, our rightful place among the peoples and nations of our world, then we must *fight* for it. Together, Jean"—he moved close—"we can *win* this war!"

His words struck a chord. She was interested.

Magneto was content.

Callisto was furious.

Followed by Pyro, she intercepted Magneto on his way back to the encampment.

"What the hell was *that*?" she demanded, and he didn't

need telepathy to see that she thought he was crazy for keeping Jean around. "Her power's totally unstable."

"Only in the wrong hands," he assured them.

Pyro obviously didn't buy it. "And you trust her? She's one of them!"

Magneto didn't even spare him a glance. "So were you, once."

"I stuck with you, all the way," Pyro protested as Magneto brushed past him. "I would've killed the professor if you gave me the chance!"

He took a quick, reflexive step back as Magneto rounded on him, consumed by rage. "The professor," he roared right in the young man's face, "was *my friend*!" He paused, for breath and for control: "Charles Xavier did more for mutants than you'll ever know. My single greatest regret is that he had to die to turn the tide."

X

"So what now?" asked Bobby Drake. It was the morning following Xavier's memorial. A bunch of kids had gathered in one of the common rooms after breakfast, to be joined by Ororo and Hank McCoy and ultimately— to a smile of warm relief from Ororo that wasn't returned—by Logan. "What do we do?"

Ororo shrugged. "I don't know, Bobby." Hank knew that none of them had really thought that far ahead. They were still too much in shock.

Hank spoke up, reluctantly, the doctor delivering the worst of news—news that seemed to be just about what everyone was expecting.

"Charles Xavier founded this school," he said. "Perhaps it should end with him?"

Ororo didn't comment, but Kitty gave a shallow nod.

"We should start calling parents," she suggested.

"What?" Bobby sounded outraged, not only at the motion on the table, but also by who it was coming from.

"She's right, Robert," Hank said. "We should tell the students they're going home."

"Most of us," Peter Rasputin reminded him, "don't *have* anywhere to go."

Bobby shot to his feet. "I can't believe this! I can't believe we're not going to fight for this place!"

Ororo didn't move from her place by the window, so it was Logan who answered Bobby's challenge.

"Charley's dead, kid," he said. "The professor is dead."

Bobby, angrily: "So *what*?"

"There is no school," Logan explained patiently, although it was clear to Hank that what he wanted far more was a session of unrestricted berserker mayhem. "There is no choice."

"There's *always* a choice!" Bobby threw his own words back at him, and then, rushing onwards: "But what do you care? This was never your home!"

Logan looked ready to reply, but instead turned to face the doorway.

Facing them was an angel.

"I'm sorry," Warren said, picking up on the vibe. "I know this is a bad time . . ." His body language and manner told Hank that he fully expected to make things worse.

"My name is Warren Worthington," he introduced himself, then with a shy, self-deprecating smile added, "the third."

Everyone knew the name. Warren plunged ahead regardless.

"I was told this was a safe place for mutants."

"It was, son," answered Hank.

"No, Henry," snapped Ororo. "It *is*."

With a long and even stride, every step proclaiming the rightness of her decision, Ororo crossed the room to the doorway leading to Xavier's study.

"Bobby," she told him as she passed, "show Mr. Worthington to a room."

She threw open the door and entered, with the rest of them following—curious, expectant, impressed, outraged—like fish caught in her net, to behold her taking her place behind the desk, as though it were hers and always had been.

"And tell all the students the school will remain open."

Hank watched her look past the assemblage to Logan, who hadn't made a move.

"This *is* our home," she told them all, but her words were mainly meant for him. "And as long as I'm here, this will be a safe haven for mutants."

There were smiles all around—even from Hank—and a muffled chorus of "Aw-*riiight*!" "Outstanding!" "Way to go, 'Ro!" From Logan, though, not a word, not even a nod. Ororo had made her decision. He made his. He left.

Upstairs, a little later, Bobby ushered Warren into a room.

"Might not be what you're used to," he semiapologized.

"It's perfect," Warren assured him.

"Yeah," Bobby nodded, comprehending the multiple meanings. "No parents."

With just those few words, they made a connection. And from it Bobby intuited at once that Warren had a lot to process, work best done in private. Telling the new arrival he'd give a yell at dinnertime, Bobby stepped out into the hall to leave the boy alone. As he closed the door, though, he caught a glimpse of Warren flexing his wings, stretching the gleaming alabaster pinions so wide they scraped the walls of the room.

With that sight came the obvious code name for so glorious a creature, that encompassed his strength and the evident courage it must have taken to break from his father—whom it was equally apparent the young man still loved—and of course his unearthly beauty.

"Welcome to Xavier's," Bobby breathed, *"Angel!"*

He left the room by a different route, to knock eventually on Rogue's door and quietly call her name, "Rogue?" And then, answered by silence, "Marie?"

It wasn't locked, and his eyes widened as the door swung open on an empty room. She hadn't taken much, and the chaos surrounding the bureau and closet told him she'd packed in a hurry. No note, no clue. *Damn her and her impulses!*

Outside, he encountered Peter and asked the obvious.

"Hey, Pete, you seen Rogue?"

"She took off."

"When? Where? *Why?*"

Peter had no clue. Bobby'd have to figure out this one on his own.

X

Logan stood before Xavier's cenotaph, replaying those final moments over and over in his memory. He hadn't moved for most of the day, but everyone at the school had the common sense to leave him be. His eyes were at half-mast, giving the impression he was dozing—but the tension in his body totally belied that. He was in full predator mode, waiting for . . . *something*—damned if he could articulate precisely what—and when it arrived he'd be ready to deal with it.

Trees rustled as his patience was rewarded. The woods were deep in shadow, and as he looked he found nothing there to see. Both trees and air seemed still, yet his ears reported the sound of movement. It was big, and coming straight for him.

He flexed his fingers, but left his claws retracted. The same instinct that alerted him to the approaching presence now assured him he was in no danger. This thing was as much the predator as he was, but it wasn't hunting tonight. At least, not him.

And just like that, within the space of a single breath, his head was filled with the scent of her.

He heard her call his name. "Logan!"

Before he could reply, his perceptions twisted inside out and he found himself tumbling through a cascade of waypoints, laying out a trail he could easily follow that led unerringly to a hidden forest encampment below a towering cliff.

"Come to me," Jean pleaded, and the force of her desperation, her need, her stark terror, drove him to his knees.

"Help me," she begged, and he realized that both sets of his claws were now extended, gleaming despite being shrouded in twilight shadows. Her doing, he sensed, a further tweaking of her perceptions, to show him what was needed.

"*Save* me," she asked of him, in the barest whisper, and then the air fell still once more and the scent of her was nothing but a memory.

He sat up, back ramrod straight, blades resting open on his thighs, legs folded under him in the Japanese manner that was an unexpected constant in his nature and the source of much speculation among the student body. How could a roughhouser from the Canadian backwoods have a real affinity for one of the most structured, mannered and *ordered* societies in history? Logan had no answers either. He simply accepted it as a part of himself, like the healing factor.

He stayed that way as the evening turned fully dark, then with uncharacteristic formality, folded both forearms across his chest, so they formed the shape of an X, and retracted his claws. With a fluid grace he rolled to his feet and laid a set of fingertips on the crest of the great stone, his eyes meeting the face emblazoned on its side. There was a little bit of humor to the way his mouth quirked; he was, after all, a man with an appreciation for irony.

"You were right, Chuck," he admitted at last. "You were always right."

Nobody heard him retrace his steps through the Mansion, but Ororo was waiting at the carriage house, where she had her loft, with the keys to his bike. There was no need for words. They parted with an embrace that carried with it an acceptance of what was, but also a promise of a future not yet even dreamed of.

Then, with a roar that woke the house as he opened the bike's throttle wide, he hit the road.

Logan had a lot of miles to go before he slept—and a promise to keep.

Chapter Eight

Some folks called it Mutie Town. Some smart-ass in the city bureaucracy slapped on the label District X. Back in the day—which in this instance was a century and a half ago—Manhattan's Lower East Side had been the tenement home to successive waves of immigrants to America's shores, starting with the Irish, then the Italians, the Jews, all the polyglot variations of country and culture in Middle Europe, followed by the Chinese and most lately, the rest of Southeast Asia. The joke in the Big Apple was that you could stroll from the Williamsburg to the Manhattan Bridge and encounter the world in small, every nationality and ethnic group currently extant upon the globe. And probably a fair sampling of the ancient ones as well. It was *that* kind of city.

The newest to arrive sort of broke the mold, in that these folks were substantially homegrown. Here, among the mean streets and hardcore neighborhoods the city would rather forget, mutants gathered to make their home. And like every immigrant group that preceded them, once established they'd begun to extend their influence beyond those initial, confining boundaries, agitating over time for the same services and respect accorded everyone else. True, they lived in a ghetto, but they also believed acceptance was only a matter of time.

Here, in the media capital of the world, Warren Worthington Jr. and Kavita Rao had established their first clinic, promising an instant escape from years of struggle and hardship, offering the chance for mutants to rejoin the rest of humanity.

Rogue had waited on line all night to reach the clinic. She'd filled out all the proper forms and been assigned a place in the waiting room. And that was how she spent her day, from that point on: sitting, watching those around her, and waiting. Same as them.

Some of the mutants appeared excited, others conflicted. The first time they called your name, it was for a session with a counselor, who outlined the nature of the procedure, the potential ramifications. For example, special care had to be taken with those mutants whose life processes involved toxic substances or harmful environments. Reverting someone with gills without the means of yanking them out of the water, pronto, was a nonstarter. Likewise a mutant with sulfuric acid for blood. If you existed in multiple dimensions, Rogue mused to herself, how can you be sure you'll end up in the right one?

The other aspect the counselor hammered home, returning to it again and again, was the fact that you couldn't change your mind. Once applied, the reversion couldn't be undone. You make the choice, you're stuck with the consequences. Being a mutant, that was fate's fault, or nature's, or God's; you could vent against those higher powers all you pleased. The cure, however, was all on you.

That's why no adolescents were being allowed to participate in these initial trials. Accepting the legal arguments put forth by attorney Vange Whedon (herself a mutant, able to morph into a dragon), head of the Mutant Rights Coalition, the feds had conceded this was too big and absolute a decision to be made *for* someone, even by loving parents wanting only the best for their children.

Rogue had done her session this morning, returned to her seat, and patiently continued to wait her turn, wishing her power applied to inanimate objects as well as people so she could lay a hand on this chair and turn herself into a statue of plastic and metal. The longer she waited, the crazier she became, content with her choice one moment, frantic the next. She thought of all she'd done with the X-Men and wondered *How could she possibly give up such a life?*

She ached for Bobby's touch and wondered why she had to wait, and then worried what would happen if things didn't work out—if he had only pretended to care for her? She had to admit there was a fundamental safety in her power. Her body was absolutely her own, and no one could lay a hand on her without suffering the consequences. Could she handle being vulnerable? Was the need that ate her up inside worth the price?

Oh God, oh *God,* what if she was wrong?

The inner door opened and a couple emerged. They'd been a mixed pair, she remembered from earlier—he a mutant, she not. Now, they were just a couple, very much in love, holding each other, cooing endearments, touching, stroking, marveling at this catalogue of new sensations that made them perpetually giddy.

The nurse overseeing the line consulted her clipboard and read off the next name.

"Marie," she called.

The name didn't register at first. Rogue was too used to being addressed by her code name. When the nurse called again, she reacted with a start, raising her hand and putting herself into a minor tumult as she gathered her gear and stepped through the indicated doorway.

X

Protestors lined the street, pro-cure and anti-, plus a group representing the self-proclaimed "Web-Nation" *Purity,* who called down a plague on both their houses, decrying the cure as a worthless smokescreen and holding fast to their core belief that the only good mutant was a dead mutant.

Opposite, and looking understandably anxious, was an unexpectedly thick crush of mutants, all apparently trying to get into the clinic at once. The police had started out by establishing and trying to enforce a line along the face of the clinic building, but the number and intensity of the protestors had gradually driven those prospective patients into a huddle of self-defense. There'd been attempts to move the protestors back, but again sheer numbers were a problem. The fact that two of the three groups consisted of individuals with every variety and degree of power didn't help. Closing the clinic and sending everyone home was no option—that decision was just as guaranteed to start a riot as attacking the protestors.

The reality of the situation was that nobody had anticipated the sheer numbers involved, on all sides. Tomorrow, they'd hopefully have a better plan. For today, which so far had gone fairly well, they'd just have to keep their fingers crossed.

Bobby couldn't believe his eyes as he had made the corner of Houston and found himself facing police lines and bodies galore. Talking really fast and using a lifetime's quota of dumb luck, he'd managed to work his way up to the clinic. Didn't hurt to bump into some friends among the cops, including the tactical commander on-scene, Inspector Lucas Bishop (a mutant and former student of Xavier's) and his senior sergeant, Charlotte Jones.

It was a gamble coming down here, but try as he might he couldn't think of where else Rogue might go. He understood that he was a large part of the reason why she might consider taking such a step, but he really couldn't comprehend why she'd go through with it; he wouldn't—couldn't—give up his power for anything. Until, thinking hard on the train ride into Grand Central, he had asked himself how *he'd* feel if their powers were switched. If he couldn't ever touch the woman he so desperately loved. He understood as well that he could promise to be faithful on a stack of Bibles, and *mean* it, and she'd still have doubts. Because, as she'd said, he was a *guy*.

But he had to believe there was another way. Or—if she was truly determined to go through with it, he would join her. Would he hate her for that, after? Would she come to resent him, in the belief that he hated her for it? Suppose things didn't work out—what then?

His head was splitting and his heart was pounding. He couldn't think anymore. The more he tried to find a way out of this maze, the more tangled and crazy he got.

In desperation, he had boiled it down to one immutable element: he loved Rogue. He would search until he found her. Everything else could wait until afterwards.

As the crowd condensed more and more into an immovable crush, Bobby wished he was much taller.

Then, he caught a familiar flash of emerald green exiting the clinic. He didn't need to see her distinctive stripe to know it was her, just knowing the way she moved was enough.

Yelling her name did no good. She had her head down, and he felt ice form around his heart at the thought she'd actually done it.

But thinking of ice gave him an idea. If he couldn't reach her with his voice, he'd deliver a message *made* of ice, writing her name between the buildings in great big letters.

He lost sight of her and tried to bull his way forward, realizing that his brilliant idea wouldn't be of much use if he put the signal up on the wrong street.

Bobby was making decent headway—when he ran into Pyro.

"Johnny?" he asked foolishly. "What are you doing here?"

"What are *you*, popsicle?" Pyro sneered back at him, making it impossible for Bobby to believe they'd ever been buds. "Getting 'cured' so you can go home to mommy and daddy?"

"Fuck you."

Pyro noticed Bobby still searching the crowd and snapped his fingers.

"Oh, I get it. Looking for your girlfriend. Figures she'd be here."

You really are an asshole, Bobby thought. Without consciously realizing it, he'd clenched his fists, his power coating them with a sheen of ice.

"Same old Bobby," Pyro chuckled, and it wasn't a compliment. Bobby wanted to wipe the smirk off the other mutant's face but there were too many bystanders, packed too close around them. "Still scared of a fight."

Bobby heard the faint click of Pyro's Zippo and saw a small ball of fire appear on the flattened palm of an out-held hand.

Oh my God, he thought, and made a grab for his former roommate as Pyro headed for the clinic.

"Stop!" he cried uselessly, knowing Pyro wouldn't listen. "John, *stop!*"

He caught at the other's sleeve, but John sidestepped between some other people, breaking the hold and using them to block Bobby's path while he worked his way closer to the building.

Bobby heard him yell, as if this were a treat, *"Fire in the hole!"* and then, Pyro let loose a sphere of fire the size of a soccer ball, arcing it through the air like a goalie clearing the net. Perfect aim, right through a ground-floor window.

It detonated like a bomb, flames punching out every door and window along that corner of the structure, casting forth a shockwave of blistering heat that knocked those nearest flat to the street and set the rest of the crowd to panicked, screaming flight.

Bobby was among those dropped by the force of the explosion, and the only one to react properly. A score of people were burning, clothes ignited by the outrush of flames, and even as he started to move towards them, a series of sharp secondary blasts shattered windows on the upper floors, sending a cascade of glass shards towards the crowd like searing-hot shrapnel.

His response was just as quick—he generated cocoons of ice to extinguish the folks who were burning, plus a wall to shield the rest from the flying glass. He could hear screams from inside the building. The fire had spread with fearful speed along the ground floor, covering the elevators and stairwells, trapping everyone who was upstairs. It was a low-rise building, the fire department could reach the upper windows and roof with their ladders—except that the blaze was growing too quickly. Pyro's fireball was composed of superheated plasma of such intensity it created an instant firestorm inside the building. Quick as New York's Bravest could possibly respond, even if it was only a matter of minutes, they'd likely find nothing but a gutted shell.

Bobby iced the roof and worked his way down from there, intentionally keeping the coating thin enough that it would almost instantly melt. It wasn't easy—he had to provide enough ice to create a constant deluge of water that would check the advance of the flames, enabling him to advance gradually upon the hyperhot core of the firestorm. Dumping ice directly on top of it would create a disaster all its own. The near-solar heat would flash the ice directly to steam, proving just as deadly to anyone it touched and doing nothing to eliminate the threat.

At the same time, he created a pair of ice slides at the other end of the building, as far removed as possible from the fire itself, allowing those trapped a means to escape.

His head quickly began to pound—he wasn't used to this much exertion. The more ice he generated to douse the fire, the more it demanded. He felt like he was trying to fill an ocean by himself. The air around him grew tinder dry, and lashes of pain laid themselves across his back and chest as the effort of channeling atmospheric moisture through his body grew exponentially.

Then, dimly, far off in the distance, he heard the grumble of thunder, and a gust of air swirled around him, as heavy with moisture as a fog. He remembered the phalanx of cameras—the day's events were being carried by every local channel and the 24/7 national news feeds. When Pyro threw his bombshell, they must have gone live globally—which he'd bet his life was exactly what Magneto had planned. At the same time, though, it must have allowed Storm to see his predicament and realize what was needed. She'd upped the humidity in the air around him to the level of a tropical rain forest, giving him more than enough resources to finish the job.

Even so, he was breathless and swaying on his feet a couple of minutes later, after it dawned on him that he'd turned the clinic building into an ice palace. He could sense no more hot spots within, and water that had been pouring from the shattered walls and windows in a flood had slowed to minor trickles. Bobby could hear sirens at last, although to him they seemed very far away. So did the people talking to him. He could see their lips moving, as the civilians in the crowd were pushed aside by reporters and police, coming together like a rugby scrum, equally determined to get to him.

At the moment, though, he had eyes only for his creation, which he had to admit was quite a sight. The entire building was covered with ice sparkling blue-white in the sun, so brightly it must have been hard for people to look at without sunglasses. Bobby himself had long ago discovered he had no problem with either snow or ice glare. The slides at one end were complemented at the other by huge sculpted mounds that had been formed by the water plunging from the building. Closest to the walls, they resembled giant African termite hills, but as he looked up and out he saw them branch into more delicate arches and pillars, spires and ramps, with stalagmites reaching up from the street intersecting with stalactites dripping down from above. A nearby light-pole was linked to the building by artfully delicate strands of ice, as were some street signs, giving the impression that some crystalline spider had been busily at work on its latest web. The sun cast the scene in flashes of diamond brilliance, but also playfully mixed in prismatic bursts of color as the ice caught its rays and refracted them, creating a succession of microrainbows to complement the much larger one forming in the supersaturated air overhead.

Another outcry from the crowd shattered his momentary reverie. A burst of fire was coursing through the air, as though from a flamethrower, to sear a symbol through the ice and into the brickface of the old tenement building: the Greek letter Ω, for Omega, the last letter in their alphabet, used to represent the end of things.

Bobby looked hard, tried to force his way towards the source of the fire, thinking he caught a glimpse of Pyro—but the crowd was too large and too spooked.

Police and journalists were already pressing his way and with fire and rescue units converging on the scene from every direction, continuing any sort of effective pursuit was a forlorn hope.

The gaggle of reporters barely got to throw a single question before their collective attention was distracted by an all-too-familiar voice booming from the speakers of a nearby radio. Waves and yells from one of the newsvans brought an instant audience, everyone pressing close enough for a view of Magneto's face as he began his broadcast, addressing them with the formal gravity of the president from the Oval Office.

"Today's attack on your 'cure' was only our first salvo. . . ." he informed the world.

"So long as this so-called cure exists, our war will rage. Your cities will not be safe. Your streets will not be safe. *You* will not be safe."

Bobby shook his head in mingled misery and frustration, painfully aware of the looks that were being split between the man on the screen and himself by the people around him, noting how they began to edge away, clearing a definable space between themselves and the mutants.

Over his shoulder, the mutants who'd come to the clinic were gathered around one of their own, who'd assumed the code name Broadband, as he generated a three-dimensional representation—plucked from the airwaves by his power—of what the rest were watching on their TV screens.

Thankfully, the firemen, paramedics, and a number of the cops, led by Bishop and Charlotte Jones, hadn't forgotten their responsibility to the injured. They finished triaging all who'd been hurt and sending them off to the hospital. If not for Bobby's instant intervention, they would tell him a little later, the consequences would have been far more awful. Instead, thanks to him, there were only a comparative handful of third-degree burns; the rest of the casualties suffered more damage to their clothes than their persons.

"You want a cure," he watched Magneto say on Broadband's life-sized generated image. "You will have it. A cure to *all* that ails you." He didn't much like the sound of that. But where Magneto was concerned, what the hell else was new?

X

At the Mansion, Storm and Hank quietly joined other students and faculty in the common room to watch the same broadcast.

"And to my fellow mutants," Magneto concluded, "I make you this offer, and this warning: Join us or stay out of our way. Enough mutant blood has been spilled already."

That was it. Silence reigned for the first two or three seconds, before one of the younger kids stuck out his forked tongue and delivered a rousing Bronx cheer.

He got the laugh he'd wanted—but only for a moment, before the broadcast switched over to the newsroom and began to present a series of reports from around the country. The incident in Lower Manhattan hadn't been an isolated attack, but part of a coordinated group of simultaneous strikes throughout the nation. There'd been no X-Man present to protect those others and the results were ruin after gutted ruin, and a casualty list—including a body count—that made many watching weep.

X

Visibly furious, the president switched off the Oval Office TV and hurled the remote into the depths of the nearest couch. He stood directly over the Great Seal and as he glared at the floor, he remembered what he'd long ago been told about the eagle. In time of peace, as now, its head faced to its right, towards the olive branches clasped in one great claw. In war, it turned the other way, towards the brace of arrows held in its left claw. If it weren't for all the furniture in the way, he was more than ready to indulge in an irrational impulse to flip the damn thing over himself.

He gave vent to his frustration. "Who in the name of all that's holy does that mad, arrogant mutant sonofabitch think he *is*? Does he really want a *war*? Does he truly believe he can *win*? Or that the world that survives will be worth living in, for *anyone*?"

"We're trying hard to track him, sir," came the response from Bolivar Tresk, along with Cockrum's sudden, bitter, cynical thought, *But that trick* never *works*. "We're working hard—"

The president indicated the TV. "Yes, I see that." He faced the much bigger man. "Work harder, Bolivar. We cannot allow this to continue. We cannot let him do this."

"Well then, sir, you know what needs to be done."

Cockrum stood before his desk, staring at the collec-

tion of files he'd been reading, all color-coded to indicate the highest level of security; even some of the men
and women now in this room weren't permitted to see
them. He seriously considered the one marked "Sen-
tinels," then decided they were better held for another,
darker day, praying as he did so that day would never
come.

Then again, he'd offered pretty much the same prayer
about today.

"Those weapons," the president told Trask. "I want
them commissioned. I want Worthington Labs secured.
I want troops in front of every clinic. Magneto is not
going to dictate terms to this White House, or infringe
on the the rights of our people."

In the background, the press secretary scribbled notes
furiously, collecting a couple of the president's phrases
to use later for sound bites.

"Anyone who wants that cure gets it," the president
reiterated, indicating that he wanted to make sure *this*
statement made print and airwaves. "We will protect
every citizen, human *or* mutant, by any means necessary."

X

Within the hour, security was in place—either FBI
SWAT teams working in conjunction with local law en-
forcement, or troops culled from the National Guard. It
was a visually impressive show of force, but, as with displays in earlier emergencies, at airports and railroad sta-
tions, the public had very real doubts as to whether a
determined attack could truly be prevented. Stopping

guys with bombs was one thing, but stopping guys who could *be* bombs, or manifest who knows what other kind of mutant power, was something else entirely.

Since New York held the greatest concentration of mutants east of the Mississippi, it was decided that the clinic here should reopen as soon as possible. The Manhattan location was a total loss, but Worthington had leased space across the river in Brooklyn: a building at the convergence of Atlantic, Flatbush and Fourth Avenues, with easy access to a half dozen subway and rail lines. The vulnerability of the location made the public security departments blanch, but the space hadn't been chosen for its defensibility. Ease of access was the main consideration. They'd just have to deal.

Antiterrorist sniper teams were deployed under cover of darkness to the surrounding rooftops and as they moved into position, their bosses began to breathe a little easier. The clinic was in the open, with high ground on every side. This gave the shooters a more than adequate series of overlapping "kill zones." Press releases identified the boots on the ground as National Guard, but that was only partly right; the detail was a mix of the National Guard and army regulars. More to the point, all of them were combat-experienced veterans with significant experience in urban population control. They knew their job and they'd follow orders. They wouldn't panic.

As they moved into position, they exchanged their M16s for shotguns that fired nonlethal bullets and gas canisters for crowd dispersal. Each man was issued a hand weapon, plastic, with backup magazines sufficient to deal with a multitude.

A secure perimeter was established around the clinic, with sandbags and fencing, and defined areas set aside for protestors, as well as for prospective patients.

The protestors were first on the scene, yelling and screaming in an attempt to intimidate the patients. They were quickly joined by their rivals, who were for the cure, an assemblage that was mainly nonmutant sapiens, with a scattering of mutants. They seemed to have the numbers, although the anticure mob definitely had the volume. The patients and their escorts were, of course, stuck in the middle.

Ororo had offered the services of the X-Men, and had very politely been rebuffed at every level of government, from the White House to City Hall. The help was appreciated, but the consensus was that the X-Men might provoke trouble more than forestall it. The subtext, unfortunately, which Ororo and Hank had recognized all too well, was that the X-Men in particular, along with mutants in general, weren't to be trusted. The team's actions in the past, including Bobby's the other day, didn't matter. Better for all concerned that they stay clear and let the proper authorities handle things.

Lucas Bishop was once more in charge of the NYPD contingent, with Charlotte Jones beside him. The seveneight, a couple of blocks away on Bergen, was her home precinct, and Prospect Heights, her home, period. Her folks lived a little farther in the other direction, in Fort Greene, so this wasn't just the job for her. This was very personal.

The protestors surged forward, against the NYPD wooden sawhorses and the baton- and shield-carrying guardsmen who backed them up. A sergeant yelled at them through his bullhorn, "Everyone, please, get back!"

Around Bishop and Charlotte, everyone moved into their proper position. In their earbugs, which tied them into the command net, the two bosses heard the status reports from all the sniper teams.

"Perimeter secure," came the report.

"Good," Bishop said. Then, into his own radio, repeated more loudly for the benefit of the troops nearby, "Let's start letting them in!"

A quartet of troopers, the biggest they could find, tucked the first clutch of mutants between them, like saplings amidst redwoods, and headed for the entrance. Watching, Charlotte remembered her dad telling her what it had been like as a boy, watching news reports from Little Rock, showing federal marshals escorting a little black girl into the first integrated school in the city, in the face of a mob of snarling, hate-filled faces spewing every cruel and hurtful catcall they could think of. She'd seen the Norman Rockwell painting as well, and hoped there was someone of equal talent and passion who could document this generation's moment of grace and courage. She was glad she had the opportunity to stand amongst their defenders, as her heart ached to see more than a few she knew—some quite well—among the protestors.

There was a construction site nearby, and some of the crowd had collected some loose bits and pieces of rubble in passing; it didn't take long for them to start throwing. The troopers used their shields as they'd been taught, linking them as the ancient Roman Legion had done to create the "turtle," putting an unbreakable roof over their heads for protection.

But the shield wasn't foolproof and not all the projectiles were deflected. One soldier went down, blood streaming from a gash below his helmet. Charlotte helped drag him clear and an NYPD uniformed officer took his place. The line bowed, retreated perhaps a step, but otherwise held.

Slowly, patiently, the snipers and their spotters swept the crowd with their high-powered lenses. Rounds chambered, safeties off, fingers rested beside the triggers, but not on them. Boring, meticulous work, maximum stress, because they couldn't relax their vigilance even a smidge, and when the time came to act, they had to be perfect. It wasn't even that warm a morning, yet, one and all, the snipers were sweating.

At Bishop's command, the line of guards advanced, step by relentless step, easing the protestors back to their original position. The order for the day, emphasized repeatedly all along the chain of command, was restraint. No screwups were acceptable, not in the face of such comprehensive media coverage, not with the whole world watching. He spared himself a ghost of a grin at the thought, because some among the protestors—although he couldn't yet tell which side—had begun that very chant, as their parents and grandparents had before them. "The Whole World Is Watching! The Whole World Is Watching!"

A stir among the anticure crowd snagged his attention. He began to respond. He noticed Charlotte turning as well, reacting to the same cop instinct, the same subconscious cues.

Someone was charging out of the crush and into the

open. Lizard skin, with legs made more for jumping than walking.

"Green light," Bishop said into his headset. "At your discretion." There wasn't an instant's thought given to the repercussions if he was wrong, and he trusted his men as he did himself.

Sniper Team One across the avenue, twelve stories up, had the best angle. Officer Zak Penn stopped chewing his gum, tapped lightly on the button that laid the scarlet dot of his laser square against the center of the mutant's back, and shifted his finger to the trigger.

The charging mutant leapt into the open, covering half the distance to the police line with the first jump and reaching a height that told them his second would put him on the roof. He had a bomb, of course. He also intended to be long gone when it detonated; he'd only need a second to drop the thing and another to be an entire block removed from the blast.

Penn made the necessary adjustments, pulled the trigger, and started chewing again while chambering the next round. He was ready for a second shot, but knew he wouldn't need it.

The mutant was barely off the ground when the projectile hit him, right on the money.

He dropped as hard as if he'd just been hit by an invisible linebacker, going into violent convulsions the moment he landed. Bishop started forward, hand on his own weapon, while Charlotte yelled for the paramedics.

But the seizure passed as quickly and abruptly as it had begun, and concern turned to astonishment as scales flaked off the man's body, revealing clean, *human* flesh underneath. His head had been crowned by a succession of bony ridges, running front to back, rising to a central crest. Now he was nearly bald, with a definite shading of hair. And as for his legs—originally they'd formed a shape something like a wild S, made for leaping huge buildings with a single bound. Not anymore. Pink feet and ordinary—*normal*—toes were what could be seen sprouting from the hem of trousers which had fit perfectly before but were now hugely oversized.

Slowly, wobbling because his balance and center of gravity had changed so markedly, struggling to get used to the new configuration of his body, the man—who'd been a mutant—rose to his feet. He stared, dumbfounded, at his hands and then lifted them and his face skyward, unleashing all his grief and rage in one monstrous bellow of denial that echoed and re-echoed throughout the suddenly silent plaza:

"Nnnnooo!"

Nobody else said a word as a couple of cops and troopers trundled forward—nothing quick or graceful about moving in all that gear—to trip him up and put him gently down so they could bind his wrists with zip ties and hustle him to the nearest police van for processing.

The protestors said nothing, did nothing, although some shot nervous looks at the neighboring rooftops, wondering what would happen next.

Off to the side, watching from the roof of their truck, which afforded the best vantage, one of the local reporters elbowed her camera guy in the ribs: "Tell me

you got that," she demanded of him and was rewarded
by a terse, satisfied nod.

X

Worthingon Jr. snapped off the TV. He couldn't bear
to watch anymore.

"What have I done?" he asked. "What have I done?"

It wasn't just the violence done to the clinics that
haunted him; in a way, he'd half-expected such a reaction, as it was emblematic of the times. What struck him
to the quick—coming on the heels of his own son's terror at the prospect of the needle—was the look on the
mutant's face as he realized what had been done to
him. Thus far, the only mutants Worthington Jr. had encountered directly were those who'd embraced what he
offered. Here was the first time he'd seen someone transformed involuntarily. The fact that he was likely a terrorist, committing a criminal act that might have gotten
people hurt or killed, didn't matter to him—which was
strange because he was a devout proponent of law and
public order. It was coming face-to-face with the realization that he'd done something irrevocable.

He remembered a movie from his youth, seen on a
day one afternoon in London, Fellini's *Satyricon*. Early
on in the movie, a man—an extra, a derelict drafted off
the streets—had actually allowed his hand to be severed
at the wrist, in a scene presenting how ancient Rome
punished criminals. He had never understood how that
person had permitted himself to be so mutilated, or how
any other rational, *decent* person could have committed
the act. What was done could never be undone, the hand
gone forever.

Just like that mutant's powers.

He remembered that tragic moment in the bathroom, beholding his son, the light of his life, slashing at himself with a boning knife, desperate to pluck away the wings sprouting from his back, unable to accept the cruel alterations in his body that would make them practical. He'd held the boy in his arms, the two of them rocking back and forth, as so much blood flooded over them that when his wife came home from work she screamed and damn near fainted, thinking husband and son had both been murdered. They'd all sobbed themselves to sleep that night, without any answers to their prayers. Why, oh *why,* had God done this to their bright and beautiful boy? Ultimately, they'd homeschooled their son because Warren hated to go outside. He had to strap his wings into a cruel harness that made him feel like he was walking around in a perpetual hammerlock, desperately afraid of what would happen if anyone found out. He broke contact with his childhood friends; he hardly left his room. Briefly, they considered consulting with Charles Xavier, but neither of them wanted their boy to be lumped in with a student body that was described in the popular press as either freaks or terrorists, or both.

Beyond that, Worthington Jr. had begun to consider the course of his son's life *after* school. Who would hire a man with wings? What work could he do? And what would this mean for any grandchildren should he ever marry?

So many hard questions, so few satisfactory answers, so much misery for all concerned. He found himself imprisoned in a box, and so he had sought a solution that was outside the box, which is what led him to Kavita.

Her research seemed to him a godsend, her discovery the ideal solution to everyone's problem.

Until this moment, when all his good works and intentions turned to ashes in his mouth.

"All I wanted to do was help," he said, a little bit lost, a little bit helpless, recalling out of nowhere the old saying about what paved the road to Hell.

"Perhaps," Dr. Rao offered, "we hadn't considered the full ramifications of the cure."

"I just . . ." Worthington Jr. said, his explanation more for his own ears than hers, "I thought this would bring us together."

Rao shook her head. "Let us hope—let us pray—it doesn't tear the world apart."

The room shook with the powerful downdraft of rotor blades as a pair of Apache attack helos circled the building, providing air cover for a Sikorsky Black Hawk troop transport that was already touching down. They heard a minor tumult in the outer office, the repetitive thunder of boots hurrying along the hallways, and then were faced by a civilian flashing a badge that identified him as FBI, accompanied by a stick of paratroopers, assigned to secure the location and especially anyone and everything relating to the cure.

Worthington's discovery was no longer his. And its fate, like those of his son, and mutantkind in general, had just been assumed by greater hands.

X

Logan knew nothing about what was happening in the world, and at the moment cared less. He was hunting.

Jean had shown him the way, but he was too innately wary to follow her trail directly. Once he found the jumping-off point, he used one of the handheld computers Kitty was fond of gimmicking together to pull a landsat overview of the scene off the Net. Cute little gizmo, he discovered, in keeping with its creator—full of surprises—it contained a miniature version of the holo-projection systems in the *Blackbird* and the Mansion, allowing him to view the target area in three dimensions rather than as a flat picture on a screen. This enabled him to follow Jean's trail virtually, a dry run that told him where he had to go, so that he could find his own way.

Normally, he'd go for the impossible route, the one nobody would think to watch. But Magneto had such a bug up his butt about the Wolverine, chances were he'd have guards posted everywhere, just for spite. The Master of Magnetism was no fool—he had to assume Logan would make a play for Jean, and establish his defenses accordingly.

So Logan found himself a backdoor that was a rugged traverse, but nowhere near impossible. It was one of a score of ways into the depths of the untracked, minimally charted mountain forest.

He came with the clothes on his back, trusting to senses and tradecraft, along with his claws, to see him safely—whatever that would mean—to the finish. No weapons, no gear. He'd sustain himself on whatever he found along the way and face the elements as he had done as a boy.

Speed was of the essence, but as he closed on his objective, it was far better to be silent. A ghost couldn't have been less conspicuous as he slipped from shadow to shadow without making a sound—not even the *shush* of clothes as he moved, the touch of boot soles to leaves on the forest floor—or leaving a sign.

Security was quite respectable. Magneto—or the flunky who replaced Mystique—knew the business. He encountered the first cadre a klick from the clearing, chose to watch them rather than engage, to get a sense of what kind of adversaries they were. Their woodcraft was lousy—they made as much noise walking as a kid busting a wilderness trail aboard his brand-new ATV. If this was the best Magneto had . . .

As it turned out, they weren't. Nasty surprises awaited him as he encountered snares and deadfalls, mostly in the obvious places, but a few sited quite ingeniously. Fortunately for Logan, he could smell the mutants who'd laid the traps and see where they'd covered their tracks. Gradually, painstakingly, he learned how his adversaries thought, and how well they worked. As he did so, he learned how best to beat them.

The home stretch came, their last line of defense—the best of their breed. These guys, he didn't want to leave on his six; they'd have to be dealt with. By this time, he had their communication protocols down pat. If he took them hard and fast, before they could get the word out, he'd have enough time before they were missed to reach Jeannie and bail. The question was, did Magneto have himself a telepath—other than Jean, of course. If he did, the psi would likely be in constant link with the sentries, and shriek the alarm at the first sign of trouble. No way of knowing for sure, he just had to throw the dice and hope for the best.

But even as he allowed himself that thought, with it came the certainty that Magneto had no psis among his new Brotherhood.

Jean, he knew; helping again. He took that for a good sign.

Two guards patrolled the woods, with another trio in the trees.

Leaves rustled. The guards responded, more wary with each approaching step, bringing rifles to bear, gearing for a fight. Nothing worth reporting yet.

He left them a footprint, and as one of them put fingers to lips to alert the others with a whistle . . .

. . . Logan blindsided him into oblivion. His partner took a swing. Logan blocked it, stabbed thumb to throat to forestall any outcry, ducked under a second swing, clipped the guy's legs out from under him, caught him as he fell, and sent him off to dreamland with his partner.

There hadn't been a lot of noise, but it was sufficient to bring the others. They came in fast from all sides, trapping Logan at their convergence.

They found their two fallen comrades, but not the man who dropped them.

They should have looked up. Pretty uncanny how well, how quickly, how quietly, a fella can claw his way up the side of a tree if there's a need.

A scrap of torn bark fluttered past one of the mutants. By the time his gaze rolled up to find the cause . . .

. . . Logan was on his way down. He dropped into the center of the trio—no claws, there was no need for blood. These weren't hardcore Brotherhood. He moved in a blur, with a focus and precision most would consider wholly unlike him. They tried their best to land both punches and kicks, but he either parried them or slipped out of the way, returning their strikes with interest, the adamantium laced through his bones impacting with more force than solid steel bars. Tough as mutant physiognomy might be, they were no match for his enhanced skeleton, or his natural strength.

Three men, three seconds, six or seven moves by all concerned, and the fight was over. They never really knew what hit them, and Logan didn't even break a sweat.

Now for the main event.

He was after Jean, and her scent took him away from the encampment, which was altogether fine with him. Mayhem wasn't on his dance card tonight, if it could be avoided. Much more fun to find a way to outthink Magneto than to play the brute, to show the old man that he wasn't the only mutant with an affinity for chess.

As Logan snaked his way along the ridgeline, a very slight shift in the wind flooded him with the scents of the mutants gathered below and tossed all his well-laid plans into the Dumpster. Thinking back over his trail, he realized that he'd been so intent on Jean and the sentries that he'd discounted the other scents filling the air—only now acknowledging that they really did *fill* the air. Carefully, taking not the slightest chance, he parted some brush along the edge of the cliff for a view of the encampment.

He had to concede that Magneto had been busy the past few days. The old man must have made a helluva case, too. He'd expected a few score, max, to rally to Magneto's cause; what lay before him easily numbered in the hundreds. Both sexes, all ages, individuals and families—not merely the ones who could fight, but the future generations they were fighting *for*.

Magneto stood upon a makeshift platform, giving a speech.

"They wish to cure us," he said, giving that sentiment and those who held it the contempt they so richly deserved. "But I say *we* are the cure, to that infirm, imperfect condition of nature called *Homo sapiens*."

They cheered.

"They have their weapons, we have ours!"

They cheered more loudly. Logan hoped Magneto, like Fidel Castro, would go on for hours. That would make his life *so* much easier.

"We will strike with a vengeance and fury this world has never witnessed. We will destroy the very *source* of this cure . . ."

It doesn't have to be this way, Logan thought, and knew as he did so that for Magneto there could be no other. He seemed as hardwired into the patterns of his life as he so firmly believed Logan was into his.

". . . and if any mutant should stand in our way, then we will use this poison against them. . . ."

Logan paused and took a moment to look long and hard at his hands, as if his skin had turned transparent and he could see the claws in their housings, tucked into his forearms, see how intricately the molecular structure of his bones had been interwoven with that of the adamantium that made them unbreakable. The process had cost him a significant portion of his bone marrow; the key element that sustained him was his healing factor. It not only healed the gashes made between his knuckles every time the blades extended and retracted, it produced red and white blood cells with incredible efficiency. Take away the healing and he was a Dead Mutant Walking.

It was not a happy thought, and a fate he was determined to avoid. He wasn't always comfortable with the X-Men, but life with them had definitely gotten interesting over the years, more than enough to keep him coming back, and maybe even to consider sticking around.

"We will end this where it all began." That caught Logan's attention. "And then, my brothers and sisters, *nothing can stop us!*"

And suppose you win, smart guy, Logan thought, *what then, eh? What about the people who're left, you just gonna make 'em "disappear"? Beat Hitler's score by a factor of a hundred or more? Can even you embrace genocide? Or do you exile everyone to Australia? Or turn them into the perpetual underclass? Is that the future you promise these folks, to become lords of an Earth populated by slaves? Look in the mirror, bub, you'll see how that scenario plays out.*

He heard a chuckle deep inside his skull, caught a flash of scarlet amidst the woods, where Jean was watching both Magneto and him.

He should have been more careful, but knew in the end it wouldn't have made any difference. He was on his way to her, quick but silent . . .

. . . when he was bounced back off his feet by an invisible wall. He thought for that first moment he'd been attacked by Jean, especially when he found himself pinned spread-eagled to a tree, unable to even wriggle.

"Here we go again," Magneto said amusedly as he approached to set him straight. "I know the stench of your adamantium from a mile away."

Logan struggled, and then grew very still as Magneto idly brandished the pistol taken from Mystique's guard. Magneto flashed his eyes from the gun to Logan, his smile broadening as they returned to the weapon. Then, obviously enjoying the moment immensely, he tucked it in his pocket.

"I didn't come here to fight you," Logan told him.

"Smart boy."

"I came for *Jean*."

"And you think I'm keeping her against her will?"

Jean turned her back on them both as Magneto pulled Logan close, using magnetic fields both to hold him in midair and to keep the X-Man utterly immobile.

"She is here," Magneto said, "because she *wants* to be."

"You have *no idea* what you're dealing with!" Logan cried out.

Magneto shook his head, battling an unhappy memory that Logan knew he was prepared to accept. A price to pay, for the old man's *greater good*. "I know full well. I saw what she did to Charles."

"You light that fire, what makes you think you can put it out?"

"Perhaps I'm like Prometheus, bringing that sacred fire to the masses?"

"I'm thinkin' more like Icarus. I don't give a rat's ass how far you fall, Lensherr, but damned if I'll see Jean fall with you."

"You truly love her." The older man shook his head, surprised by the revelation, and clearly saddened.

"I'm not leaving without her."

Magneto pulled Logan right up to him and the look he gave the other man was actually sympathetic.

"Yes," he said. "You are."

He placed his hand flat against Logan's chest and gave a gentle push.

Logan finally came to rest just this side of the horizon from where he'd started, close on twenty miles, through an entire forest and a fair share of boulders and quite likely a mountaintop. He'd lost track of his progress early on, and when he landed he didn't move. His body was brutally torn, flesh as much in rags and tatters as his clothes, and while his bones arrived unscathed, the rest of him was as close to the end as could be imagined. His spleen was ruptured, liver speared by a broken branch. His lungs were intact within the rib cage but the diaphragm needed to pump them was savagely torn. His heart could still beat but what was the point, since a huge gash across the top of one thigh had severed the femoral artery. Any one of those injuries was an absolute guarantee of death. The combination of them all . . .

. . . only made his healing take quite a bit longer than usual—it was also a real pain.

Miles away, hearing him scream, knowing how he felt—both in terms of the healing and, far more importantly, about her—Jean Grey hugged her knees to her breast and stared into the heart of the campfire.

She wept.

X

Logan looked like hell when he returned to the Mansion. He felt a whole helluva lot worse. He hadn't waited for the healing to run its full course. As soon as he'd woken, as soon as he could move, he found his bike and hit the road, stopping at a biker dive just long enough to pull a *Terminator* and relieve one of the gentlemen present of his leathers. And then, once the dust settled, he put in a quick call to the feds to come deal with the crystal meth lab percolating out back.

He'd ridden all day, all night, and he was just getting warmed up.

"Storm!" he bellowed, slapping the double doors of the formal entryway open so hard he damn near popped them off the hinges.

"We have problems," he announced.

"You found her," Ororo said, assuming things hadn't gone well. Hank joined them as Logan shook his head, indicating that was an understatement.

"I sure did."

"Still with Magneto?"

"Locked at the hip, but I'm not sure they're walkin' the same road. 'Ro, she led me right to her. She knew I was coming, she wanted me there—but when Magneto caught me, she walked away."

"I told you!"

He shook his head violently. "It's not that simple."

'Ro shelved the argument for another time and her thought echoed Logan's: *If we make it that far.* "Where are they, Logan?"

"On the move. Sonofabitch has raised himself an army!"

"You're saying you saw Magneto?" asked Hank, who got ignored for his trouble.

"I know where they're going, 'Ro," Logan told her. "We've gotta get there. We're the only ones with a chance to stop him."

Storm nodded, understanding the double meaning to what Logan said, that the struggle with Magneto wouldn't be the one that truly mattered.

As they left the foyer, Hank McCoy pulled out his cellphone and tapped 1 on his speed dial. Originally, that slot had held Xavier's number, but as Hank came to realize when he accepted his cabinet post, there are certain phone numbers, and certain people in this country, who take second place to no one.

It rang once, and was answered by the best switchboard in the world.

"This is Hank McCoy," he said, even though they knew that already with caller ID. "Patch me through to the president."

X

David Cockrum was in the Situation Room with his senior security and battle staff, monitoring in real time an ongoing military special op.

"Seven minutes to contact," Bolivar Trask told him.

The president nodded as Trask gestured towards a satellite image of Magneto's encampment. "Magneto's base of operations."

A straight line ran northwest through the trees from

the vicinity of the camp to a distance of over twenty miles. Cockrum asked about it.

"We're not altogether sure, sir," Trask replied. "The original best guess was some kind of projectile, consistent with something being kicked out of a rail gun. It's a stunt that's certainly within Magneto's power and capabilities. But when we checked out the terminal point with a recce team, they reported finding a fair amount of blood, and what they tell me was a trail of physical evidence. Near as they're willing to hazard, somebody landed there, got up and walked a couple of miles down to the highway, where it seems a bike was stashed. Next we hear, there's been a helluva bar fight nearby, one guy versus the local outlaws. Seems he wanted some clothes. Seems he also found a drug lab the DEA's been after for quite a while."

Cockrum quirked his eyebrows. He was tired of waiting for Trask's punch line.

"It was the Wolverine, sir. Start to finish. We lost track of him at the bar, but I just got a flash from the NSA that our Keyhole surveillance satellite tasked to monitor Xavier's mansion got a photo of him rolling in about ten minutes ago."

"Jesus" was all Cockrum could say, considering the ramifications of what Trask just told him, thinking first *What the hell is that guy* made *of?* And then, with relief, *Thank God he's on* our *side.* And then last, anxiously, *Dear God, I* hope *he's on our side.* Finally, as a way of covering those worries, he asked, "Bolivar, how did we find Magneto's base?"

Trask indicated another subordinate display, presenting a quite lovely, well-dressed woman, Caucasian, blond. She sat in the conference room of a United States attorney, her lawyer at her side, and signed an affidavit.

"She gave us everything we wanted, and more."

Almost as if she'd heard Trask speak, the woman looked directly up at the monitor. Mystique may have lost her ability to change shapes, but Cockrum still couldn't shake the certainty that she could see him through the video feed.

" 'Hell hath no fury,' " he mused to himself, " 'like a woman scorned.' "

An aide whispered in Trask's ear and the secretary picked up the phone.

"Not a great time, Hank," he said brusquely.

"I have reason to believe Magneto is en route to attack Worthington Labs," Hank told him. "He intends to destroy the source of the cure."

Nice of you to call, old buddy, Trask thought. *You're just a day late and a dollar short.* Aloud: "We're well aware of his plans, Hank, we're taking all appropriate measures."

"Bolivar," Hank demanded, "what does that mean?"

You're out of the loop, Henry, Trask thought, *you quit the team. What gives you the right to an answer?* But aloud: "We're moving on him as we speak. It'll all be over soon."

He hung up. The president looked, obviously catching enough of the conversation to guess who'd called. Cockrum gave a shallow nod that told Trask he trusted his judgment in dealing with it.

Trask pointed to the main screen. "It's starting, sir."

Technology gave them a multitude of perspectives. From a network of satellites overhead came real-time streaming video. Direct imaging was useless after dark, and the natural cover of the forest canopy made it even worse. However, enhanced infrared presented the scene in eerie shadings and surprising detail. Targets were coded red, incoming troops in blue, with the overall scene neatly and comprehensively labeled by the attending computer.

At the same time, there were a whole host of secondary displays projecting a multitude of feeds from minicams attached to the soldiers' helmets, each labeled with the identity and rank of the wearer and his or her position, which in turn was repeated on the master display.

The army had fielded an entire brigade of special ops, totaling over three thousand troops in a multilevel cordon around the encampment, to ensure that—regardless of powers—none would escape. Because intel, courtesy of Mystique, told them women and children were present on-site, the rules of engagement called for nonlethal force. However, as with all military plans, there were built-in escalators. The president knew when he signed the orders, even though it made him heartsick, that if things went south, people were going to die.

"No contact," came a scratchy voice out of the room's main speakers, the computer identifying the officer as Colonel Simon Kinberg, leading the attack. "All units in position." One of the secondary screens relayed the data from his on-scene scanner. "I mark one hundred plus unfriendlies."

"That's the number Mystique gave us," Trask crowed. "Everybody's home."

"Tell them," said the president, "it's a go."

"This is Team Leader to Bravo One," said Kinberg.

"We are green. Repeat, we are greenlight to go. 'Mr. and Mrs. Smith' on the flip."

"What's that mean?" Cockrum asked.

"Hit 'em hard and elegant and with a smile, like there's no tomorrow."

The first wave charged from every side, each approach angled so as to avoid clashing with the others' fields of fire. Laser sights traced myriad lines of scarlet and green through the air, questing for their targets, finding none.

In the Situation Room, they heard a hoarse profanity from Kinberg and saw on their display the same thing he did: one after another, the target heat signatures were disappearing from the screen.

The speaker filled with a chorus of startled voices, radiating confusion and alarm. No one was sure what was happening, and everyone suspected a trap.

One contact remained, utterly solid, holding up his hands and grinning ear to ear to find himself dotted with scores of laser points.

A soldier shoved a lens in his face, popped the flash, and within seconds the prisoner's identity card dominated the main display: James Madrox, code-named the Multiple Man.

True to form, he remained nonviolent to the last.

"It's a goddamn decoy!" Kinberg bellowed in complete frustration.

Cockrum could see that Trask was in an altogether opposite mood to their lone prisoner, looking like he wished to indulge in a lengthy session of ultraviolence.

The president spoke to him in concern: "Bolivar, if Magneto's not there, then where the hell *is* he?"

Trask looked at the phone. The president looked at him. Trask grabbed the handset, but all he got was Hank's voice mail. And when he called Xavier's school, it was the same.

X

A crowd waited at the entrance to the hanger: Bobby, Kitty, Colossus, Angel, even McCoy. Storm was a bit behind, waiting by the *Blackbird*.

Logan rolled his shoulders, trying to settle his uniform more comfortably. He preferred not to wear it, so it had never been broken in. Not like Ororo's, which felt like kid gloves. The others were all suited up as well.

Kitty was grinning—she'd obviously saved a quip for this special occasion. "Remember how you told Bobby our uniforms were on order?" *Little girl,* he thought, *you weren't even flamin'* there! "Well, guess what just came in the mail!"

"We're coming with," Bobby announced.

Logan snorted, his way of telling them in no uncertain terms, *The hell you are!*

"We trained for this," Peter Rasputin said, backing up his friend. "We're ready."

"Best offense is a good defense, right?" Ororo smiled from the plane, clearly enjoying every moment of Logan's comeuppance.

Warren III stepped forward, visibly shy but refusing to give in to his fear. "They say Magneto's going after my father," he said, his voice shaking as much with outrage as nerve. "My *father*! He may be wrong, sir, but he's not evil. I'm not going to leave him out there alone."

Serious now, Ororo added to what Angel said, "This is our fight, Logan. Not just yours."

He sighed. He didn't want them to learn the realities of his life this way. Or ever.

"This isn't gonna be like class," he told them, looking one after the other in the eye, hoping they could see on his face, in his own eyes, what he was talking about, "or the Danger Room. It's gonna be real battle. With blood and tears . . . and death."

They were kids. Even if they thought they understood what he was talking about, they had no proper frame of reference. Hell, deep down inside, they *knew* they'd live forever; that's why armies preferred their recruits young. Things like this could only be learned the hard way. It was a part of life that mirrored Worthington's cure, in that once you crossed this Rubicon, you could never go back. What you saw, what you did, would stay with you forever.

"As much as we've lost in the last few days, that's nothing compared to what's on the line."

Nobody moved. Nobody even blinked.

"We get on that plane, we're not students and teachers anymore. We're not kids and grown-ups. We're soldiers."

"We're X-Men," Bobby corrected. "All of us."

He nodded, gestured to the *Blackbird*.

"Get in, then. Let's go."

He had to look twice at McCoy's uniform. He'd seen pictures in the archives and was thankful the school had moved on to something better. The design was form-fitting, akin to spandex, a dark brown leather pants-and-jacket combo, although the top was short-sleeved, with yellow bands on the shoulders. The X symbol was stitched in yellow and brown on the left front breast of the jacket.

Logan had reviewed the specs. The old suits had environmental properties similar to the current ones, protecting the wearer from extremes of weather and environment. They were in fact body armor, proof against a significant array of projectile and edged weapons; they could even handle shots from directed energy beams. All told, they were remarkably efficient uniforms. They were just incredibly, unforgivably ugly. And as a chaser, in case he thought it couldn't get any worse, it was clear that McCoy had outgrown the whole thing; the jacket looked like it was holding on for dear life, barely zipping over the Beast's massive furry chest. The pants were so tight that a belt wasn't necessary, and his huge blue feet protruded from the flared pant legs. Unfortunately, even Logan had to admit to himself that McCoy looked pretty formidable in his outdated uniform, despite the trouble he was having fitting into it.

"Christ on a cracker," Logan exclaimed, still wondering how McCoy put the damn thing on, and also how he kept his fur from binding, "is that a joke?"

Hank actually looked offended. He'd apparently worn this proudly in his day. "My old uniform. Still fits . . . almost."

"And I thought black leather was bad."

He scented her, even though she hung back out of sight in the hallway. She wasn't trying to hide from him—she knew better—just from the others aboard the plane.

"You almost missed the flight, darlin'," Logan told Rogue, rounding the corner to join her. "C'mon, girl, get suited up, we're on a clock here."

She shook her head. "No, Logan, I'm not goin'."

He looked down, having heard from Ororo what Bobby had seen in Manhattan the other day. But her hands were still gloved.

She smiled, like she'd lost something precious.

"Couldn't go through with it," she told him with a shake of her head.

"So," he prompted, suggesting with the gesture that she head into the hangar.

"You don't know what it's like, Logan, to be afraid of your powers . . . afraid to get close to anyone . . . to know you can never go home again—"

He held up his right hand, showing it to her the way he had when they'd first met. She'd asked him then, "Does it hurt?" Meaning, *when the claws come out?* His reply, for the first and only time in his life, for reasons he still couldn't fathom, allowing someone outside to see what this had cost him: "Yup."

"Yeah, Marie," he told her very quietly. "I do."

"No," Rogue protested, "you don't. You can control your power." She faltered, remembering the times she'd seen him go berserk, most significantly the night William Stryker's mercenaries had attacked the Mansion. She and Bobby and Pyro had been cornered, and capture was certain. Until Logan leapt from the gallery above with a terrible cry she'd never forget. She never really saw how many soldiers confronted them—the hallway was dark, things happened so fast. There were a lot, that was certain, and heavily armed. With startling suddenness, they were all dead. Only Logan was left standing, his jeans and T-shirt and face splattered with lives he had just taken. Single-handedly, he'd more than decimated Stryker's command. None of the casualties were wounded, and more than a few were in pieces. But the true horror of that moment came when he looked towards the children he'd come to save—and didn't recognize them. They faced the very real possibility that he was so lost in his killing frenzy that he would do the same to them. But he hadn't. The man in his soul grabbed hold of the monster and regained control.

"I can't," she confessed in a broken voice, barely more than a whisper.

"Logan," she heard Bobby call from the hangar. "Aren't we in a hurry?"

"But I can't run away, either," she finished, sounding a little bit bemused to discover something bright and indomitable amidst the desolation of her spirit, something that had set down roots too deep to be dislodged, that was determined to grow. "I thought that was the answer then"—she paused to look in Bobby's direction as though she could see right through the wall—"and now. Not my brightest idea, I guess." She'd never really considered herself particularly strong, or brave, and here she was evolving into someone that was both. It made her smile, just a little.

"Controlling the powers has nothing to do with bein' afraid, Marie," Logan said, acknowledging the change within her by deliberately using her real name again, instead of the one she chose for herself. "Of the powers themselves, of getting close to someone, or never going home. If it matters, you find a way. If this doesn't work for you, find something better."

She leaned up close to his cheek, sparing him a kiss so fleeting that he barely felt the thrill of her power grabbing for his, yet he'd never experienced anything more heartfelt.

"Workin' on it, bub."

"So I see," he agreed, and added, "They're a smart and sneaky bunch here, Marie. Give 'em a decent chance to prove it. Throw 'em a challenge."

She gave Logan a lazy, lopsided, little bit sassy smile that reminded him just how much she'd changed—grown—from the adolescent river rat who'd hitched her way from the Gulf to Laughlin City, Alberta, the unofficial end of the road.

"I'll get changed," she assured him.

"I'll tell 'Ro."

But she surprised him by saying, "I'm still not comin'."

Prompted, she explained, "Someone's gotta look after the kids, don't you think? Wouldn't be the first time Magneto's faked us out."

"Figure you can handle trouble, if it comes?"

She tossed him a look she had to have learned from him. "Ain't that what Rogues do best, sugar?"

"That's my girl."

"Always. Hey," she called as he headed for the *Blackbird*, "you go kick the Bad Guy's butt, Mister!" He nodded, but she wasn't done with him just yet. "And you make sure you find a way to save the girl, hear? We're countin' on you."

Come back with your shield, victorious, the queens of ancient Sparta had told their kings when they marched off to war, *or on it.*

He tossed her a farewell salute and a nod that was both jaunty and deadly serious.

And within the minute, as Rogue pulled her leather uniform from its locker, the complex shook with the rumble of the *Blackbird*'s huge engines, quickly fading to silence as the plane rose into the air and sped away.

All the lockers around her were empty, all of the X-Men were gone. She didn't mind being alone, but she'd count the seconds until their safe return.

Chapter Nine

Jean Grey hated her dreams.

They were full of fire and passion, of a violence as primal and lasting as Creation itself. They took her to places beyond imagination, that somehow she knew were as real as her own life. Because, perhaps, they were aspects of her own life.

Xavier had been a frequent guest that fateful summer when he recruited her, but after the first meeting, she'd rarely seen Erik Lensherr, sensing a growing sadness in Xavier's relations with his old friend. Something was not right between them and the passage of time only made the breach wider and deeper. She was aware of it even though outwardly he was as charming and relaxed as ever. He and the 'rents would talk for hours, about a multitude of subjects, as he helped Elaine cook, or shared an afternoon ball game on the tube with John. He had no great love for baseball but he faked it well, and he actually learned some new recipes from Mom. Of course, whether the subject was history or art, current events or philosophy, it was really all about Jean. To learn about her, he was determined to learn about the forces that shaped her, her home and her parents. Moreover, since he'd be taking her out of that home, away from those parents, they had to know they could trust him absolutely.

This, she understood then as now, was where he and Magneto parted company. Magneto might have experienced a momentary pang of regret at the sundering of familial bonds, but for him such a sacrifice was necessary for the common good. Xavier wanted—needed—her parents to share the journey of her life, so none of them would be afraid.

For Magneto, fear was the defining element of his world. For Charles, it had always been hope.

He had always viewed Jean as the embodiment of that hope.

Yet she had slain him. And Scott.

And she had slain the ones she most loved.

To anyone looking, which was basically just Magneto, she appeared utterly normal. Yet the core of the Brotherhood kept well clear of her. Even John Allerdyce, who'd been her student, and Callisto, who professed to fear nothing. She made them nervous. Especially penned together in the plane carrying them westward to their final destiny.

She smiled to herself at the thought of Callisto trying to take Mystique's place by Magneto's side. Mystique was the closest thing to fearless Jean had ever encountered, this side of Logan. As likely as not, she'd have simply sidled up beside Jean for a gal-chat, spiced along the way by the occasional metamorphosis into whatever form would get most irritatingly under Jean's skin. Mystique's nature was to push everything to its limit; the greater the danger, the more she enjoyed it. Jean envied her that freedom and wondered if losing those powers would make a difference.

Jean had been all alone in that big, empty house at the beginning, although she quickly found herself irresistibly intrigued by all the work being done belowground as Xavier and Magneto built the hidden complex where much of the real work of the school would be accomplished. Later, as the rest of what would become the founding class trickled in, she made new friends.

At first, they numbered but four: herself, Ororo Munroe, Henry McCoy and Scott Summers. Despite herself, she discovered in Ororo a kindred spirit to fill the aching void left by the death of Annie Malcolm. In Hank, she found someone who could make her laugh, no matter what, who could challenge her intellect as no other, and best of all, who taught her how to attempt the triple somersault on the trapeze. She never succeeded—her personal best was a perfect double and an "almost made it"—but the work taught her how to delight in her physicality. And not to be so scared.

She fell a lot, and that's why she wore a harness, but with practice, as her telekinesis grew stronger, she discovered she could slow her plummet with a thought so that she landed easily on her feet. And later still, to stop herself in midair. And finally, to push herself back up to where she started, so she could try again.

Ororo taught her how to fly, sustaining herself aloft with a combination of her own telekinesis and her friend's winds.

As for Scott . . .

. . . he taught her love. Which she thought was enough.

Until Logan came along.

She'd told Logan bad boys were for dating, for a fling, for being naughty, but you *married* the good guy. And he'd said in a way that thrilled her to the core that he could be the good guy. Scott was love, Logan was passion.

Just thinking about him made her heart race, which set their plane to trembling just a little, prompting startled glances at the little trickles of fiery energy that popped into view along the periphery of everyone's vision, like the monster forever lurking *just* beyond the campfire's glow.

They were right to be nervous. *She* was terrified.

Had Magneto pinpointed the rational reason for her being here? Probably, and he'd no doubt concluded in his arrogance that it was worth the risk and that when the time came he could properly manage her. But she still had too many ties with the X-Men, and she'd already struck them two blows to the heart, without meaning either. To see Ororo or Kitty, Hank or Logan—*Logan*—fall the same way . . .

She shook her head violently, the plane bucked, and the pilot warned them they were entering a field of turbulence, telling everyone to strap in.

Better, she'd decided, to be a potential threat to Magneto. Serve him right if things went wrong.

She covered her eyes, liking less and less the patterns her thoughts were falling into. She was a doctor, and she'd sworn the Hippocratic oath to "do no harm." She was a scientist, whose absolute province was the *rational* mind.

The events since her resurrection sure had blown both those views of herself all to hell.

Resurrection.

Even by X-Men standards, she was dancing *way* out on the edge.

Outwardly, her hands were rock steady in her lap, her face almost serene as she gazed out towards the watching stars. Within, though, she trembled like a child quailing in the face of parental rage, so terrorized by the force of the wave of emotions breaking over them that the only outlet is barely coherent tears.

In desperation, within her mind's eye, she forced herself to her feet and envisioned about herself the bowl shape of a medical theater, claiming for herself the air of a physician conducting rounds.

Break things down. Regain perspective, and thereby, control. Climb the steps one at a time, see where you're led.

Her leg ached murderously as she dragged herself from the belly of the Blackbird. *She'd used her telekinesis to knit the broken bones together, telepathically stealing the "how" of it from Logan's backbrain, but wasn't comfortable enough in her knowledge to do the job of healing as quickly and perfectly. Or maybe it was always this miserable for him and he'd long ago stopped giving a damn.*

She had seconds to act, to create a barrier to keep the onrushing flood at bay while lifting the X-Men completely clear. It occurred to her that she could rise with the plane, that she could put a protective bubble around herself to survive the torrent, that she might try a lifeline— she faced a whole menu of options that allowed her to survive. Yet she considered not a one.

The passion was rising in her, glorious and hungry;

the more she drew on her power, the more there was for her to claim, increasingly desperate to be unleashed. It was a song more ageless than the stars, dating from the moment of their birth, when Creation came into being as an inconceivable outrush of matter and energy. Water turned incandescent at her touch, the ground at her feet fused instantly to trinitite glass, as if seared by the breath of the sun itself. Stellar prominences danced in her eyes, over her skin, filling her with a yearning as inexpressible as it was unfulfilled.

She said her farewells, through Xavier, hoping he would understand, aware that even his brain and insight were limited in their perceptions of what she was experiencing. Very much, and she had to smile, like trying to explain the sensoral totality of telepathy to the headblind. She felt Scott's agony as he charged the hatch, was grateful beyond measure when Logan held him back. As bad in some ways, far worse in others, was the sharp and keening cry of anguish that Logan kept to himself. Two hearts were being savaged by her sacrifice; what made the moment bearable for her was the recognition that now she'd no longer have to choose between them.

In truth, she wanted . . . needed . . . desired them both. The plane flew, the water loomed. Time for her to go. This was for the best, she knew. She was human, that was how her story should end.

So strong an instant before, she shattered with the impact of a million tons of water, crushed and broken, stripped of anything that might resemble the woman she had been.

Yet she went on from there.

She really should have known better. Damnably, of course, X-Men were too bloody stubborn to go out so easily.

Her own perceptions splintered.

She found herself cast adrift from the world—still a part of things as they happened yet increasingly apart from them, experiencing the totality of thought and emotion with an intensity that was as new to her as it was exhilarating, yet equally aware of them as an audience might be, safely removed from all consequences.

From each of her friends, in turn, her touch brought forth sensations of grief, of fury, of confusion, of aching and irredeemable loss. Some were as loose from their moorings as she, while others became their bedrock.

She sensed William Stryker—defiant to the moment of final oblivion—while his son claimed refuge within a threat that would prove more lasting and deadly than he had ever been. Buried in the catacombs, a product of the original industrial plant, it was not yet functional but no longer dormant.

Much the same was true of Yuriko Oyama, Lady Deathstrike, trapped and helpless beneath countless tons of rubble in the augmentation chamber, yet sustained by a spark that—like Wolverine's—refused to be extinguished.

She skimmed the residual essence of the slain troopers scattered through the complex and what remained of those who'd preceded them—a number that horrified her—dating back to the days when Alkali Lake had been a thriving community of Black Ops medical research. If karma had any meaning, this cursed place was well and truly haunted and would remain so always.

In her mind's eye, Jean opened her arms and sped away from all she knew, to eagerly embrace the far greater All that awaited her.

Splinters became prisms, reflecting a myriad of possibilities, the lives that might have been, or perhaps actually were elsewhere: she saw herself older, younger, with a daughter, alone unto death. Living a life of unbearable routine in a world where mutants did not exist, doing precisely the same where mutants were the norm. She called herself Marvel Girl and favored an X-Men costume of emerald green and breathtaking brevity. She saw her own grave, tasted grace, ruled Hellfire; she shuffled the deck of existence and cast forth every imaginable permutation of herself.

She flew across the face of Forever, on wings so wide they reached from the beginning to the end of All.

She heard humming, in absent delight, a song her father favored when she was little, played to the point of her mother's distraction, his own way of celebrating the promise of the future represented by his children. She tried her very best, remaining painfully, perpetually aware that Grace Slick would always do it better, "You are the crown of creation . . ."

Worlds, whole dimensions, screamed violently to an end, others slipped unnoticed into being. Life was forever a cycle, each ending a beginning somewhere else, the story of every individual, no matter how seemingly inconsequential, forming its own thread in the tapestry that philosophers called the scheme of things.

She ached with the yearning to know more, to be more, chafed at the sense it wasn't yet her time, impatient as any child to run when barely able to stand, no

*sense whatsoever of the cost when she fell, no compre-
hension yet that none stood by to help and comfort her,
that she had reached that point in fate where she must
prove herself able to act on her own.*

Or, she thought, blinking furiously as her thoughts
settled back to the world of the now, a growing pressure
in her ears telling her the aircraft was descending at a
rate dictated by stealth and expedience rather than the
comfort of its passengers, *I could just be mad.*

At the moment, she figured, it was a toss-up which
was better.

It made her wonder, though, as she had since that
fateful day when Xavier and Magneto first came calling,
what it *really* meant to be the "next step in evolution."

She sagged back in her chair and creased her lips into
a real smile as she reconsidered one of the images from
her daydream: *an emerald green off-the-shoulder mini-
dress.*

She stretched and let her gaze travel down the long,
lean length of her legs. Definitely not her style, even when
she'd been young enough to dare anything and damn
the consequences. The Hellfire *leather,* though, that had
definite possibilities.

Scott, she knew, would have loved the mini. And been
tempted by the leather.

Logan, she knew, cared nothing for the trappings. He
loved *her.* Enough to do what Xavier could not and
Scott would not.

Sometimes, the soul had to sit in judgment of the
heart.

X

Jean always loved San Francisco. New York was about power, an expression of humanity's dominance over its world; aside from the harbor, the view was nothing but pillars of steel and stone and glass. The City by the Bay however, while amply represented by the works of man, one of which—the Golden Gate—loomed below them, was dominated more by those of nature. What you saw back east, strolling along the waterfront of Manhattan, were more buildings, as both New Jersey and Brooklyn took it upon themselves to ape the island that separated them.

Here, there was brilliant blue water to behold, and the island of Alcatraz to catch the eye, unless you preferred to look a little more seaward to the heights of Tiburon and Mt. Tam beyond.

The X-Men had spent some time here, and a memorable night had been lost to Ororo and Jean, Scott and Hank, starting in Chinatown—Hank ordered, since he spoke both the language and local dialect. They strolled downhill to the Bay and cruised the piers, closing two or three bars before calling it a night with the dawn just below the horizon, sun on the barest brink of rising, with the sky equally split between shadow and light, enjoying crab fresh off the boat with cocktail sauce so hot with horseradish they thought they'd instantly combust.

It was the kind of madcap, "dare ya" night that found Ororo and Jean staring across a table at each other, going shot for shot with the owner's private stock of tequila, while the guys kept score and debated who'd get to carry whom home.

Ororo had reached out an elegant hand, taking gentle hold of one of Jean's and drawing it to the center of the table, cupping it palm upwards. Jean shivered ever so slightly as a swirl of intensely icy air passed around her neck and dived towards that upheld hand, and then she had felt a decidedly warmer zephyr race around the other side of her, like the caress of someone's breath.

The two streamers of air had collided, intertwined, fought for dominance, and Jean blinked with surprise at an actinic flash, so sudden she had no chance to react, so intense it scattered spots all across her vision. That same instant, she had felt as much as heard an equally intense but wholly contained boom of thunder.

Clouds had then begun to form over the table, thin streaks that quickly merged and grew into big-bellied cumuli and from there into the anvil-topped monsters of cumulonimbus, creating a pillar of force and energy that reached barely a foot above Ororo's hand. Outside, with the vastness of the atmosphere to play with, this thundercloud would have easily topped forty thousand feet. Jean had smelled and tasted ozone, and the static electricity generated by the tiny cloud had raised the hairs all the way up her extended arm. Another bolt of lightning had followed, from deep within the cloud, joined by a minor drumroll of thunder that went wholly unnoticed against the backdrop of conversation and the maxed-out jukebox by all save the four mutants.

Then, she had giggled and almost jumped as the first raindrop struck her palm.

The sensation of the cool water had been a delight against her skin, which felt exceptionally hot, and strangely separated from the rest of her, as if she were running an impossible fever. Jean had deepened the cup

of her fingers to form a bowl, watched it fill, turned her
hand over to let the rain work its wonders on the other
side.

The guys had grinned ear to ear, but Ororo wasn't so
thrilled, as not a drop of water fell—either from the
back of Jean's hand or the inverted palm. The simple exercise would have been to form a telekinetic barrier—a
bowl of energy. But Jean was in a mood to show off, so
she'd tried the much harder route of binding the molecular structure of the water more tightly together, creating such surface tension that it had behaved more like a
solid than a liquid, but without crystallizing into ice.
Moreover, she'd locked it into place against her own
flesh.

Fascinated, Jean had leaned a little closer, and without realizing what was happening her focus sharpened
to pinpoint intensity so that she was presented with a
view of a single, solitary raindrop, suspended in midair
by her telekinesis, partway between the cloud and her
hand.

As she had bored in on the drop that caught her attention, it quickly separated into component molecules,
to atoms of hydrogen and oxygen and from there to ag-
glomerations of charms and quarks, muons and gluons.
This was always more Hank's side of the street than
hers, and without conscious awareness she had plucked
from him the information she needed to give names to
what she beheld and provide a clue to the next destination on her journey.

Time then lost meaning for her, perception stretching
it like taffy as long as she needed. The others had seen
her eager and radiant smile, her sparkling eyes, the tilt of
her head as she found herself lost in wonderment, en-

compassing perhaps a fraction of a moment of elapsed objective time. By contrast, Jean could have sworn she was engrossed for hours.

She'd never had so much fun.

Too much fun.

Inexplicably, she had felt a sudden chill, and reacted with a desire for warmth, drawing in the myriad dots of energy that surrounded her, hoping to draw energy from them to restore herself.

Too little, too late—wrong power, wrong solution.

It hadn't been her telekinesis she had to worry about, but her telepathy.

She'd allowed herself to become so caught up in exploring the subatomic quantum world within Ororo's raindrop that her natural psi-screens had slipped loose from her control. Like a single loose thread unraveling an entire tapestry, her telepathic window on the world around her had become ever more porous.

The first thoughts that had come to her were nothing special, raised no flags of warning: she tagged thirty-eight people in the bar, pretty fair business considering the hour, twenty-one men, seventeen women.

A number were couples, some of them committed, others just friends, some just for the night, others looking for something more. Many were single, a few by choice; some were looking, others didn't care. She had beheld varying degrees of inebriation, stone-cold sober to slight buzz to one guy falling down drunk and another dead asleep in a booth at the back.

She had sensed lots of conversation, mainly inconsequential, not a whole lot of actual communication, the facile exchange of words used too much as a shield against intimacy. The true intimacy was reserved to looks, or touch, the lazy smile that sparked a drop of the eyes, a slight flush, an electric tingle racing along the surface of the skin, occasionally delightedly to the core of the being.

But lurking in the background like a shadow mugger she had felt frustration, loneliness, boredom, excitement, anticipation, desire. There were dreams galore—within reach or just beyond, unfulfilled, even unrecognized.

She had detected the sharp intensity of predators on the hunt, and the equally sharp taste of those being hunted, all tangled together with the primal needs and fears of rejection, of acceptance, of success, of commitment.

And that had been just the surface.

Each person had a history that bundled all the experiences of their lives within the labyrinth of their psyche. Each backstory led Jean down paths that were winding and twisted, branching as randomly—yet in their own way, on their own terms, as logically—as the tributaries of the Mississippi, taking her to parts of each and every person that they likely never even dreamed existed, to the deepest secrets of the subconscious, their fundamental selves, never meant to be revealed. To the thoughts that were forbidden for a reason.

The emotions crashing against her then were as fascinating as the quantum microverse. By the time she had realized how far she'd gone, she couldn't tear her inner eyes away, and she didn't want to.

The curse of her telepathy: not only did it strip reality of its walls, it seemed to mandate that every observation, every experience be unforgettable. Now, sitting on the plane, the harder she tried, the more the memories thrust themselves into her face. There were so many, crowding in on her like passengers on a rush-hour subway. Her mouth twisted at the power some of them had to thrill her—not always the ones she welcomed. At the power others had to shame her, because even if she atoned for the fault, she couldn't escape the memory of the original moment.

There was so much more darkness than light. The darkness was the natural state of things. And yet the alternative terrified her so much more, because it was a light that seemed to Jean to come from the fire in her soul, the transcendent and all-consuming passion that had destroyed Scott and Xavier, and that terrified her so much more.

It would be so easy to drown. She felt that way with Annie, felt that way at Alkali Lake.

She closed her eyes, opened them wide at the sound of a familiar voice, to behold another moment of memory, one from that very same night.

A game of pool, her against Scott, telekinesis versus optic blasts.

There had been tables in the back of the bar, in surprisingly good shape. She honestly couldn't tell how she'd gotten to her feet, much less made it the dozen slightly wobbly steps to the game room, but once she arrived there she had been determined not to disgrace herself.

Scott always had that effect on her. Whenever she found herself in the riptide of her telepathy, his presence was like a sea anchor to her, steadying her against the fierce current, giving her the opportunity to collect herself and regain her inner focus.

A gentleman always, Scott had offered her the break. This was their own private version of the game of pool, played with powers instead of cues. She had smirked and slapped the cue ball with her thoughts, hoping to clear the table with a single shot. That wasn't impossible—it merely required pinpoint and simultaneous manipulation of every ball on the table. She couldn't, for example, use her powers to drag the balls over to the pockets and drop them in; back at the beginning they'd agreed that would be way too easy. For this stunt, the contact had to be one smooth, continuous flow from ball to ball, off one another and the rail to their final resting places. She had to play angles and forces in the blink of an eye—and, as the saying went, let the balls fall where they may.

She'd actually succeeded, more than once. But not that night.

Six balls had dropped, and from the lazy gunfighter smile on Scott's face she knew he wasn't about to show her any mercy.

He had prowled the table with surpassing grace, a lithe physicality that was rarely associated with Scott, yet was as much a part of him as it was of Logan. They had that in common—they were both hunters. Scott always had an uncanny knack for seeing the patterns of things and of people, which made him as formidable at poker as he was at chess. Nowhere was that more evident than in a pool hall; pool was all about spatial geometry. He'd taken advantage of the shadows in the back to switch his sunglasses for his visor, which allowed him better control over his eyebeams. He had proceeded to unleash his optic blasts in precise and fractional bursts, minute flashes of scarlet neon from his eyes that barely registered even in the darkness at the back of the bar. He'd tap a ball here, nudge it there, using sufficient force to move it properly without damaging the felt it rested on.

He had run the table, the bastard, and she loved him for it. He grinned when he was done. Because it had been a private moment, because it was just him and her, he let down all his usual defenses and for one of those rare, precious, delicious instants had just let himself be *himself*. He was strong and confident, tempered by the wounds and losses he'd suffered in his life, made whole by the love he felt for her. And she in return had felt an aching need that drove her around the table and into his arms for a kiss she wanted to last forever.

He'd looked at her just the same way when she'd killed him.

She wanted to scream, and she wished for the power, the will, to reach inside her own skull with fingers turned to obsidian claws and tear out the offending memories, to gut her head until it was a hollow shell, just to give herself some lasting peace.

Then, in memory, something happened that was . . . *different*.

Scott broke their kiss, which is what had happened. And then they'd returned to their hotel arm in arm and put the DO NOT DISTURB sign on the door, and proceeded to fulfill a great many of their teammates' more scandalous and fantastical suppositions.

But instead, the memory shifted, and changed, and now quite seriously, he told her: *"Stop!"*

She blinked.

"Be the teacher, Jean. Show us the way," he went on.

She blinked again.

"Growth is change, change can be chaos. It isn't always peaceful, and there's always a price."

"Too damn high," she told him now, in this memory that had somehow warped into something entirely different, taking refuge in acting as drunk as she remembered feeling that night. "I don't want to pay." She turned away from the table. "I don't want to play."

He pulled her back, using that strength of body and will that always had the capacity to surprise her. None of the X-Men had really understood how much he meant to the team until he was gone. Especially her.

"What's done is done," he told her, gently wiping away the tears that burst unbidden from her eyes.

"I killed you."

He gave her that damn smile again and shrugged. *"I'm still here."*

She blinked, uncomprehending.

"Perfect memory, coupled to the power to transcend all the rules and realities."

"You're a figment of my damn imagination!"

He sighed. *"Whatever I am, wherever I come from, I'm a part of you."* He stroked the tip of his thumb lightly across her lips as his hands cupped her face, and she responded in kind by leaning her body against his, marveling at how well they fit.

"Power is responsibility," he told her gently. *"Responsibility is choice."*

Her own lessons. She didn't want to hear them.

"Have it your own way, then," he said, and before she knew what he was doing, thought and action so close together—virtually one—that even her telepathy wasn't able to warn her, he wrenched off his visor.

Twin spears of force struck her wholly unrestrained with an impact sufficient to punch a hole straight through the base of a granite mountain. She flew backwards as if she'd been shot from a catapult, screaming with rage as she crashed against a wall that should have broken with the blow, but miraculously held.

The fire blazed within her eyes as she fought back, taking the energies Scott hurled at her and making them her own, using that strength to establish a shield and force the continuing blasts away from her body and back towards their source.

It wasn't easy. Even when they'd fought at Alkali Lake, when Scott had been mind-controlled by Stryker into becoming the X-Men's adversary, the fact that he'd been shooting through his visor maintained an upper safety limit on his power level. This time, all those governors had been cast aside.

She gathered her own power and prepared to strike back.

Only—just like that, he closed his eyes.

The sudden absence of pressure caught her as much by surprise as his initial attack. She was pushing so hard against that titanic resistance that she was thrown immediately off-balance and couldn't stop herself from pitching to the floor in an undignified sprawl.

As she shoved herself up, she found him beside her, visor once more in place, the picture of loving solicitude. She reacted with fury and slapped him aside, putting some distance between them as she moved against the wall, the better to let him see the fire in her eyes.

He was no more afraid of her now than he'd been at Alkali.

"I can't help myself," he told her as he had told her long ago, and tapped a couple of fingers against his temple. *"Something's not quite . . . right in here, a bit that's broken, that we never found a way to repair."* She'd done the MRI and CAT scans after they'd met. It was a crucial bit of organic brain damage dating from a childhood accident. In a way, it was much like what had happened with her and Annie; both she and Scott had suffered a trauma that catalyzed their powers ahead of schedule. Each had had to deal with the lasting consequences.

"I can't turn off my optic blasts," he continued, *"and you have access to more raw power than you ever imagined. Question is, my love, does the power control you? Or . . . ?"*

Xavier's final question, his final plea.

Charles hadn't been afraid, either, but more—surprised. And in a way that suggested he beheld a frontier of infinite possibilities, not the end of his life but a whole new beginning.

"You have a choice, Jean," Scott told her.

It was time.

Chapter
Ten

"Welcome," the tour guide announced, "to the northern anchor of the Golden Gate Bridge."

The big Prevost bus was pulled off to the side of the road, onto a paved overlook that provided a sweeping sea-level panorama of the Bay, with a spectacular view of San Francisco and Alcatraz. Almost a full load, a little shy of fifty tourists, mainland Chinese on holiday, had come to view the sights and visit relatives who'd emigrated generations ago. There was a lot more variety in clothes than the guide remembered from previous tours and a significant improvement both in general style and quality. It was fascinating to him how much like everyone else they'd become, surprisingly indistinguishable in outward affect from their counterparts from Des Moines. Made sense in a way; for all he knew, they *made* a lot of the clothes heartland America wore— why shouldn't they wear them as well? Generational splits certainly transcended national and societal boundaries, that much was obvious: the older folks were totally excited, the parents looked harried, torn between caring for *their* parents and their kids, while the kids, who ran the spectrum from very early teens to barely twenties, clearly wanted to be anywhere but here. On their own, they might have found this fun, but stuck in this crowd, they were determined to proclaim their independence by radiating ennui.

"If you look in this direction," he said, leading them around the front of the bus for a better look, "you'll see the foundation anchors for the north tower. The bridge was the brainchild of engineer Joseph Strauss, and executed by architect Irving Morrow—who we have to thank both for the Art Deco design touches and the bridge's distinctive and unique color—along with engineer Charles Alton Ellis and designer Leon Moissieff. Construction began on the fifth of January, 1933, and the bridge itself was completed in April, 1937, and officially opened a month later, in May. It's one point seven miles from end to end, with a central span of forty-two hundred feet rising two hundred twenty feet above mean high water. The two towers that support the roadway stand seven hundred forty-six feet high, ninety feet above Golden Gate Strait.

"Couple of more fun facts before we move on," he continued, preening ever so slightly as a number of cameras turned his way. "Each of those anchorages, the one here in Marin and its counterpart over there at Fort Point, weigh better than sixty thousand tons. The total weight of the bridge—soup to nuts—is just shy of nine hundred thousand tons. Each main cable is about a mile and a third in length, a yard in diameter, and is made up of twenty-seven thousand separate strands of galvanized wire. The total weight of the main cables, the suspender cables, and all the bits that hold them together is nearly twenty-five thousand tons.

"There are a couple of bigger bridges in the world," he finished proudly, "but none more beautiful. Take your time with pictures but save some film, because I guarantee that the view from the Marin headlands," he pointed up the road ahead, "will take your breath away. It's the shot you see in all the movies, but take it from me, the reality is even better!"

X

"Are we *there* yet?" Georgina wailed, delivering a pretty solid kick to the back of the driver's seat, and for the umpteenth time since they'd hit the road, all of twenty minutes ago, Allan Ryerson wondered why he'd taken the plunge when the salesman had suggested the Mercedes SUV with the integral video-game monitors and DVD player—it seemed to be no help at all with keeping the kids quiet.

He tossed a glance at Blair, who returned a semihelpless shrug and twisted around to remind her daughter yet again not to bother daddy when he was driving, which Allan very much appreciated, as the bridge was a bit more crowded than usual. Out of the corner of his eye he could see Tim huddled in his own seat, taking refuge intermittently between his Playstation controller and his stash of comics, wanting nothing to do with his kid sister's demands for attention and the parental outburst they were sure to provoke.

Allan felt a bump down by the small of his back and figured for that first fleeting moment that Gee Gee had again ignored her mother, and given him another boot. But it happened again and he thought of potholes and speed bumps or that perhaps he'd drifted over a line of lane-separating cat's-eyes.

Then, impossibly, terrifyingly, the bridge gave a sudden and violent sideways lurch. His tires squealed as Allan fought for control, instinctively stomping on the brake as he registered taillights flashing scarlet all across his field of vision as every other driver in view did the same. He fishtailed slightly— eyes wide and staring into the rearview mirror, praying the guy on his tail was just as much on the ball—and he registered a deep rumble, like a convoy of fully loaded super dump trucks passing close at hand. He skidded laterally and wailed inside as he heard the telltale crunch of contact with the SUV to his immediate right. The repair cost would likely be obscene, and even if insurance covered the bill his rates would skyrocket, assuming the company didn't cancel his policy outright. Then he cried out in shock, Gee Gee screamed, and Blair cried his name, as a pickup on the other side collided with enough force to shower him with glass. He was dimly aware of someone in the other car calling out over and over, "I'm sorry, I'm sorry, I'm sorry," but he had more important things to terrify him as they were hit one last time, from behind.

The shaking around them was getting worse, cars bouncing on every side like toys. The constant contact was horrible; metal ground together, and sprung bits of plate and bumper got tangled so that doors torqued out of line and locks were jammed. Something whizzed across his line of sight and slammed into the hood of the SUV next to them with a terrific *bang!* He stared at it, uncomprehending, for what seemed like a long while, trying to place the origin of an object colored so bright a red. Then, after what had really been only a second or so, his mind made the proper connection and he paled with recognition and craned his neck around for a view of the south support tower they'd been passing when this nightmare began.

It was a rivet.

The shaking was popping the rivets that held the bridge together.

There was only one thing with force enough to do that, and from the way everyone who was able was piling from their cars and racing pell-mell for shore, he wasn't the only one to come to such an obvious—especially for San Franciscans—conclusion.

Gee Gee gave it voice, with a shrill scream: *"Daddy, it's an* earthquake!*"*

Allan tried his door, but it wouldn't budge. He looked to Blair, but knew at once that hers was just as jammed. He knew the passenger doors most likely wouldn't work either. And with the truck jammed up tight against their rear bumper, they wouldn't be able to get out that way.

No sunroof—an option he'd passed on to chisel down the price. His own window was shattered, but there wasn't enough clearance for him to wriggle through. The best hope, the only hope, was to smash the windshield.

Everyone around him was making noise: Gee Gee was howling in terror, Blair struggling with her seat belt, twisting herself between the seats, the better to reach her babies, while Tim was nonstop with questions— "What's happening, Dad? What're we gonna do, Dad? Are we gonna die, Dad?"

Allan's breath caught in his throat—*What was happening up ahead?*

"I . . ." he started, then worked his lips and tongue, partly to moisten his mouth, partly to remind himself how to speak. He spoke more loudly this time, to make himself heard. "I don't think it's an earthquake."

He craned upwards in his seat as best he could to give

himself a better look, then gasped in astonishment as a Hummer up ahead bounced into the air as though shot from a catapult.

It didn't go far, but it wasn't alone. Allan found himself reminded of the most memorable scene from *The Ten Commandments*, the parting of the Red Sea—only in this instance it was cars being shunted aside instead of water. An invisible wedge was moving down the center-line of the roadway from the Marin shore, blasting aside everything in its path and piling vehicles up with the careless abandon of a kid who's been asked to clear away his toys.

He could see people now, a crowd following the lead of a tall and commanding figure wearing a formal-looking coat that seemed to Allan some kind of uniform. The crown of his head gleamed in the waning light of day, and for a second, watching, Allan was puzzled—until he recognized it as a helmet, and then saw more clearly the kinds of people that trailed behind him. And Allan knew with an icy stab of terror who they were facing.

The man was Magneto, the mutant terrorist described on the news as the Master of Magnetism.

Close behind Magneto were two men and two women. The women, one a tall redhead, the other darker, both wore leather like it was a second skin. One of the men was slight and surprisingly young, and as he approached, Allan could see he was playing with a Zippo lighter, constantly flipping it open and shut, open and shut. The other was a mountain with limbs, so monumentally massive he put even the most powerfully built pro wrestler to shame, the armor he wore making him even more impressive.

Behind them came a crowd of mixed folks, some who

looked like average people but others who were outright monsters—a hundred strong.

Around the Ryersons, everyone who could was scrambling from their cars and fleeing for shore. He wanted nothing more than to join them, but try as he might—he pounding with his fists and Blair kicking with her foot—they couldn't pop the damn windshield. Then, startlingly, provoking more cries from the children, and a yelp from Blair as she found herself tugged off balance, everything inside the vehicle that contained even a scrap of ferrous metal began to rise to the ceiling. Blair's problem was her belt, composed of interlocking steel links, and she dangled semi-helplessly until Allan was able to release the buckle and help her twist free. She ended up huddled in the back with the kids, and he wished he could join them.

Something heavy hit the roof, the first in a series of impacts that reminded Allan of a prairie hailstorm, until the shattering of glass demonstrated that what was falling here was considerably heavier.

He heard a terrible *snap* from overhead, and cried a primal and atavistic wordless protest—rage, defiance, denial, despair—as it was followed by a high-pitched and metallic *twang* and then a tremendous crash, as one of the great suspension cables landed alongside them.

Allan was crying, his family was crying, Blair sat with the kids clutched close, and even though he couldn't hear a word for all the din that enveloped them, he could see her mouth forming the words of the Lord's Prayer. She believed they were going to die. He was sure they would, too—but even as the thought occurred to him it was banished by another, just as profound and far stronger, the certainty that they would not. He would not allow it. Hopeless as things seemed, utterly crazy and impossible as it sounded, he would find a way to save his family.

Magneto was very close. Allan could see him with perfect clarity as the man raised his arms high.

It was a grand and theatrical gesture . . .

. . . and it achieved an immediate, equivalent response . . .

. . . as the Golden Gate Bridge was torn free from its northern anchors.

Magneto turned to his troops, every inch a conqueror, and all of them save one cheered him accordingly.

The redhead looked bored.

X

On the Marin side, the tour group ran for their lives. They didn't bother with the bus. A piece of concrete from overhead that was twice its size had squashed it flat and the air was filled with debris of every material and size, peppering both water and shore with shrapnel. Some of the group tried to pause to take proper photos, while others simply held their cellphones and digital cameras over their shoulders and shot on the run, hoping something appropriately dramatic would develop that they could use to make their fortune. The guide heard screams he knew would haunt him until the day he died, which he prayed with all his might would not be today, and was thankful he couldn't see what caused them. He was the last up the hill, making it his business to look after his passengers, assuming the same sense of responsibility assigned to the captain of a ship or an aircraft. The ground was shaking, the air thick with a choking cloud of dust; even if he could find breath enough to speak, it was likely impossible to make himself heard over the sheer volume of noise.

Something caught him behind the legs and slapped him down, hard enough to bloody his nose. He didn't know what it was, and didn't care; he was being sucked and dragged downslope. He scrabbled for handholds, broke nails on tarmac, cried out with shock as he was doused in bitterly cold water, and then regretted the impulse as his mouth filled with salt water that made him gag, on the brink of drowning.

Just as suddenly, just as violently, he found himself jerked clear of the flood, his arms draped across the shoulders of his rescuers, while other hands clutched at his belt to keep him upright. Without prompting, he found the means to propel his legs into action and kept pace with the men on either side as they scurried clear of the maelstrom.

They probably climbed a hundred feet without pause, moving at a rapid, relentless clip, before they reached a bend in the road that seemed to be a safe vantage spot.

When the guide's vision cleared, as he tried to stammer thanks to men who'd hear none of it, he couldn't believe his eyes. He'd been felled by a titanic wave caused when the entire north tower of the bridge moved past them and into the bay, as though pivoting on some monumental axis.

In the distance, he saw what seemed to him like minor puffs of smoke from the San Francisco base of the bridge. Close-up, he knew, for those in the Presidio with a grandstand seat—as he and his tourists had over here—there'd be nothing "minor" about it at all. Whatever had wrenched the bridge from its Marin moorings was doing the same across the Golden Gate.

Something flicked across his peripheral vision and he caught sight of a TV news helicopter buzzing the scene, taking advantage of what little light remained to broad cast the event live.

But even as the helicopter approached, it twisted into sudden and unexpected evasive action as one impossible event was eclipsed by another. Freed of all its anchors, from both shores and the foundations of the towers, the Golden Gate Bridge rose silently and majestically into the air, to proceed in stately procession deeper into the bay, leaving in its wake a trail of tumbling cars and collapsing superstructure from either end, like Hansel and Gretel depositing breadcrumbs so they might find their way home.

X

Magneto placed one foot on the coaming of the bridge walkway and leaned forward on bent knee, surveying the way ahead with cool confidence and no small amount of pride, like a shipmaster bringing his vessel into harbor.

"Charles always wanted to build bridges," he commented.

And Jean thought, *It's always about Charles. Every action, every decision, you measure against him, as though you can't accept the rightness of your cause until you prove him wrong.*

As though sensing the tenor of her thoughts, he turned to face her, indicating their fast-approaching destination—the former prison island of Alcatraz.

"Once that cure is gone, nothing can hold you back. *Nothing*."

And Jean thought, *Silly, foolish man, you talk as if that's a good thing.*

She couldn't deny, though, how much she was tempted, and she knew the intoxication of the moment, the anticipation of what was to follow, showed in her eyes, on her face.

Aloud, with a smile he should have found dangerous, she said, "I know."

She closed her eyes, released her power, took a count of the souls on the bridge, and those awaiting them on the island. If Magneto asked for their disposition, she'd tell him. Otherwise, she decided to hold her peace.

She wondered if she should tell him the X-Men had arrived.

X

Everyone crowded the flight deck for a view of the bridge as Ororo brought the *Blackbird* over the bay in a wide, sweeping turn that allowed them all to see what was happening. Further aft, at Hank's tech station, every screen on the main display revealed a variation of the same event, pulled from all the local TV channels, plus the national and international news networks. Far more than the incidents at the Worthington clinics, this was something the whole world was indeed watching.

"Oh my stars and garters," Hank murmured, taking refuge in a catchphrase he hadn't used for years. It went with the costume.

Kitty, sitting in the right seat, announced in response to a flashing telltale on her panel, "We're being painted,

TraCon Doppler radar from Oakland and San Francisco International." She tapped a control, refining the sweep. "But—I'm getting some Q-band activity, high range, reads as an E2C Hawkeye AWACS off the *Teddy Roosevelt,* establishing a target portrait for possible air strikes."

Ororo tapped a code into the center control console, between her and Kitty. "Going to stealth mode."

From outside, the great black aircraft, already difficult to see in the gathering darkness, shimmered and then vanished, both to the naked eye and to all forms of electronic detection.

"On your toes, people," Ororo said quietly. "Everyone back to your places and strap in. Henry, Kitty," she added, "we're depending on you now. This airspace is likely to get more than a little bit crowded and since we can't be seen, we can't be evaded. It's up to you two to keep us from any collisions."

"A circumstance most devoutly to be avoided, ma'am," Hank agreed with mock solemnity, while Kitty, in the midst of tossing him a slightly jaundiced look, simply nodded.

X

In its way, M-day, as this would come to be called when it was all over, proved as significant and memorable a start to the twenty-first century for the City by the Bay as its fabled earthquake had been for the twentieth. It was certainly the kind of thing that nobody present ever forgot, especially those "privileged" enough to actually watch it unfold firsthand.

It had been just a normal Friday afternoon, with everyone going about their average and altogether ordinary pursuits, closing out the workweek, preparing for the weekend. Most folks downtown weren't even aware of anything amiss, at first; Magneto's seizure of the bridge occurred so fast, and the action itself was so incredibly unbelievable, that even with a helicopter on the scene, broadcasting live, it still took a little bit of time for the word to spread, and for it to be taken seriously.

Imagine the moment, riding the cable car up and over the crest of Russian Hill, thinking about what to do for dinner, bills to pay, aching back, walking the dog, watching cable, gazing out at the familiar sight of Alcatraz—the mind perhaps not quite registering what the eyes behold, the sight of this magnificent feat of engineering, one of the marvels of human history, gliding effortlessly across the waves.

In that, appearances truly were deceiving, because for Magneto the traverse was proving anything but effortless. *Lifting* this mass of better than a half million tons was but the first challenge, and moving it was nothing compared to the necessity of keeping the entire structure together.

Jean watched impassively, gauging the strain he was placing on his body, impressed by his determination. This would have been no small feat for him in his prime, and yet Magneto had first manifested his power in the Nazi death camp at Auschwitz, better than sixty years before.

She shrugged inside, tempted to let him succeed or falter on his own; if the world was truly a place defined by Darwin's dictum of survival of the fittest, shouldn't those same rules apply to him as to the sapien humanity he desired to supplant? But even as she acknowledged that consideration she found herself establishing a link between the two of them, on a level so slight he couldn't possibly be aware of it, but which allowed her to share her own energies with him, granting him a sufficient reservoir of strength to complete his task.

The bridge passed Fort Mason, depositing as it did so a few more stray cars from the end of the roadway, a line of near misses across Aquatic Park, leading to a couple of direct hits smack into the belly of a Scarab cigarette boat moored at Hyde Street Pier, along with the working trawler tied up just beyond it, and lastly some dot-com zillionaire's Lamborghini doing a swan dive right through the roof of a waterfront restaurant at the Cannery, to finish out its days as the centerpiece of the bar.

By this point, people down along the shore had gotten the message and were clearing the area as quickly as they could, especially as it became increasingly obvious that the bridge was about to make a landing.

The sound it made, and the effect it had on the city when Magneto brought it to rest, reminded many of the last great earthquake. The noise struck like a physical blow and while the ground trembled only for a moment, the shock wave was sufficient to break a fair share of windows and, far more annoyingly, trigger hundreds if not thousands of car alarms along the entire breadth of downtown.

Once the bridge had settled into place, with the tower a ways offshore and what remained of the roadway extending far enough to flatten a line of waterfront structures, people regained enough confidence to gather and watch what happened next as the other tower was brought into line with Alcatraz, and then deposited.

The bottom depths there weren't anywhere near consistent with those at the mouth of the bay itself, so the bridge ended up canted at a dramatic and awkward angle, tilting downward from city to island, with one end of the roadway suspended at a decent height above the shoreline while the other wasn't all that much higher than the water itself.

Magneto hadn't really cared much about the people underneath the bridge as he maneuvered it into place. He had no actual intent of killing anyone. He just didn't have the energy to spare and besides, they were only sapiens. They were functionally irrelevant to the future he was trying to bring about, and the sooner they were shuffled off the evolutionary stage the more merciful it would be for them. As for the troops assigned to the island—this was the risk, and price, that came with the uniform.

The journey concluded a bit more abruptly than Magneto would have preferred. He was a man of sublime precision, as much as Xavier, and it irked him to miscalculate the final descent so that the bridge crashed to rest with a jolt severe enough to knock everyone standing off their feet. Only he and Jean remained upright.

He shook off the hand she'd used to steady him and, as though to prove his might to all present, immediately levitated above the crowd, giving them all a grandstand view as he hovered to the forefront of the bridge and used his powers to partially collapse that end of the roadway, combining it with a gathering of debris from the crushed barracks to form an easily negotiable ramp from bridge to island. Beyond, at the highest point, rose the cellblocks.

X

In the White House Situation Room, Bolivar Trask was the first to take notice of what was happening. Only minutes had passed from Magneto's initial incursion onto the bridge, and the news was still making its way up the government information tree. What caught Trask's eye was a hard to watch visual on one of the TV monitors tuned to Fox News, what caught his ear was an anchor reduced to stammering incredulity.

He wondered as he spoke if his own voice sounded the same.

"Mr. President," he said quietly, in that unimaginably matter-of-fact voice that one calls upon to announce the imminent end of the world, "I think you should see this."

Even as David Cockrum turned to look at the screen, some techs in their cubbyholes had worked magic of their own, projecting network news feeds on subordinate screens while saving the main display for a Keyhole KH-13 surveillance satellite-view of the scene from orbit, enhancing the image to take into account the fact that it was almost nighttime.

There was a gap across Golden Gate Strait, as glaring as the suddenly toothless space in a hockey player's mouth after a close encounter with a puck. And there was a landlink connecting the island of Alcatraz with the city on its doorstep.

"My God," the president said in a whisper.

And then, because that was his job, he called his military advisors to order and started planning how to deal with it.

X

Allan Ryerson could barely believe he was still alive. In all the confusion, as the bridge swung across the bay and then crashed spectacularly to rest, the surrounding cars had shifted away enough for him to force open his door. But now that they could escape, he wasn't sure it was such a great idea.

A couple of car-lengths ahead of him, Magneto descended once more to the roadway. Now that the sun had set, and with the power to the roadway lights severed when the bridge was torn from its moorings, it was dangerously difficult to see. The only illumination came from the city behind them, the ambient radiance cast by its apartments and skyscrapers, which barely lit up the opposite end of the bridge. The way ahead, to Alcatraz, was shrouded in total darkness.

Magneto didn't seem bothered by this in the slightest. He glowed, just a little, outlined in a pale blue corona like a minor display of Saint Elmo's fire. Allan yelped as his SUV's lights came on, along with those of every other car that remained on the bridge. The vehicles had been arranged with purpose, so that their headlights created a more than sufficient pool of illumination that stretched the length of the bridge and extended out onto the island.

Allan couldn't help staring, awestruck and impressed. Acknowledging his reaction, Magneto inclined his head and allowed Allan one of those practiced, professional smiles favored by British royalty.

Blair was far more practical. She slapped the door lock closed and protectively gathered her children about her.

That actually made Magneto chuckle—although there was a haunted aspect to the shadowed eyes beneath the brow of his helmet that Allan would never forget, and which belied the outward and very real humor of the moment.

Magneto's memory was not as pristine and absolute as a telepath's, but there were certain instances that could not be excised. Looking at Blair Ryerson reminded him of one, from an age he wished he could forget, when he was huddled in the arms of a woman who wasn't his mother, yet who was determined to protect him just the same, crammed into the corner of a cattle car trundling through the bleak wilderness of a Polish winter, from one camp of misery to another.

Auschwitz wasn't up and running as a death camp in those days. They were among the first inmates, the ones who had to help construct the facilities, and that spared them the fate of those who followed, those sent to the gas chambers. They were simply worked to death, under that damnable legend *Arbeit Macht Frei*—Work Makes Freedom.

"Never again," Magneto breathed to himself, turning violently from the past—his own and humanity's—and waving his makeshift army of revolution towards what he was determined to make a bright and shining future.

* * *

Jean watched Erik take the lead, more aware of his thoughts and what they meant than he was, and she took a moment to sweep her gaze across the family in their Mercedes GL500. They were confused, they were afraid, they were angry at the wanton assault—and yet, there was no hate.

What to make of that, she wondered, and suggested with another thought that this was no fit place for them. And just to make it easier, she used a little twist of telekinesis to make sure all their car doors opened freely.

The moment Jean passed, Allan Ryerson burst from the driver's seat, wrenching open the sliding door beside his daughter and gathering Gee Gee into his arms while Blair and Tim tumbled free, Tim still clutching his handful of comics like they were a talisman, and Blair holding on to him just as tightly, for the same reason. Gee Gee started howling. They'd left her stuffed bear, and Allan handed her off to Blair, made a frantic dash back to the car, cursing a blue streak as he tore through the clutter until he found the animal. Then he gathered his family and they fled for their lives.

Jean watched them go. Only when she was positive they were safely on shore did she turn to follow Magneto.

X

On the island, frantic radio calls for help went unanswered, as all the emergency frequencies were occluded by sleet storms of impenetrable static. The same applied to video and cellular links, and internal communications were also crashed, as was every computer on the island, from network superservers to handheld PDAs. The lights were still on, but that was more for the convenience of the invading force than any defenders.

In his office, which used to be the warden's, with a view that overlooked the entire prison, Warren Worthington Jr. and Kavita Rao stood at the window and stared straight down the roadway of the Golden Gate Bridge and into the faces of the mutants who'd come to destroy their life's work.

Deep within the main cell house, on the opposite side of the island, in his room which afforded him his favorite view of the great bridge, young Jimmy—code-named Leech—took one last look at the yawning empty space where it used to be before burying himself in a cocoon of quilts and covers and stuffed animals of his own beneath the bed.

Back on the bridge, Magneto led the way, Callisto by his side, flanked in a shallow arrowhead formation by Pyro and Juggernaut on one side, Arclight and Kid Omega on the other.

Jean, as always, was a little bit behind.

Callisto advanced a few steps, taking point, casting her perceptive net across the whole of the island.

"Boy's in the back," she announced with satisfaction. "Southwest corner of the big building." She pointed to the squat, massive structure of the cell house.

"Well then," Magneto informed them, "this place has long since outlived its purpose. Let's take it down to the nails."

He reversed position and raised his hands.

At that signal, the mass of mutants who'd been following surged forward with a great, accompanying cry, a dozen fliers assuming the vanguard, scattering in combat pairs across the rock while twenty more streaked after them across the ground.

Juggernaut began to follow, but Magneto motioned him back.

"In chess," he said meditatively, "the pawns go first."

Jean shook her head. *Scott wouldn't have been so dismissive; for him, for Charles, even pawns had value.* But they were dead. It was left to Magneto to seize the day, and lay claim to the future.

In a sequence of bounds, a young woman whose mutation made her mostly lizard, with the predatory speed and power of a Komodo dragon, raced through the ruined barracks, up a wall, leapt to a rooftop and from there to the lighthouse—where she took a perch at the top, using eyes that saw as well by night as by day, and a forked tongue even better at finding prey, to scout the way ahead. The eyes saw nothing untoward.

The danger tasted by her tongue came too late.

Even as Komodo raised the alarm, troopers arose from hidden ambush points, and grenadiers on all sides unleashed a volley from shoulder-mounted missile launchers. Football-shaped projectiles, smaller than regulation balls, more akin to the ones given to grade-schoolers, arced through the air, detonating over the roadbed of the bridge where it met the island, filling the air with a cloud of minute flechettes the size of toothpicks.

At first it seemed like a joke, like being attacked by gnats. The darts were so fine they could slip through the weave of an ordinary cotton shirt, though the heavier thickness and construction of a jacket or military-issued cloth could quite easily deflect them. Even when they struck home, they barely stung. Some of the mutants didn't even realize they'd been hit. But the mutants in the first wave were the target of a score of projectiles from which came uncountable numbers of darts, enough to carpet the roadbed in a veritable lawn of plastic, many exploding upwards as well, to strike any of the fliers overhead.

Everyone froze for a moment, expecting—assuming—the worst.

Komodo plucked one dart from her neck.

"It's a dud," she crowed, convulsively sweeping all the others she could reach from her skin, furious with herself for being so spooked when the bombs had been launched. She had been sure they were goners.

"Keep up the attack!" she yelled, and bared her teeth ferociously, deciding it was time to run down some soldiers and scare them just the same as she'd been.

But then—with staggering suddenness—her snarl twisted into a rictus of pain. Komodo wanted to cry out in denial, she wanted to beg for mercy, because she remembered what she'd seen on TV, how it had been with the mutant in Brooklyn, and knew it was the same now with her. A cascade of pain stole away both breath and thought and she collapsed to hands and knees on the observation platform, watching in anguish as her skin rippled like a pond of water with fish fighting over bait right beneath the surface. Her hands lost their webbing, her skin its bright pattern. She screamed, wanting to hurl herself to the rocks below, better to end everything than endure such misery—not simply the agony of transformation, for she knew much worse was to come as her bones reshaped themselves back to their original baseline sapien configuration, but the awful fate of living with the memory of what she'd been, the certain knowledge that those days were gone forever.

She reached for the lowest bar of the railing, pushed with her feet against the wall behind her, but she didn't move. She had no strength. In every respect, save perhaps for weeping, she was done.

Overhead, some of the fliers who hadn't been hit made frantic, diving grasps for their fellows who had, reflexively trying to save their falling friends. Some they caught, some they missed, some yanked free of the hands that held them, and the night was broken by the sound of dull, scattered impacts, like sacks of meat striking the earth.

Thirty-five mutants had been hit.

Thirty-five men and women—although some might better be called boys and girls, they were so young—in varying stages of devolution, took their place.

"That," remarked Magneto from his summit on the bridge, "is why the pawns go first." He shook his head. "Humans and their guns."

Ahead and below, mop-up teams emerged into view—a full company of regular army, evenly split between those equipped with the dart weapons and those with riot gear, plus a contingent of medics to deal with any wounded. A Humvee rolled into the courtyard, sporting a water cannon to help the riot troops deal with the prisoners while the combat platoon took up new positions to prepare for the expected second wave.

A lieutenant spoke into his radio, tried again, then tossed the set aside in disgust; electronics were useless. Using hand signals, he passed word to his platoon sergeants and squad leaders to begin their advance. These were tough, experienced professionals, veterans one and all, who'd learned their trade in urban warfare.

Magneto faced Jean.

"Destroy them," he told her.

She ignored him, concentrating her attention—at least in part—on the view ahead, as the last airborne mutants were picked off by snipers.

"Jean," Magneto snapped commandingly, in a tone of exceptional harshness, *"do as I say!"*

She let him see a hint of the fire in her eyes, in her soul.

"You sound like him again."

He met her gaze without fear.

From the island, the lieutenant's voice rang out: *"Fire!"*

A volley of missiles arced towards the bridge.

Magneto snatched up a pair of cars and brought them together well ahead of him to form a barrier, instantly flattening and expanding the metal fabric of the vehicles to form a bowl-shaped shield that enveloped the bombs the instant they detonated, to ensure not a single dart escaped.

Just as quickly, he rounded on Arclight, a tall and rawboned woman who looked as though she'd just stepped out of an ancient Hellenic portrait of some Amazon warrior battling before the walls of Troy.

"Can you control your shock waves," he demanded, "to target those weapons and destroy them all at once?"

She looked dismissively towards the advancing troops.

"You find the right wavelength," she replied, "everything breaks."

"Amen to that," agreed Juggernaut.

Arclight popped another stick of Beeman's gum into her mouth to complement the one she was already chewing, then moved a few steps clear of the others to stand alone in the center of the roadway, seemingly intent on making herself the ideal, irresistible target. This was why Magneto had let her experiment with one of the weapons they'd claimed from the transport guards—to find the precise frequency to destroy them.

As soldiers moved warily into view—understanding full well that while Magneto couldn't affect their weapons, there was nothing to stop him from using the very bridge against them—Arclight clapped her hands together. The air before her shook with the generation of a localized sonic boom, and visible ripples marked the progress of its energy-charged shock waves as they rolled outward towards the oncoming troops, who responded by bringing their guns up to fire.

Before a single dart could be unleashed, the shock wave was on them, shattering each and every plastic pistol and rifle they held. Stunned, the soldiers watched the darts they held clatter uselessly to the ground.

The shock waves continued their advance across the entire island, doing the same to every plastic weapon on the Rock.

As the soldiers on the bridge hastily withdrew to join their fellows on the island, Arclight turned to Juggernaut, hand upheld, and he slapped it in a high five.

X

"What about jets?" demanded President Cockrum of the Chairman of the Joint Chiefs. "Tanks? There's an aircraft carrier just offshore. Can't the *Teddy Roosevelt* launch an air strike?"

Bolivar Trask shook his head. "Magneto'll turn them into scrap metal."

Cockrum pounded his fist on the table in frustration. "Where the hell are our ground troops? We have to be able to do *something*!"

X

With the paramount threat neutralized, Magneto led his troops ashore. Jean remained at her perch on the bridge, head cocked to one side as though listening to a conversation only she could hear.

The X-Men weren't attempting to mask their thoughts, although they had tech aboard the *Blackbird* that would allow them to try. Ororo was testing her, Jean knew: would she reveal the X-Men's approach to Magneto? Ororo wanted to determine now, before the situation escalated, where Jean's loyalties lay.

Truth be told, Jean still wasn't sure.

Magneto looked, searching for the source of a sound that shouldn't be there—the muted roar of a pair of jet engines. Jean allowed herself a rueful smile. Apparently, the sound baffles weren't quite properly tuned.

"We have visitors," he warned.

Ororo announced her arrival with lightning, a bolt powerful enough to illuminate the island bright as day, dazzling those who saw it almost to the point of blindness and opening a crater in the ground.

In quick succession came three more, bracketing Magneto's cadre of mutants on all sides as Ororo streaked into view from a point only Magneto could perceive atop the main building of the prison.

* * *

While this was happening, in those precious seconds that their adversaries were reeling from Ororo's assault, the X-Men took the field.

Hank McCoy leapt impossibly from roof to wall to roof to wall to wall, bouncing effortlessly back and forth as he made his way to a landing in the yard.

Peter Rasputin simply dropped, full metal body, like a solid steel rock—despite the risk that represented against the powers of Magneto—to make a nifty crater of his own.

Logan slid down the face of the building, using his claws to thrust into the masonry wall and slow his descent.

Kitty Pryde came down with Bobby Drake in her arms, phasing the pair of them so that when they reached ground level, they simply disappeared into the earth. A moment or so later, they popped right back up, like corks on a wave. Kitty, with Bobby by her side, clambered to the surface. She was grinning with delight. He looked ready to hurl.

"Don't *ever* do that again."

She rolled her eyes. Some guys were just plain useless.

The lieutenant commanding the force on Alcatraz recognized McCoy, despite his outlandish getup, and couldn't help staring. Presidential cabinet officers don't generally take the field of combat, much less clad in formfitting costumes.

"Pull back your troops, Lieutenant," McCoy told him, with the full authority that only someone used to having the ear of the president can muster. "Let the X-men handle this."

"Sir," the lieutenant swallowed, well aware of what McCoy was asking and not altogether sure his men would follow, "this is our post, sir. Six of you, sixty-five of them. Those odds suck! We can help."

Hank acknowledged the offer, knowing what it meant for sapien troops to volunteer to stand shoulder-to-shoulder with mutants, allowing himself the hopeful thought *Perhaps some lasting good might come from this mess.*

"You've done your part and more, Lieutenant," he told the young man. "Go. Now. That's an order."

Hank had no place in the officer's chain of command, but such was the natural force of his voice that the lieutenant responded with a crisp salute and did as he was told.

"Mind you," Hank mused to Logan by his side, "given those odds, he does have a point."

Logan snorted. Hank considered that for someone like the Wolverine, with his temperament and capabilities, he probably thought of this as a fair fight.

"Get together, people," Logan told them. "Side by side. Whatever comes, we hold the line. We defend this place, and the people in it, at all costs."

Magneto shook his head.

"Traitors to their own cause." *Forgive me, Charles,* he thought. *For the cause we both champion, I must destroy these children you hold most dear.* "We must finish them," he told his mutants, and both tone and expression left no doubt as to what he meant by "finish." As far as he was concerned, this battle would be to the death. He would ask no quarter, nor grant any in return. "Every last one."

He turned his eyes to Jean, who met his gaze but made no other move.

At Magneto's signal, his mutants charged. A phalanx of almost forty against a line of five.

Logan didn't wait for them to reach him; for him the best defense was always offense.

Ten came for him, and he took them down without breaking a major sweat, without even popping his claws.

He was quick, but that was just the start of it. His healing factor gave Logan a reaction time that was significantly greater than the average sapien, *or* the average mutant. He rarely needed to think as he fought, on any conscious level; his body—working through backbrain and instinct and physical memory—did that for him. He reacted to the slightest of cues, on levels more subtle than most hunting dogs, which allowed him to begin his counter at virtually the same time, so it seemed to his adversaries as though he was reading their minds, anticipating their every attack.

For his opponents, it was even worse when bodies actually made contact. The Wolverine's skeleton was laced with adamantium, and striking him was akin to hitting bars of a metal far stronger than steel. Punching him in the jaw invariably broke a hand and the same applied to any blunt force object like a cudgel. When he struck back, it usually took only a single blow for *lights-out*.

The claws were a last resort, his ultimate weapon. He finished this initial engagement without needing them, save for a sideways slash through a lighting stanchion to drop it as a temporary barrier between one group of combatants and the next.

McCoy was even faster in speed and reaction time. Unlike Logan, he possessed an unnatural grace that made him seem almost weightless. He seemed utterly at home on any surface, floor or ceiling, vertical or horizontal, stationary or mobile. Even masonry in midcollapse could be turned into a momentary perch or pivot point that allowed McCoy to move from one opponent to the next without the slightest pause, as though the entire engagement had been choreographed. Combined with an acrobatic agility that would make an Olympian gymnast weep, the Beast was nearly untouchable, definitely unbeatable.

Hank caught a punch in one hand, flipped the man head over heels into the two beside him, leapt for a wall, bounced off the head of another mutant, yanked him into the air, grabbed a pole, and used momentum to make a 360-degree pivot in time to slam a foot into the now-falling mutant's belly before dropping back into the heart of the fray. And all the while, his face was split by a grin of true delight, as he reveled in a true and outrageous physicality that had been straightjacketed for far too long within his bespoke Savile Row suits, strapped down as cruelly as young Warren Worthington's wings.

Twenty of Magneto's crew in as many seconds. That was the score when Hank and Logan came together, back-to-back, at skirmish's end.

"We've cut their numbers by a third," Hank crowed.

"Thought you were a pacifist," Logan growled, looking for Magneto, crying out in his mind for Jean, thinking, *This was* way *too easy.*

"As Churchill said, 'There must come a time when all men must—' "

The second wave came, as many as the first, but much nastier to look at.

McCoy shrugged. "You get the point," he said, and leapt back into the fray.

Ororo rose skyward at the same time, eyes flaring white as she gathered winds and power to her, pulling moisture from sea and air to generate a massive cloud formation just off the island's shore.

Thunder shook the rocky island, and a series of sympathetic, almost electronic *twangs*, like the plucked strings of an untuned guitar, sounded along the length of the bridge as the boom established a cascade of vibrations across the suspender cables.

In the space of a few heartbeats, Ororo ramped up her storm to better than Category Five on the Saffir-Simpson Hurricane Scale, and unleashed its full fury into the heart of the attackers, striking them with wind-driven rain that knocked some off their feet and left the rest too dazed and disoriented to cope with the storm surge that followed, a wave that rose to twice their height and swept the battlefield clean of debris and combatants.

Because of the close quarters of the combat, Ororo had to come down low to wield her weather with the necessary precision of force and placement. There were no fliers left among Magneto's troops, no sign yet of any energy casters like Pyro, so she thought her position fairly secure.

Callisto proved her wrong, demonstrating a strength and agility—and daring—that was on par with McCoy as she scrambled up one of the suspender cables and hurled herself at Storm with headlong abandon.

Ororo sensed the shift in the air that heralded the other woman's approach, but had to make sure her weather was safely under control, costing her the split second needed to properly respond to Callisto's attack. The woman had a knife and raked it across Ororo's body, scoring the leather of her uniform and leaving a trail of fire in its wake that told Ororo she'd drawn blood. The impact followed a moment later, as Callisto wrapped both legs around the taller woman for an anchor, hammering at her with a clenched fist while trying again and again with the knife for more blood. Being up in the air clearly didn't faze her in the slightest; she must have simply assumed that Storm's power would keep them aloft until Callisto killed her or she got too distracted to maintain it. Either way, they'd fall, and she knew that Callisto would try to make sure that Storm landed on the bottom.

Ororo refused to fall. She did the reverse and shot the pair of them better than a mile straight up in the blink of an eye. Callisto paid no attention, instead cracking her forehead against Storm's hard enough to revert the silver eyes back to normal. As they started to tumble, as shock severed Storm's link with the winds that propelled them aloft, Callisto hammered at her with her fist, to the throat, the head, the face, to whatever part of her she could reach. She'd find her own way to survive, she had no doubt, just so Storm didn't. She was good at that.

She tried stabbing as well, but Storm caught that hand in hers, using the greater length of her arm to keep it well clear.

Callisto squeezed her thighs together, as hard as she could, and was rewarded by a grunt of pain from her foe.

She grinned—this was her moment—and wrenched her knife hand loose. Callisto didn't try stabbing, she knew Storm would block her, but instead flipped the blade end over end towards her own waiting left hand. She'd go for a quick grab, and a quicker stab to the other woman's unprotected flank, end of story. She'd never know what hit her.

But her fingers closed empty . . .

. . . and Callisto felt an awful mix of fire and ice course through her own chest, which suddenly refused to draw in any more air.

Uncomprehending, she dropped her gaze, to behold the hilt of her weapon just below her breast, a perfectly placed thrust to the heart.

She looked back into Ororo's eyes and saw a hardness in them that put her own inner armor to shame. Storm had plucked the knife from midair—Callisto couldn't believe she had such speed in her—and delivered the final blow to Callisto instead, without a moment's hesitation, without a shred of mercy.

She tried to speak, tasted blood, felt her face twist into an unaccustomed expression that was a silent plea for salvation. She'd never in her mutant life considered the possibility of dying. Facing it at last, she was terrified.

As her eyes closed, her head lolled, and her legs lost their grip. The face before her remained unrelenting.

But when Callisto fell, Ororo caught her.

She'd come of age in a war zone, in a place and at a time where girls were generally considered of no consequence, and learned to defend herself long before her mutant powers manifested.

Killing came easy.

That's why she strove to find a better way.

X

Back on Alcatraz, further along the line, Bobby found himself confronted by a behemoth who called himself Phat for reasons that were grossly obvious. The files held in the Mansion mentioned a mutant who worked in a carnival, with a similar physique, who called himself the Blob, but Fred J. Dukes was a matinee idol compared to this guy. Phat's footsteps set off tremors through the rock and threatened to bring down whatever walls of the barracks still remained upright.

Bobby tried freezing the ground to upend him, but Phat was so massive that the ice merely shattered underfoot.

Fortunately, he was no speed demon, and Bobby had little trouble ducking and dodging his grabs. There wasn't a whole lot of wiggle room and the fight around them was devolving into a madcap melee. None of the X-Men could afford to devote themselves overlong to a single adversary, for fear of becoming vulnerable to someone else.

Desperation produced inspiration and, instead of a sheet of ice, Bobby chose to form a pillar instead, to enfold the other man. This way, except perhaps by tripping, Phat couldn't bring his weight effectively to bear. And if he should manage to fall, Bobby was determined to build an ice mountain on top of him, to make sure he wouldn't soon get up.

Phat still managed two or three more steps before the ice locked him in place. Despite Bobby's efforts, he was still struggling and Bobby knew that if he eased off, even a little, the other mutant would quickly break free. *Made sense, damn it, that a creature of such obscene bulk would have muscles to match; how else could he* move, how else could he get his heart and circulatory system to function properly?

Then Colossus was there, landing a single punch to Phat's jaw that broke the foot-thick encasement of ice as if it were nothing, and *still* connected with power enough to shatter the mutant's consciousness before he hit the ground.

The big Russian turned at once to aid Kitty, who really didn't need it against the woman with the axe. Time and again, the woman slashed her blade through the girl's ghostly body without doing the slightest harm, while Kitty bobbed and weaved and backpedaled until she came within Peter's reach.

A single backhand, not even full force, knocked the woman twenty feet and out of the fight.

There were a couple of quick glances from side to side and the briefest exchange of smiles back to Logan, who acknowledged that they were doing well.

At Logan's signal to the lieutenant, the soldiers moved onto the scene, taking the fallen mutants into custody.

Up on the bridge, Pyro glared across the way at Bobby, chomping at the bit to confront his former roommate.

Magneto would have none of it.

"Not yet," he said to the young man, in a tone that allowed neither argument nor defiance. "Stay by my side."

Instead, Magneto turned to the Juggernaut.

"Mr. Marko," he called out. "You have the coordinates from Callisto. The boy we seek is in the main cell house." He pointed to the very top of the Rock. "Up there. Get inside. Find the boy. Kill him."

Age didn't matter, the fact that he was a mutant didn't matter—no more than it had when he was prepared to sacrifice Rogue years before at Liberty Island. If it was necessary for the cause, that was all that mattered to Magneto.

As for Cain Marko, he really couldn't care less. He just loved to smash things.

Buildings were fun, people better—and X-Men would be best of all.

He dropped his head, angling his torso forward as best he could so that his conical helmet appeared a bit like a massive cannon shell plowing through the air. The sloping roadway allowed him to build up a decent amount of speed, and he was fairly confident that nothing below would be able to even slow him down, much less bring him to a halt.

Squads of troopers were the first to fall, solid hits that made him feel the same satisfaction as when he threw a strike in bowling, with bodies flying as wildly as tenpins.

A Humvee rolled from cover and deployed its water cannon, which had about as much effect as a kid's water pistol. Juggernaut struck the vehicle more solidly than any battering ram, shattering it on contact and bouncing all the bits and pieces off the surrounding walls.

Logan popped his claws, figuring they might do some good against the onrushing giant—what good was unstoppable momentum if you had no legs left to run with?—but he was at the wrong end of the yard, with too many bodies to fight between him and Juggernaut.

Colossus was much closer, and he made the interception on his own, without a signal from the others, setting himself right in the charging man's path.

Juggernaut accepted the challenge and picked up his pace. Peter set himself, and cocked a fist.

He threw a great punch, but it never got the chance to land. Juggernaut body-slammed him right off his feet, turning the massive strength of the X-Man against his teammates, deflecting the armored Russian into a nearby wall that was already on its last bricks, forcing Beast to scramble to yank Iceman clear as the entire edifice crashed to the ground.

By then, of course, he was on his way to the cell house.

"He's going for the boy," McCoy yelled.

"Not if I get there first," Kitty yelled back over her shoulder, for she'd started running the moment Juggernaut bounced Colossus aside.

Juggernaut couldn't be stopped. Neither could she—only she was a lot less messy about it. Kitty phased straight into the body of the rocky island, and the hill that formed the foundation of the cell house.

X

Warren Worthington Jr., gun in hand, and Kavita Rao were running for their lives, and for the future. She was terrified—because they were in a headlong flight *towards* the sounds of battle, rather than away, scrambling through the rotted, shadowy warrens of the old prison in a desperate attempt to reach Jimmy's room and take him with them.

"We need . . . to get . . . the boy," Worthington spat out between gasps, as his body mercilessly reminded him of the twin tolls of age and the good life. He'd thought himself in perfectly fine shape, only to have the last few minutes puncture that balloon forever.

Not so far away, and coming closer, he could hear a series of hollow *booms,* followed by the *shush* of collapsing masonry; it made him think someone was taking a wrecking ball to the building. Didn't much like the sound of that.

"There he is," came a shout from a gallery overhead.

Before they could move, find an escape, bring the gun to bear, the mutants were upon them, led by Kid Omega. Kavita shrieked in reflexive terror as the three mutants— Psylocke, Arclight, and Kid Omega—surrounded them.

"You're the guy that invented the 'cure,' am I right?" the female known as Psylocke demanded.

Worthington faced her, surprised to discover that while he was scared almost out of his mind, it didn't really show. Outwardly, he appeared altogether calm.

"Yes," he replied. "I am."

"That's what I thought," she said, displaying a gorgeous smile that was filled with both mischief and menace.

"Psylocke, what about her?" asked one of the others, giving Kavita a rough shake. She was crying, praying, lost within herself with the certainty of her imminent doom.

"She's the brains," Psylocke said. "He's the money. Kill her."

Worthington stared at Kavita in horror, two sets of wide-open eyes momentarily locking glances. He tried to reach out to her, only to find himself yanked roughly away.

Over his shoulder, he saw the other boy deploy quills across his shoulders and down his arms. A single flex of the forearm hurled a demonstration set into the neighboring wall with the force of a nail gun.

As Worthington was tossed around a corner, his captors not caring if they raised bruises or broke bones, he saw the mutant reach for Kavita and heard her last, despairing howl.

Kitty had no time to spare. She was surrounded by three mutants of her own. She went solid for them, spinning side kicks to the face, backed by the strength of a dancer's leg, bouncing one guy into the next, shaking both up enough for her to complete the pivot and punch the third in the belly, dropping him at last with a knee to the nose.

The others made uncoordinated grabs for her but she stepped right through them and turned solid from behind to give them her version of the Vulcan neck pinch.

Everyone was down but breathing. There was no time to do more because the sound of smashing walls was far too close for comfort, and her lead over the Juggernaut was perhaps a wall away from vanishing.

As if on cue, he thundered into view below, scattering chunks of masonry, bars that were more like spears, into his path as he lumbered the length of the tier.

Saving grace—the boy he was after wasn't on the ground floor.

Up he came, without slackening pace, each step bowing the metal stairs as if they were tin, while Kitty sprinted along the gallery to catch him.

She phased him with her, so that his next step— instead of landing solidly on the metal grating—plunged right through. She'd meant to leave him there, dangling from his midsection, deck and body inextricably merged until she came back to pull him free, but he proved quicker and more on the ball than she'd anticipated.

The instant he sensed the unique tingling that came from her nervous system interrupting his, he slammed his great hands down on the gallery with force enough to tear this entire section loose from its mountings and pitch both himself and Kitty to the main floor below.

They landed close enough together for him to make another grab at her, which failed as she went reflexively ghost—only to discover that was precisely what he wanted, as he used that momentary intangibility to wrench himself free of the deck grating.

Not only quick, but cunning. And now, really pissed off.

Thank Heaven, she thought, *at least* something's *going right!*

Kitty bolted. As hoped for, he followed.

She couldn't give the others an update; one of the major repercussions of her power was that it shorted out any electric circuit she passed through. Total murder on circuit boards, which was appropriately ironic for a natural gearhead. Advantage, she could neutralize surveillance systems, electronic locks, even people, with just the right touch. Problem, put a radio on her, it died.

She couldn't call for help, which meant she was on her own.

She considered a Wile E. Coyote stratagem, maybe leading Juggernaut around in circles until he'd undermined the body of the prison so much that it collapsed on top of him. Then decided, from recent experience, that not only was he probably a tad too smart for that, but the crash wouldn't stop him.

Now she understood the nickname. His power made Cain Marko unstoppable.

She'd reached a wholly refurbished section of the prison that managed to make the great, gray edifice look quite comfortable. Fresh paint, modern furniture, total climate control; it reminded her of the wealthy of days gone by who transported stately manors or castles—or London Bridge—from Europe to rebuild them brick by brick over here. In this case, if she hadn't known better she'd have figured she was standing in any top-flight lab in the world.

The floor trembled, the echo of collapsing walls reached her, and she was galvanized into action. She'd lost her lead again.

Kitty phased through the nearest doorway, then raced from room to room, assuming that sooner or later she'd get lucky.

Figures. The room she wanted was the last, at the end of the hall, with a spectacular corner view of the now-empty straits. She made a face. It was some interior designer's vision of what a kid's room should look like, with all the personality of a magazine layout.

The boy was huddled under the bed, clutching a stuffed animal that was almost as big as he was to his chest.

She really didn't have the time, but she spared him her most reassuring smile anyway.

"I'm Kitty," she said, holding out a hand. Another crash. Wouldn't be much longer. "I'm one of the X-Men. We're the good guys."

"I know," he said, "I've seen you on TV. I'm Jimmy," he continued. "But they call me Leech."

Nice name, she thought, casting shame on whoever was responsible for it.

"What's happening?" he asked, terrified through and through.

"I'll tell you later," she said, motioning him towards her. "Right now, Jimmy, we've got to get you out of here."

She caught his hand and yanked him into her arms, shoving herself towards the nearest wall.

Major mistake. She led with her head and for a moment, as stars did a fandango across her mind's eye, she thought she'd broken it for sure. Cracked it wide, just like Zeus, only instead of Athena springing forth full grown, she was losing brain cells by the multitude.

Damnation—the shock actually made her cry.

"What *happened*?" she yowled, pressing the heel of her free hand to her battered forehead.

"Your powers won't work around me. That's *my* power."

She couldn't help grinning: "Honey-bunny," she told him hurriedly, "Rogue's just gonna *love* you."

Enter Juggernaut, beyond rage.

"Come over here," Kitty said loudly to Jimmy, making a show of putting him behind her, flat against the wall. They both looked trapped.

Jimmy dropped to his seat on the floor, staring through Kitty's legs at the man-mountain who faced them.

Juggernaut savored the moment.

"Two for the price of one," he growled delightedly, forgetting that Kitty could always phase herself to safety. Or perhaps assuming that maybe she'd run out of gas, that she couldn't play the ghost any longer. Or maybe she was staying solid to protect the brat.

The reason didn't matter to Juggernaut, only the result, which in this case would mean blood—theirs.

He dropped his head to ramming position and kicked himself into gear.

Kitty waited until the very last possible moment as he barreled towards her, building up an impressive head of speed for such a small space. She couldn't afford to misplay this in the slightest, as she had no illusions about her ability to face Juggernaut in a fair fight. For all her strength and skills, she'd be a toothpick in his hands.

He was almost on her when she dropped, a boneless puppet with severed strings, right to the floor to cover Jimmy's body with her own as Juggernaut . . .

. . . crashed full tilt into the wall.

Put a hole in it, too—right through the Sheetrock that formed the outer wall of the refurbished room to the two-foot-thick granite underneath, reinforced by concrete and brick and steel.

Kitty gathered Jimmy close against her and shoved them both along the floor between Juggernaut's legs until they were well clear of him. She'd heard a monstrous *crack!* on impact but wasn't yet willing to put any faith in that as she levered herself back to her feet, keeping hold of Jimmy, ready to start running again if needed.

Juggernaut was starting to wobble. Stiff legs turned spongy, his butt popped a bit back from the wall as gravity exerted its hold, and he was done. His eyes were open, wide as could be, but the pupils were wholly dilated. Nobody home at all inside that skull.

Kitty pumped a fist and laughed aloud as Jimmy echoed her.

She started towards the entry hole Juggernaut had

made, then changed her mind. She had a better idea, something she hadn't had to do since she turned thirteen.

Leading Jimmy by the hand, she reached for the handle . . .

. . . and opened the door.

Chapter
Eleven

The two mutants laughed as they hustled Worthington Jr. to the roof of the cell house. It was a sheer drop, four stories, to the ground, but since the building came dangerously close to the edge of the island itself, a hefty shove—which his captors were more than physically capable of—would send him plummeting down the cliff to the rocks over a hundred feet below.

"You still think we need a cure?" Psylocke demanded.

Worthington couldn't answer, even if he wanted to, his throat closed by a mixture of stark terror and absurd pride as the strangest memory coursed through his head, one of the climactic scenes from *The Lion in Winter*: three young princes, facing execution as traitors to the Crown. Young Prince Richard, still building his reputation as the Lionheart of legend, intends to meet his end with courage—he won't beg for his life. His brother Geoffrey thinks him a fool, as if it matters how a man dies. Richard's final words: *When the fall is all that's left, it* matters.

Worthington's insides were ice. He feared that he would lose control and shame himself, and he knew that's what the mutants wanted, why Kid Omega kept mimicking—with fearful accuracy—that last, awful cry from Kavita. But at the same time, he found himself gathered in a strange and unexpected cocoon of calm, as though he was suddenly snuggling deep within an emotional comforter. He was measuring the last moments of being with each step across the roof. He could hear the sounds of battle but they seemed very far away, and since the two mutants paid them no mind, he assumed their side was winning. The wind off the bay seemed refreshingly cool on his skin, sharp enough blowing straight into his face that it brought tears to his eyes; the air was as crisp and clear as he'd ever seen it. He was so used to seeing the straits framed by the towers of the Golden Gate that seeing it open like this made him think of a door being suddenly flung wide, leaving him with an unreal sense of liberation.

The mutants made no effort to match their pace to his. They liked it when he stumbled, even though they wouldn't let him fall. They were in a rush, talking about places to go, things to do.

"Well, guess what, Warren," Psylocke told him, getting right up in his face. "It's time to cure *you*!"

They shoved, harder than he expected . . .

. . . and his arms flailed reflexively, pinwheeling as he shot out and well away from the prison wall.

He cried, *"No!"* but that was an automatic denial. At the same time, he found himself cataloguing the sensations, body remembering his training and experience as a skydiver to shift from the shock of his violent launch into the limbs akimbo pose of flight.

If I only had a 'chute, he thought. And then he recalled the classic joke about the man who leapt from the top of the Empire State Building. As he passed each floor, people heard him say, "So far, so good."

So far, so good.

He was falling faster. He wouldn't clear the rocks, and he wondered how much it would hurt, how long he'd feel it before final oblivion.

And then, his son caught him.

There was a terrific shock of contact, then an even stronger jerk as the boy's great wings beat at the air, both to arrest the older, larger man's headlong fall and to gather sufficient lift to maneuver. Warren had stooped like a diving hawk, dropping with the speed of a race car to tackle his father and grapple him with arms and legs, making sure not to hurt him, wrapping himself around his father as he used to do as a little boy.

It was a tremendous effort and for the first frantic moments it didn't look like he'd be successful. Angel cried out in very real pain, his voice breaking with the strain; there was fire across his shoulders, down his arms and spine, and he suddenly feared his wings could not withstand the strain of lifting someone twice his weight.

Adrenaline surged through his system as he refused to accept the possibility of defeat, his beating wings generating a pulse of ground effect sufficient to give him just enough lift to skim the crest of the rocks and transform his crazed descent into a semblance of level flight, barely a tall man's height above the waves.

Worthington got his feet wet as they skimmed a couple of crests, but that was all as Warren kept beating his wings, startling the gulls and pelicans out for their own daily excursions.

Out of the corner of his eye, Worthington caught sight of his son's face, in profile, taut with the effort of keeping them aloft—and yet, also transported with a fierce and primal joy the father would never himself feel. He looked to the birds that joined them, then back at his son who was as much a part of their world as of Worthington's own, and he felt a tremendous sorrow. This was not something to be feared, or to be denied—the fact that his son had wings, that he was a mutant, that he could *fly*—but to be celebrated.

Perhaps others might feel differently. Perhaps there were powers that should be neutralized, as there were sure to be people who should not be allowed to keep them. That was a question for each individual and the society they were a part of. With mutants, as with all people, the judgment should be one of action and character, not genome. He didn't regret his part in creating the cure, although he would always bear the burden of Kavita's death, and of the harm that had come from his actions. What was wrong, however, were his reasons for it: the shame of having what he thought was a freak for a son, and the fear of what that represented for the future.

"Thank you," he breathed.

It broke his heart, in the best of ways, to behold the smile his son gave him in answer.

"You're my dad," Warren told him, as though that represented the answer to everything.

"And you're my *son*," Worthington replied, as proudly as he was able.

X

Back on Alcatraz, the ground battle was winding down. Storm had rejoined the team. Beast was facing the last few of Magneto's fighters still left standing. One had extensible limbs, grabbing for Hank with rubber-band arms. The burly X-Man bobbed and weaved, leapt and twisted, with seemingly aimless abandon, staying out of the other's reach as he bounded from wall to pillar to post until he had the poor mutant all tangled up with himself.

Before the mutant could sort himself out, Hank concentrated on his companions, springing off fingertips to flatten one with a foot to the face, while using prehensile toes to grasp his mate and pitch him better than twenty feet into Rubber Band Guy. Another leap dropped him into the middle of the impromptu scrum, and a quick flurry of blows dealt with them once and for all.

He was sure somebody would have a minicam, if not among the mutants then certainly the soldiers, and that it was only a matter of time before images of the battle were all over the Internet. So much for his political career. He looked down at himself, clad in his old brown leather suit that was a size too small, and figured he'd come across as a laughingstock.

Or maybe not. The uniform may leave something to be desired as a fashion statement, but the moves were as good as ever. Seeing the X-Man battling side by side with the army, defending the people against a common foe, might do some good. The clothes might make the man, as the saying went, but the *deeds* defined him.

Speaking of deeds . . .

Logan, up by the bridge, where the roadway met the island, was duking it out with a multilimbed mutant whose body was covered in a protective carapace that gave him some of the aspects of a lobster. Nothing funny about what he could do, though, as the bodies of a clutch of troopers scattered about him testified. He had a weapon in every hand and the muscles to make a single blow lethal. Near misses shattered concrete and bent steel and the number of appendages took away the advantage of Logan's speed. Logan could dodge one or two limbs, but not all of them. Fortunately, his unbreakable skeleton kept him from serious harm. *Un*fortunately, he was still vulnerable to strikes against the unprotected portions of his anatomy, and was taking some heavy hits to the belly.

That wasn't the worst of it, though. Logan used his claws to lop off an arm. There was minimal blood and he fell back quickly as the mutant redoubled his efforts with the limbs that remained.

Even as Hank watched, the scientist in him utterly fascinated, a bud appeared at the base of the severed limb, regenerating at such accelerated speed that it was fully functional well before it regained its original size. Comparing all the arms, Hank noted that none of them were precisely the same, which told him this process had been ongoing throughout the fight.

Logan, however, was done playing. Hank feared he would simply kill the mutant. That would certainly fit Wolverine's well-deserved reputation, but he discovered that the X-Man was not without his own brand of rough humor as Logan hauled off and kicked his adversary soundly between the legs.

The mutant went to his knees, gasping, face instantly

pale purple with shock, all hands going reflexively to his crotch, none left to protect his jaw from the follow-up punch that Logan delivered to end their engagement.

"Well," Hank muttered, to himself he thought, until a quick turn of Logan's head his way reminded him of just how keen the other man's ears really were, "that's one way to do it."

A few of Magneto's fighters remained, but they collectively chose the so-called better part of valor and began a helter-skelter withdrawal back to the bridge. On Alcatraz itself, there was just some mopping up left to do.

X

Warren took his father home, to the big house on Russian Hill. He thought this would be a safe place, but the bridge was almost close enough to touch. He stayed low to the rooftops as he made his way across the city. There'd been time now for the army to respond to the day's events and the air was becoming increasingly crowded with gunships, observation helos and remote, pilotless drones, both for battlefield surveillance and for attack. Some were armed with conventional ordnance but Warren suspected that more than a few would be carrying air-launched versions of the missiles the Alcatraz troops had used against Magneto's forces. He didn't want to be dropped by "friendly fire."

His father looked at him after they had landed and moved a step or so back, intrigued despite himself by the new, confident way his son stood in front of him.

Warren grinned shyly, his expression darkening just a tad as he remembered the harness he used to wear to hide his wings and he vowed to himself, *Never again,* "I've learned to fold the wings pretty good."

"I'm sorry for that, Warren, truly."

"I know, Dad. I know you always meant well."

"Son . . . thank you."

Warren shifted on his feet. Worthingtons were never good with displays of emotion, especially between men. Ideally, that's what spouses were for. But Worthington Jr. wasn't done.

"Warren, I . . ." The words came slowly because they came hard, because they came from the father's heart and from his soul. "I have never been more proud of you. I hope I can become half the man you've shown me you are today."

"Dad," Warren began, but instead of words he stepped forward and put both arms and wings around his father in the kind of embrace they hadn't shared since he was a boy.

"I've got to go," he said, when they stepped apart once more. "I'm one of the X-Men now. I've got to help."

"Take care of yourself, boy."

"See you soon!"

And with that, he was gone, rising majestically into the air with a casual sweep of the wings that reminded his father of sketches his son used to make when he was still a boy, long before he'd begun to change. He read comics in those days, and like many fans, created his own characters. His favorite, and here Worthington had to wonder if even then on some deep subconscious level Warren had known what was in store for him, was a winged avenger that he christened Archangel. The suit had been too garish for words, and the pose and body had been cribbed from da Vinci.

Watching his son now, Worthington Jr. saw that dream made real, in all its glory.

X

Jean's mouth twisted as she caught that faint pulse of awe and wonder and pride from Worthington Jr., and the determination of young Warren to stand by his new friends. At that age, she'd been much the same, yearning to be a part of something greater than herself, to be of value, to be—a star.

The battle was rushing to its end, and Magneto's side was losing. Quite badly.

Not a surprise to her, since she knew what they were up against. Magneto invariably underestimated the X-Men, unable to see how they compensated for the weaknesses of each of them as individuals through team-work, which involved self-sacrifice. Mutant to mutant, Magneto's forces were stronger by far, but that was how they fought, utterly solo. Each of them demanded center stage as a matter of right; they didn't care to subordinate to the group—whereas in the X-Men, Xavier created a whole that transcended the sum of its parts.

The mainland shore was awash in colored light, alternating flashes of red and white announcing the presence of just about every emergency vehicle in the city, and likely every police car in the Bay Area. Not to mention the military.

There was significant armor on scene, but the tanks and self-propelled guns were keeping their distance, as were the helicopters, out of respect for Magneto's power. From the cityside came such an avalanche of thoughts and emotions, hundreds of thousands of citizens in varying states of anxiety and rage and outright panic that even Jean found herself staggered. She could block them easily enough, but the overwhelming volume made it increasingly difficult to discriminate the ones she needed to single out from the unending background clutter.

So she set aside her primary power and used her eyes instead, catching hints of movement that gradually resolved into an extended line of skirmishers, making their wary way onto the bridge, advancing towards the shoreside tower.

She considered stopping them, turning off their brains, shutting down the engines on the helicopters . . .

. . . and stepped back from that abyss with a gasp.

She was a *doctor,* she swore an *oath*: To *do no harm!*

And thought, bitterly: *Fat lot of good that did Charles—or Scott.*

Magneto wasn't happy with the turn of events, and responded characteristically. He turned to Pyro.

"It's time to end this war," he announced.

There were easily a few hundred cars on the roadway. With a flick of the wrist, Magneto hurled one skyward as if it had just been shot, rocket-propelled, from a catapult.

"Incoming!" Logan yelled, as the vehicle shot over his and Ororo's heads. *"Take cover!"*

Instead, Colossus strode forward and met the falling vehicle with a punch sufficient to bounce it clear of the island, to land in the bay with a nice splash.

Magneto gave a cue to Pyro, who flicked his lighter aflame, and launched a volley of cars this time.

As they cleared the bridge, climbing to the apogee of their trajectories, Pyro hit each and every one with a fireball, igniting their gas tanks and using his own control over fire to amplify them until they blazed hotter than any blast furnace.

The sight was eerily beautiful, like watching falling stars.

Pyro grinned, ear to ear, because he was just getting started.

Magneto had launched a half dozen cars. Pyro detonated them in a random and staggered order, one high in the air as a distraction, some much closer to spray the scene with incandescent shrapnel and flaming gasoline, the remainder as ground bursts. One impact and explosion chopped the base out from under a guard tower, toppling the three-story structure and forcing a number of troops out into the open where they could be bombarded with white hot metal and living fire.

One car struck Colossus dead on, driving him to the ground. Even as he fought his way back to his feet and pitched the wreckage into the water, Pyro surrounded him with flame, attacking him with salamander-streamers from the other burning cars with such intensity that the armored X-Man quickly began to glow red hot himself, radiating such incredible heat that he became a danger to anyone close by. He stepped too close to a pile of wreckage and the wood there instantly and spectacularly burst into flame, which Pyro turned against him. During his time at Xavier's school, they'd often speculated about the big Russian's resistance to heat—just how good *was* that armor—but no one had ever subjected him to anything approaching the ultimate test, even in the Danger Room. Professor Xavier felt it was far too dangerous.

Time, Pyro figured, *for me to take Mr. Muscle where the prof was too scared to go.*

More cars led to more fire, and Pyro ran streamers from one blaze to the next, building a fence across the battlefield that allowed no one to escape, gradually building the intensity to the point where it could explode into a firestorm capable of incinerating the island. Anyone not incinerated outright would suffocate as the great fire sucked all the oxygen away from ground level. By the time he was done, there'd be nothing left to mark the presence of any of the island's defenders, not bones—except perhaps the Wolverine's—not even ashes.

Afterwards, for fun, maybe he'd start to work on San Francisco itself, by carving his name across the city in letters ten blocks high.

Amidst the growing holocaust, Bobby yelled to Logan, *"What can we do?"*

He looked to Storm, who shook her head.

"John and Magneto are working together," she replied, refusing as she always did to use the code name John Allerdyce had adopted. "Creating a fire dome over the island high enough to deal with any rain I can bring to bear, combined with a magnetic field that cripples my control over the weather. I can't manifest a storm powerful enough to do us any good, *or* any lightning."

Logan growled, "Sonsofbitches picked the perfect time to quit being divas."

Then he paused, eyes caught by some loose cartridges from the soldiers' dart guns that hadn't been destroyed by Arclight's earlier attack.

"Okay," he said, shuffling the elements of his plan together like a deck of cards, thinking fast, dealing out orders faster, "they work as a team, we work better."

He held out his hand, with the ampoules he'd gathered. Ororo picked up the cue as if they were both telepaths.

"Best defense is a good offense?"

He grinned and thought she looked good enough to kiss, and she thought how much she'd like him to try.

"Yo, popsicle," he called to Bobby.

"Don't call me that!"

"Make me—but first, you figure you can take out your old bud?"

Bobby gave Pyro a long, hard look. In all their sessions in the Danger Room, every test of their powers, John had come out on top. He knew Pyro was counting on that.

He also knew they had no alternative. He was already gasping, and each harsh breath left his mouth and throat dry, his chest aching. Maybe a minute more, they'd likely be breathing flame.

He signaled Logan. He was good to go.

"Furball," Logan turned to Beast, who wasn't handling the ovenlike environment well at all, "can you still move in that suit?"

"If it'll take me off this griddle!"

" 'Ro," and he reached out to lay surprisingly gentle fingers against her cheek, thumb stroking an invisible piece of grit from beneath her eye, in a gesture so light and tender that she barely felt it, yet which sent an unexpected surge of electricity the length of her spine, straight to the core of her being. "I know it'll be hard, but we need some cover."

Her eyes danced back at his, accepting the challenge, and they turned from a warm and welcoming brown to a blue that started as deep as the most magnificent sky before paling to an arctic blue-white. He felt the hairs on his body rise, saw that McCoy felt the same—although there was a special undercurrent to the sensations *he* felt that he would always keep to himself—as Storm brought her energies to bear, smelt and tasted the faintest hint of ozone.

One of the remarkable sights of San Francisco is that, looking west late in the day, it appears as though an impossibly huge mountain wall has filled the seaward horizon. It's a view that never fails to impress, hearkening back to the days of the Ice Age, when great glaciers swept south from the pole to blanket the northern hemisphere.

Now Ororo drew on that distant phalanx of fog, and used it as the primer to call forth a localized bank of the same from all around the island and the nearer base of the Golden Gate.

Pyro's excitement had gotten the better of him, and he was totally swept away by the rush of battle. He had moved ahead faster than Magneto, who was still on the main body of the bridge.

Magneto called a warning as the fog swirled up around them, closing him off from the sight of his adversaries, but Pyro couldn't hear him above the crash of falling cars and the roar of flames. He couldn't use radio, either, even though the units had been constructed to be resistant to his magnetism; the same forces he was employing to inhibit military communications and Ororo's weather powers created an impenetrable sea of static. If he scaled back enough to reach Pyro, Storm would be able to bring more substantial resources to bear.

Obviously, the X-Men were up to something. But he had no doubt that when they made their move he'd crush them.

He sent another car in their general direction, Pyro ignited it . . .

. . . but this time, a *whoosh* of ice extinguished the flames before they had a chance to get properly burning. The car was quickly coated, made so cold that when it crashed to the ground it shattered to bits, its metal components turned instantly brittle as dry twigs.

Before them, silhouetted against the background of Pyro's flames, which still imprisoned the sapien troops, stood Bobby Drake.

Magneto stepped up beside his protégé.

"Are you a god," he asked, as he had the day he'd recruited Pyro away from the X-Men, well aware that once upon a time the two young men had been the best of friends, "or an insect?"

Pyro stepped away from Magneto and bounded down to the courtyard, to face Bobby gunfighter to gunfighter, every element of expression and body language proclaiming that he had no doubt as to how this fight would end, and that he was looking forward to enjoying every delicious minute.

From the surrounding fire, he hurled twin pillars of flame at his former roommate.

True to his code name, Iceman parried as he had every

time they'd fought in the past, with barriers of ice. Pyro shrugged and upped the ante, aware as he did that as he poured more and more concentration and energy into his confrontation with Bobby, he was allowing the barrier walls he'd created to fade away and the troops he enclosed to race for fresh shelter. He wasn't bothered, though. Once he was done here he'd simply stoke the flames to an even higher intensity than before. The poor saps were just prolonging the inevitable, just like Iceman . . .

. . . whose ice was melting at a rather distressing rate, allowing the flames to approach ever closer. He was sweating buckets. Soon he'd be burning.

"Same old Bobby," mocked Pyro, deciding the time had come to put his former friend out of his misery. "Maybe you should go back to school."

"You can't do this!"

"I do what I please, a-hole. Can you stop me?"

"How could you join Magneto?"

"Simple. He's right. Xavier's wrong. Not to mention dead." Pyro shook his head in anger more than pity. "God, you and Rogue are such a matched set, I am *so* glad I let that train wreck pass me by.

"Don't you *get* it? While Xavier talked about sharing, the so-called human race was turning the Earth into a cesspool. They're so busy ruining their present they're not giving a thought to the future. They don't give good god-*damn* about their children, or their children's children; it's all about today. Well, we represent tomorrow—we're here today and we want to make sure we have a decent home to inherit. If that means evicting the current tenants . . . hey, get with the program, popsicle, or get deleted."

"I won't let that happen."

Pyro smirked. "Yeah, right. Is this some kind of joke, putting you in the field against me? I mean, remember all those scraps we had in the Danger Room, about which of us had the better power, fire or ice? Who always came out on top?"

He advanced on Bobby, pushing his flames to their limit, and was satisfied to see Iceman hammered to his knees. Still, battered though he was, Bobby refused to yield. The flames were close, but he was still fighting back, with more strength and determination than Pyro would have given him credit for.

"Drop a mountain of ice on me, Bobby boy, my fire'll melt it to vapor in a flash." Arrogant *snap* of the fingers for emphasis.

"Hey," he continued, "when you're icing, do you burn like normal folks, or make like the Wicked Witch of the West?" He adopted a singsong parody of the classic moment from *The Wizard of Oz*, " 'I'm melting, I'm *melting*!' "

Pyro shook his head. "Dude, you gotta stop thinkin' we're still buds. We were never friends, Bobby, just classmates for a while. That story's done. In this new one, I take no prisoners."

Bobby'd always known that, just refused to accept it, hoping against hope that sooner or later things would work out. He was on hands and knees, alive through sheer mulish stubbornness, staring at the ground without seeing as he focused solely on enduring this torment as long as he was able, to buy his fellow X-Men the time they needed.

He'd miss last good-byes with Marie, with Rogue,

that was his sole regret that mattered. Calling them a train wreck was utter bullshit, as if Pyro'd ever done any better.

His eyes narrowed as the visual information they were transmitting finally made its presence felt inside Bobby's somewhat heat-addled brain. His ice barriers were melting, no surprise there, but while much of it was indeed incandescing into gas, there were puddles of water all around him. And now that he was paying proper attention, he could see that even though he was sweating, every exhalation of breath brought with it a puffball cloud of condensed air. He wasn't simply generating cold, *he* was cold.

Connections closed on levels far below his conscious mind, memories of discussions he'd had with Jean Grey on the nature of his power, of mutation, of where it might lead him. She and the professor always talked about things happening in the natural course of time, but he no longer had time to wait. He had to make things happen *right now*.

The puddles crystallized, the crystallization flashed from one to the next, building linkages of ice as Pyro did with fire.

They touched his nearest finger.

"You were always too much in love with your own mouth, Johnny," Bobby said, getting a shrug in return. "Too damn busy being you to pay attention to basic science."

"What's that supposed to mean?"

"Entropy." His finger was coated with ice, yet it bent just like normal, the process of transformation accelerating as it swept up his arm. The sleeve of his uniform shattered to splinters as if it had just been plunged into liquid oxygen, revealing a perfectly formed arm of ice underneath. He couldn't help grinning at the look on Pyro's face now, as the rest of his jacket fell apart, even if his humor was partly to cover for his acute embarassment. He didn't want to think about what was coming when his pants shattered. If this was the way his power manifested from here on, they were definitely going to have to find him at the very least a set of cold-resistant briefs.

"Even molecules get tired, Johnny. They slow down, they get *cold*. The default state of the universe isn't fire, it's *ice*."

The flames couldn't harm him. His new skin was better than armor.

Pyro didn't believe it. "This isn't fair. This isn't right! Every time we tangled in the Danger Room, every evaluation of our powers and skills, I was always better!"

Bobby lunged forward, grabbing both of Pyro's hands in his.

"I learned some new lessons."

He iced the other man's arms all the way to the elbows, the intense cold striking Pyro with the shock of being plunged into a midwinter ocean, creating a paralysis of thought and action. Before Pyro could recover his wits, Bobby let him have it with a solid punch to the jaw.

Lights out at the source, no willpower to sustain the superstorm of fire he'd created. And since that blaze had been so unimaginably fierce to begin with, it had consumed all the readily available fuel, leaving only Pyro's power to keep it burning.

There was a discernible *pop* of imploding air, as the flames vanished and cooler atmosphere rushed in to take their place, and the stench of charred debris. But otherwise . . .

. . . the island was still, fog-draped and dark once more.

Logan tapped Colossus on the shoulder. "Okay, Tin-man, time for that fastball special." Colossus took some steps back from Iceman—he'd been using the other X-Man's cold to bleed off some of the heat from his armor, and he was still uncomfortably warm to the touch, but no longer glowing. Logan could handle that. Peter grasped the Wolverine by the belt.

"Make it a strike," Logan challenged him.

Colossus made it a bullet, right on the mark.

Of course, Magneto sensed him coming.

Without even sparing a glance, he raised a hand and successive waves of magnetic force punched the X-Man into the roadway more than hard enough to make an impression.

Magneto didn't bother being gentle. He used Logan's body to create a trench right down to the underlying steel as he reeled him in the rest of the way.

"I warned you," he chided, ever so gently, ever so finally, making abundantly clear they would not dance this particular dance again.

Logan had no eyes for him, only for Jean, on her perch above and behind the Master of Magnetism. There was nothing of the woman he remembered and loved in her stance or affect. She looked at them as at a strange and alien—and *lesser*—species, the way a scientist might examine some new species of microbe. She perhaps found them intriguing, but there was no emotional contact to bind them.

The first line of troops from shore were close enough to take action. Logan started to yell a warning to Jean to watch out, to the soldiers to stand down, anything to head off what he feared was to come, but they were operating on hair triggers.

They shot on sight, at her and Magneto both—and if Logan got clipped in the cross fire, them's the breaks, pal. Every combat engagement has its regrettable collateral damage.

He shouldn't have worried. None of the darts even came close. Jean stopped them all, less than an inch shy of contact.

Her eyes flashed celestial fire and the darts turned to dust.

Satisfied he had nothing to fear from the military, Magneto addressed his full attention to Logan.

"You never learn, do you?" he mock lamented, raising a hand to separate Logan from his adamantium once and for all.

"Actually," Logan replied quite pleasantly, "I do."

Too late, Magneto sensed another presence. He spun around, and the fog around him cleared, revealing the form of the Beast—almost invisible against the night thanks to his dark fur and uniform—hanging upside down from one of the suspender cables.

Hank flashed fangs in a grin and flicked a finger at the X-Men's oldest adversary.

Magneto felt a sting across his cheek and the fingers

he clasped there came away colored with the merest thread of blood.

In shock, he took a step away from the Beast. His legs lost all strength. He collapsed to hands and knees in the face of agony such as he had never imagined, much less experienced.

Around Logan, all sense of pressure and pain faded. He rose to one knee beside the man who'd been about to kill him. His right fist was close enough—it would be no effort at all to pop his claws and put an end to Magneto. Hank had the same thought, he saw, and was gripped by the same ambivalence. Some adversaries, perhaps, ought *not* to be spared.

Once, Logan suspected he'd have done just that, without a second thought or an ounce of regret. Thankfully, that man, those days, were lost—Logan didn't mind in the least. He much preferred the man he was becoming and the way he was starting to live his life. Xavier would have his legacy.

Magneto sunk back on his heels, dazed with horror as he groped for his helmet, only to have it fall from fingers suddenly gone nerveless.

Watching him, Logan realized the true kindness would have been a quick, clean death, but he shook his head to banish the impulse. He had to learn from the mistakes of his past; if Magneto was worthy of Charles Xavier's friendship, he'd have to do the same. And perhaps find a way to atone for the harm he'd caused that had brought him to this place.

"I'm . . ." Magneto said, unable to go further.

"One of them," Logan finished for him. "It should have never come to this."

Then came the screams.

Another wave of soldiers had attacked, and this time Jean didn't bother with just their weapons, she erased the men as well.

"*Jean!*" Logan called, imperative to get her attention before things could turn any worse. In that regard, he'd reckoned without Magneto, who spoke the moment Jean made eye contact with them all.

"You see, my child," he said in a voice that could barely be heard but with thoughts that rang out like a clarion call. "Look at me. Look into their hearts. This is what *they* want. For *all* of us."

She didn't like that idea.

"Jean," Logan called again, making his way to her.

She unfolded her arms from where she perched, spreading them wide with stately and majestic grace, and gazed at Logan with eyes no longer even remotely human. They were black eyes, doll's eyes, predator's eyes, and deep in the heart of them burned the fires of Creation itself.

Energy pulsed from her body, spiraling outward across bay and city in successive waves that churned the water more powerfully than any storm of nature. She rose from her perch and descended from bridge to island, Logan springing after her, waving to McCoy to follow. He did, gathering Magneto into his arms and then making most of the trip upside down, using his feet as hands to bound along the suspender cables.

Jean was hovering above the center of the courtyard that had been the main battlefield, streamers of fiery energy swirling faster and farther from her body as though she were becoming the core of her own galaxy. She was certainly blazing brightly enough, generating so much radiance that even sunglasses would have been little help.

Waves crashed furiously against the shore of the island, against the base of the bridge's towers, but the water didn't recede from those impacts. Instead, impossibly, the water began to pour *up* into the air, as though some great suction pump was evacuating the entire bay. Much the same effect was happening to the island as well, as everything not nailed down—debris, weapons, tools and the like—shot skyward so suddenly it was as if gravity were reversing itself. Thus far, people weren't being affected, but it didn't take much imagination to conclude that probably wouldn't last much longer.

"Everyone off the island!" Logan bellowed from the ramp. *"Now!"*

Jimmy and Kitty emerged from the cell house. For a brief moment, surveying the situation, Kitty considered turning Jimmy loose on Jean. Locking eyes briefly with Logan, she realized with a start that he was considering much the same, and rejecting it, just as she was. Jimmy was a kid, he had no place here. Even if he was willing, both of them knew Jean's telepathy would give her enough warning to finish him before he got close enough to affect her. Waving off the other X-Men, Kitty made a beeline for the bridge, pausing as she did to inform the army lieutenant about Juggernaut lying unconscious in Jimmy's cell.

Given the situation, she doubted anyone was going to go collect him.

Bobby ignored her signals as he approached with John Allerdyce slung in a fireman's carry over his shoulders. He'd definitely undergone some major changes since she saw him last. Kitty couldn't help wondering if they were permanent. He had much the same questions, made all the more pertinent by the absence of Professor Xavier or Doctor Grey to help him find the answers. Within a dozen or so paces of her, his ice shell began to flake away, revealing the skin underneath; he also started blushing as furiously as anyone she'd ever seen, for reasons that became scandalously obvious a couple of steps later. By the time he was by her side, he was well beyond mortification, staring straight ahead as she struggled to do the same, thankful for this moment of utter absurdity to counterpoint what seemed like the imminent end of the world.

Colossus scooped up as many of Magneto's fallen fighters as he could carry, passing them off to troopers as they established a rough line through the ruins and up the ramp. Angel saw Iceman's predicament from overhead and later made himself a friend for life by finding Bobby a pair of pants.

Twenty meters away, bursts of power fell from Jean with increasing strength and frequency, creating what could only be described as *tears* in the fabric of the universe. Magneto, whose training and research in the fields of subatomic physics were rivaled only by his erstwhile ability to manipulate the forces found there, shook his head in wonderment and utter weariness. He was spent in soul, far more than he ever had been in the flesh, more so even than at Auschwitz. He had only one moment in his life to measure against this one, the death of his beloved firstborn, his only child, his Anya, and the horror he had seen in the eyes of his wife, Magda, whom he'd saved from the camps but who could not bear to look at him, stay with him, once she'd beheld the vengeance he'd taken against those who'd kept him from saving his daughter.

"What have I done?" he breathed.

"More to the point," Logan demanded of him, "what's *she* doing?"

"Discorporating the planet," was the reply. "Stripping existence around her down to its primal component states."

"Why?"

Magneto snorted. "Because she can."

"Your rationale, bub."

"It's what Charles understood that I didn't: the true meaning of the *next* step in evolution. For us, for all our powers, we're talking little more than baby steps; for her, seven league boots. I don't believe she can handle the transition."

"Time for you to go," Logan told him.

"I'd like to stay."

"For this," Logan's voice was brutal, "you lost the right."

"I'm sorry," Magneto told him.

"Yeah."

A trooper grabbed Magneto's arms and hustled him up the ramp to be swallowed by the fleeing crowd. Logan didn't watch, didn't much care; with his powers gone, Magneto was significantly neutered as a threat. If Logan needed to find him, he'd do so.

Assuming the world survived.

"It's not Jean," Ororo cried out to him as she tried to pull him away as well. He didn't bother telling her she was wrong. "Not anymore. Nothing can stop her, Logan. *Nothing!*"

He looked at her and quirked his mouth into a semblance of a smile, as from a man about to embrace the Gorgon in its lair. "I'm the only one who can get close."

She didn't need to ask what would happen next. Instead she let her eyes reveal her heart and leapt quickly aloft before her tears could betray her. No matter how tonight ended, if they lived to see the dawn, they would lose something supremely precious.

His insides churned as Logan turned back to face Jean. He knew that he was being bombarded by lethal levels of radiation. Wasn't on purpose, he knew that as well, she was broadcasting energies like a star coming into being. That insight wasn't something he'd think of—the flavor of it was purely Jean and it gave him a breath of hope. If she could still reach him on that kind of deep subconscious level, he could find a way to pull her all the way back.

"I hear you, darlin'," he said, and took his first step, "I know you're still there."

The ground was coming apart. It wasn't a case of rock being shattered to dust and the dust dissolving, she was shredding the component molecules, manipulating the states of existence so that what was solid and opaque one instant became utterly transparent the next, allowing him to see straight down to the core of the world. The patches of earth became utterly nonexistent after that, forcing him to progress in hopscotch fashion, following his instincts—which in turn followed cues he grew increasingly certain came from Jean herself—towards his goal.

Jean turned to him and his own molecules began discorporating, his skin literally (painlessly, thank God) boiling away. The adamantium was partly what saved him, because it possessed the tightest molecular binding of any substance conceivable. Given time and will, she could deconstruct it the way she was shredding everything else, but right now her mind was focused on greater things.

The metal provided an anchor for his physical being and at the same time, the outrush of power from her acted as an amplifier for his own abilities. He hadn't seen Scott die, but he could guess what happened. She amplified his optic blasts, so much that he damn near shattered an entire mountain, but all that really did was complete the energy loop back to her. Blasting at her actually made her stronger, and meanwhile Scott had no defense against the discorporation process. Same with Xavier. His telepathy must have been heightened to an unimaginable extent, but even if it put him on a level above her, he could not match her telekinetic powers and he couldn't repair the damage she was doing to him.

Logan, of course, was another critter altogether.

The harder she hit him, the more efficiently his body healed. She couldn't kill him, only make him stronger. If she really wanted him gone, there were ways to accomplish it. Throw him away for instance; he had no doubt, at her level, she could put him into orbit with a thought. If he was still here, it was for a reason.

He loved her. He wasn't going to fail.

The buildings were going, and it came to him that he was watching in slow motion the awful and absolute annihilation that occurred at ground zero of a thermonuclear blast.

He went blind as his eyes melted, could see again an instant later, the process speeding up to such an extent that obliteration and reconstruction became virtually instantaneous processes. He reached for her, his arm stripped to bare gleaming bone, the great claws visible and quiescent in their housings.

The linkages were intact. Careless of her not to sever them.

He had no lungs to breathe with, no heart to beat, no blood to pump, no body to sustain. He was little more than artificial frame, the ghost of a nervous system, an agglomeration of self and will within the bunker of his unbreachable skull. Yet he would not fall. He would not stop.

She turned those monster onyx eyes on him and there was no recognition of him to be seen in them.

"You would die for them?" Her voice resounded in his soul. If he'd had a body the effect would have left him gasping, face-to-face at last with the truth of the ancient understanding that angels are as terrible to behold as they are beautiful.

"Not for them."

She started to smile, preening satisfaction, thinking she'd found the flaw in him that would allow her to discard him once and for all.

"For *you*!"

He didn't merely say that with words. He couldn't. No face, no tongue, no lungs, no anything. She was a telepath. He gave her his thoughts. But of course, because she was a telepath, she got much, much more than words.

He loved her, had from the first; he gave her that, too, and all it meant for him. Life had been a simple thing for Logan before Jean Grey. He did as he pleased, took what he wanted, didn't consider the consequences or repercussions. Nobody had ever cared much for him because he made it plain he wouldn't care for them in return.

Rogue had been the chink in that armor, and Jean had torn it open wide, so much so that he couldn't go back to the old ways even if he wanted to. And knowing her, loving her, knowing that she loved him in return—even if she'd pledged herself to Scott—made him never want to again, no matter how much the new way hurt.

He gave her his dreams, he gave her his hopes. He understood that she could see what he likely never would, the creature he had been, and stood upright and proud to be judged against the *man* he had become.

Amidst the fire in her eyes, he saw a flash of green.

"Save me, Logan," he heard her say, and felt her hands gently cup his face and draw him close, bodies closer, lips aching to touch in a last and loving kiss.

SNIKT!

She spasmed against him, clutching him to her as if she could merge her essence with his and make them one coherent being. Or maybe it was a desperate attempt to gain access to his healing power. Didn't much matter because again, the adamantium got in the way.

One hand, all three claws. There was no margin for error, or mercy.

"That's better," he heard her say with satisfaction, and beheld her eyes still full of fire, but stripped of the dark rage that had fueled her actions. There was the warmth he remembered, the sense of completion he felt during those fleeting times they'd shared together, the native generosity of spirit that was more than he figured anyone deserved, especially him.

"Stop selling yourself short, bub."

She smiled, that wry curl of one side of her lip that he'd always known was just for him, that marked them as kindred souls.

"Oh Logan," she breathed. He could no longer sustain her weight, his body was still too much of a mess, so down they went in a clumsy heap with her in his lap, reversing the pose of a Pietà. "Where I am, where I'm going," and she couldn't help gathering him into her thoughts, to share the moment so he wouldn't sorrow for her. He was glad his senses were still a shadow of what they should be because even that fleeting glimpse filled him with such wonder and pure, primal joy that much more would have been the end of him.

If this was but the merest taste of what Jean had tapped into, small wonder she was overwhelmed.

"Be well," he told her.

She had no final words for him. She didn't need them.

He had no regrets, because this last moment was a lifetime for them both.

There was a final pulse of energy, surging from her to set right as much as she could. It washed over him like the gentle glow of a spring morning, lighting him as much within as without.

The water pulled from the bay began to return, as a softly falling rain.

The moon appeared through the dispersing fog and cast the scene in strokes of silver and shadow.

He cradled Jean close, rocking slightly back and forth in time to his heartbeat as it reasserted itself, savoring the myriad scents of the island as he gained once more the capacity to breathe, acknowledged to himself the presence of his friends, as first Ororo, then Kitty, and the others returned to Alcatraz.

He was weary to the bone, ravaged in body and soul. He felt reborn.

Epilogue

"Mutation: it is the key to human evolution."

X

When Ororo thought of Scott, or Jean, or as now, Charles, it was as though they were still with her, their words as fresh as if they'd just been spoken, the expressions making her believe they'd only just parted and would surely be seeing one another soon. Within her they were as alive as ever, and when reality reminded her that they weren't, her response wasn't what you'd expect. She didn't feel at all sad. They were gone, but they'd never be forgotten.

A magnificent oak overlooked what was now called the Memorial Garden. When Ororo first arrived at the school she'd chosen it for her private place, an acknowledgment of far too many nights in her youth when she'd had to scramble for a branch to keep from becoming some four-footed beast's dinner. This is where she often came to think, and to write, which never came easily.

She didn't believe Charles would object to her borrowing some of his words for her own. It applied to the both of them.

"When I was young and foolish," she spoke aloud, scribbling the words on her pad, "and feeling totally cast out from the world, I used to wonder if there were others like me, and dream of the future we might create."

He couldn't walk when he had recruited her, and never told any of them—except probably Jean—how he'd lost the use of his legs. True to form, he'd bought himself a Land Rover, fitted it for hands-only driving, and headed out across the savanna. He hadn't gone alone, of course; Jean was by his side. Ororo wasn't a very trusting soul, living in the shadow of Kilimanjaro and playing up local superstitions and legends to keep herself safe. She'd been learning the use of her powers by trial and error and inadvertently done far more harm than good, trying to help her own people by ending their drought only to cause an even worse one in the neighboring country. She believed Xavier's words, but it was Jean's smile that won her over. By the time they returned to Westchester, the two girls were the best of friends.

"Then," Ororo continued writing, setting aside her reflections, "I actually encountered some, and aspects of that dream turned out not to be so pleasant.

"As with every era in human history—perhaps even natural history—good seems ever balanced by evil. The higher and more glorious the summit of our aspirations, the fouler and more insatiable the abyss we leave behind.

"That's why Xavier's has always been, and I shall hope and pray always remains, a *school*.

"While we X-Men exist to protect humanity from those who dwell in the abyss, this school is ever focused on the summit.

"Why humanity is fractured, why some have enhanced genes and others not, none of us can say. But that should not, *must* not, matter, for fundamentally we all come from the same stock. We are all born of this world, composed of the same raw materials as the cosmos itself. A potentially magnificent family of sentient beings.

"We strive because we must, that is reality. But *why* we strive must *never* be forgotten."

Her eyes flicked across the three memorials: Xavier's in the center, flanked by Scott and Jean. There were fresh flowers below each one.

"The yearnings—the hopes—that bind us together as a species must be greater and more lasting than the petty conflicts that drive us apart. We are all of us brothers and sisters, parents and children. And ultimately, the character of each and every person, and the deeds that flow from it, must matter more than the color of their skin, or the structure of their genome.

"That is our dream. This school, and we X-Men, exist to help make it a reality."

"Not so bad," commented a voice from right beside her. A sideways glance revealed Kitty, standing nonchalantly on empty air, her easy manner wholly belied by the hooded eyes that surveyed the three markers.

"I'm terrified," Ororo remarked.

"You get the big office, Headmistress," Kitty zinged quietly, "you get the headaches to go with."

"I think I liked our lives better when we were semi-outlaws."

"Everything changes, 'Ro. Ain't evolution a bitch?"

Ororo cocked a disapproving eyebrow. Friends they

might be and teammates as well, but they were also Head and student and certain proprieties had to be observed. Rules that were good enough for Charles Xavier were just as good for his first successor.

Kitty air-walked down a flight of invisible steps that brought her to the three cenotaphs. Ororo swung herself from her perch with a silent grace she'd learned when she was younger than Kitty, training to be a thief. For her, that outlaw past was more than a mere phrase.

"I miss them," Kitty said simply.

Ororo draped an arm across the girl's shoulders and pulled her close. "Me, too," she replied, her voice going briefly husky. "Every day."

X

"It has enabled us to evolve from a single-celled organism into the dominant species on the planet."

X

Bells sounded throughout the great, old house, and the hallways of its lower two floors exploded with life and activity, as scores of young people made their way from class to class. The student population was double what it had been before Xavier's death, and there was a deliberate mix now of mutant and sapien, as the school began to establish a reputation not only as the world's foremost facility for the teaching and investigation of mutant abilities but as an academic institution in its own right.

X

"This process is slow, normally taking thousands and thousands of years."

X

Hank McCoy sat perched over the teacher's desk as the students filed in, hanging upside down from a trapeze bar installed by Nightcrawler. No one stared, as this was actually one of his more restrained poses.

On his desk, his laptop was open, its webcam oriented to pick him up where he was hanging. He wore a headset. None of the students could see the screen, which was just as well since he was finishing a conversation with the president.

"I appreciate the offer, sir," he told David Cockrum, "but I truly believe that my place is here. For the present anyway, this is where I can do the most good."

"I understand." Then Cockrum broke his train of thought with a shake of the head. "Henry, for God's sake, have pity on the rest of us. Do you have any notion of how disconcerting it is to talk to someone who's hanging upside down?"

"You look perfectly fine to me, sir," McCoy replied, blandly deadpan.

"Have it your own way, then. I'm taking your advice about Alicia Vargas. I'll be sending her name up to the Senate for confirmation as the new Secretary of Mutant Affairs."

"Couldn't do better, sir."

"Actually, I could, if the fella I have in mind weren't so damn stubborn. Any time you want a job, Henry!"

"Due respect, sir, the government job I find myself fantasizing about isn't really yours to give."

Cockrum snorted. "Give a man his second term, will you? Be well, Henry."

"Best to Paty, sir."

"By the way," the president said just before breaking contact, "a very young lady just walked through the wall behind you. Does that happen often?"

"Do you really want to know?"

Both men chuckled. The screen went dark. As McCoy twisted himself lithely to his chair, he noticed that Kitty had left something for him to look at: a fairly professional-looking poster, a head shot of her looking quite grown-up, below the words: ELECT CHICAGO'S PRYDE.

He cocked an eyebrow, and she returned a conspiratorial grin; evidently he wasn't the only one harboring presidential fantasies.

X

"But every few hundred millennia . . . evolution leaps forward."

X

Hank called the class to order, and set aside the text he'd originally intended using. With a wicked smile, he plucked up a well-read copy of *Ethics,* by Benedict de Spinoza.

"So long as a man imagines that he cannot do this or that," McCoy read, his well-rounded, theatrical tones instantly quieting the room and gathering in everyone's attention, "so long is he determined not to do it: and consequently, so long is it impossible to him that he should do it." He paused a moment to let the words sink in. "So, class, how do we integrate such a philosophy into *our* modern world? What for us constitutes 'impossible?' Ms. Pryde, shall we start with you?"

X

"That is why I created a school for gifted youngsters . . ."

X

"Also in today's news, spokesmen for Warren Worthington Jr. announced this morning that the last of their mutant clinics has been closed. Established only a few months ago to distribute what was trumpeted as a 'cure' for the so-called mutator gene that is present in a significant and growing segment of the global population, the clinics were the cause of considerable controversy during those early days. However, with Worthington's subsequent acknowledgment and acceptance of his own son as a mutant, popular support and interest in that cure has substantially evaporated, as has the need for the clinics."

X

"This world will continue long after we are all laid to rest. And while our bodies may be gone . . . our lessons are eternal."

X

Bobby Drake rose quickly, a little clumsily, to his feet as Rogue slipped through the doorway into his room.

His smile was bright, hers as shy as ever.

"Hey," he said in greeting. "I heard you went home to visit your folks."

"Been so long," she replied, with a nervous toss of the head, "I figured they'd forgot all about me."

"No such luck?"

"Go figure."

"Probably make a whole lot more sense when you're in their shoes."

"That'll be the damn day."

"So," he began.

"So," she echoed, making him wish he was back on Alcatraz going toe-to-toe with Pyro.

"Kitty wants to be president," he told her brightly, grasping frantically for anything to use to make conversation. "She wants us to be her brain trust."

Her look presented her thoughts on that score with painful eloquence.

"You don't—" he began, but she cut him off.

"Got no doubts about her, sugar," she said, allowing a lazy smile. "That's a slam dunk. It's this 'brain trust' thing that's got me worried."

"So," he tried again, after a pause.

She took a breath, crossed a Rubicon, pulled her hands from behind her back.

Her sweater was long-sleeved, but she'd pushed the sleeves up to her elbow. She wore gloves.

"I'm sorry, Bobby," she said, her Bayou accent much

more pronounced, the way it always was when she was majorly stressed. "I . . ."

"Rogue," he started, "Marie, it's okay."

She smiled softly, counterpointing it with a slightly acid look that came totally from the girl he loved. "I know," she told him, with a slight subtext: *dummy!* "It's what *I* wanted."

She held out her hand and he took it.

And for the longest time, sitting side by side in the bay window that afforded one of the better views of the estate, that was all they did.

X

At the end of the long underground hallway was a door that was easily the size of a bank vault, more imposing than anything you'd find protecting the United States Gold Depository at Fort Knox.

As they approached, it slid silently open, to admit the seven of them—four girls, three boys—to another world. They stepped across the threshold into nighttime darkness and found themselves amidst the ruins of what had once been a city.

"Where's the door?" one of the boys asked, and they all turned as one to behold the same bleak vista behind them as before. One of the girls stepped forward, arm outstretched, and looked perplexed when she encountered only empty air.

"Ain't that easy," Logan told them, flicking a thumb across the tip of his match to strike it alight and then setting the flame to the end of his cigar. He stood at the crest of a pile of rubble, dressed in X-Men combat leathers, as were Kitty and Colossus among the group below. The rest wore the standard training uniform of gold and indigo. The yellow was intense on purpose; the kids were supposed to be seen.

"Pryde," he said, calling the roll, narrowing his eyes at the sight of Kitty's uniform, with pants riding dangerously low and her bolero jacket cut high and tight, showing off her superbly toned dancer's body to the best effect she could. Girl was putting *way* too much faith in her phasing power to keep her from getting in trouble; he'd have to find a way around that. "Rasputin."

He moved on to the newbies, a pair of very long, very lean drinks of water, one of each sex, blond mountain boy from the coal-mining hollers of eastern Kentucky, and a raven-haired Cheyenne out of Wyoming. "Sam Guthrie, Danielle Moonstar."

Dark-haired fella was next, hanging back in the shadows, playing with a couple of cards, surprisingly hard to see despite the Day-Glo design of his uniform. Logan sensed at first sight this "Gambit" would be trouble, which suited him just fine. "Remy LeBeau?" No spoken answer, just a curt nod of the head and the flash of eyes that glowed red in the darkness.

The last was a woman identified as Sage. Dark hair, dark eyes, a pair of marks falling from the outer corner of each eye that made it seem as though someone had tattooed a line of tears down her cheek, although in the light allowed them now they looked much more like blood. She held herself perfectly still, giving away nothing, the epitome of graceful control, and with a single glance she caused every hackle to rise on the back of Logan's neck. Instantly, he revised his estimate of the class. The Cajun with the cards and the attitude would be trouble; this girl was dangerous.

He spared a glance up and behind him, over his shoulder at the observation blister mounted in the ceiling, sensing without seeing the presence of Ororo, overseeing his first training class. He knew she was smiling, enjoying every moment of his discomfiture, but also trusting him to do the job right.

"Okay, firstly, this isn't a game. Anyone thinks different, go out back and sit a spell by the memorials. The world could be a nasty place before we came along; the presence of mutants, with powers, has just upped the ante into the stratosphere. Most of the kids upstairs, they'll leave this place with a degree and a future, and that'll pretty much be the end of it. Mutant or not, they'll go on with their lives. You lot, you're cut from a different cloth. Here's where we see what you're made of."

He took a long, contemplative drag on his cigar. "It's gonna seem like this is all about ducking and dodging, staying in line . . .

". . . but what it's really about is . . . being a part of something. Not just a team. More than that."

He made a face, certain he could hear Ororo laughing at him. The quick look Sage split between him and the blister—which by rights she shouldn't have been able to see—made him wonder if she could hear her, too. Definitely *very* dangerous.

"Anyway," one last puff and he tossed the cigar aside, "I'm not one for speeches. Or theory. Around here, we pretty much learn by doing. So—let's get started."

And on that cue, all hell broke loose.

X

His favorite spot was atop Corona Heights, just above the Castro, where a natural outcrop of rock known as Arthur's Seat afforded a truly magnificent view of San Francisco.

If he looked over his shoulder, he could see the red and white spidery tripod of the Sutro Tower, a gigantic communications mast that dominated the western heights, like some Martian invader out of H. G. Wells. Downtown and to the left the skyline was completely transformed by the Golden Gate that now linked the city with Alcatraz.

The disruption caused by the bridge's removal had been nothing short of monumental, and commuter traffic patterns had proved to be the least of it. Canny entrepreneurs were already attempting to fill the breach with large, fast hydrofoil ferries, such as were used up north in Seattle and Vancouver; the problem was terminals, either in Tiburon and Sausalito or here in the city proper. Pedestrian passengers could be accommodated except that they needed somewhere to park over there and access to mass transit over here. Driving around the bay—from 101 to the Richmond–San Rafael Bridge that separated San Francisco Bay from San Pedro and then down Interstate 80 to the "Governor Norton" Bay Bridge—was certainly feasible, if you didn't mind a two- or three-hour drive each way. Housing prices in Marin had crashed and both the mayor and the governor in Sacramento were shrieking for federal disaster relief. On talk radio and blogs, the trial balloon was being floated—with a vengeance—that since mutants had made the mess, they should bear the responsibility of cleaning it up.

How hard could it be? they speculated ad nauseum. After all, it took only one of them—albeit the self-styled Master of Magnetism—who was said to be no spring chicken either, to move the bridge in the first place. Surely a bunch of them could replace it, or at least make the rebuilding go more quickly and cheaply? Or, failing that, why not find Magneto himself and force him to make restitution? Sure, the X-Men claimed that he'd fallen victim to the Worthington Cure and had been permanently stripped of his powers, but aren't the X-Men muties, too? How can we believe them? How can we trust them, really?

That was the argument, across airwaves and bandwidths, day in and day out, each side, mutant and sapien, yelling at the other without regard to logic or the slightest effort to consider the other opinions.

Someday, eventually, a new bridge would span the straits. In the meantime, the city and its people would cope, as they had a century ago after their equally famous earthquake. For now, though, they had a perfectly wonderful and unique new tourist attraction.

Sightings of actual mutants were still surprisingly rare, with every paparazzi and amateur with a long lens searching the sky for a shot of the newly christened Angel out for a flight. The fact that he was at school back east didn't seem to faze them; they still kept a perpetual stakeout on the Worthington town house. Some of the more enterprising professionals had thought to sneak onto Xavier's property in New York, for shots of the young man and any other muties they could find. They spent a night straight out of *Blair Witch* lost in the woods, and fled to the coast on the earliest flight, never to speak to anyone of what happened.

The only such photo to actually see print came from an amateur birder and made the cover of *Audubon*.

The world proceeded much as it always had.

The FBI had Magneto at the top of its Most Wanted list and every intelligence service in the world had the word out to find him. There were the usual chorus of rumors that he was dead, as well as those which maintained he'd never existed, that it was all a hoax perpetrated by the X-Men to make their reputation.

He enjoyed the stories immensely, dividing his thirst for news between the *New York Times* and the *Economist*. TV wasn't for him; the drama was too harsh and the comedies weren't terribly funny. Having endured so much of the reality, he had no stomach for pretend violence.

Hollywood went big budget on *The Battle of Alcatraz,* with one of Britain's finest Shakespearean actors, a knight no less, tapped to play the role of Magneto. It was scheduled to premiere in San Francisco in May.

Somehow, he meant to find a way to see it.

He'd always been a careful man. He'd scattered his resources across the globe, so that regardless of whatever setbacks he encountered along the way, he'd be able to sustain himself and start again. This was the first time he'd had to do so without the use of his powers.

He had a job, working one of the trawlers that still pulled out of Fisherman's Wharf every other week; he'd been "adopted" somewhat by *Arcadia*'s skipper, Aleytys Forrester. She cooked him meals, he taught her Greek. She asked him no questions, he told him no lies.

In many respects, he was in the best physical shape of his life.

He was surprisingly at peace while he remained awake. His nights, of course, were haunted.

His custom was to nurse a large muffin—freshly baked, organic and obscenely delicious—and a tall cup of dark, rich coffee over a book, basking in the sun until the afternoon fog rolled down off the heights to shepherd him home.

Occasionally, though, in remembrance of happier days, he'd take a seat at the chess table down below the knob of Arthur's Seat and play a game with Charles in his head. It wasn't exactly kosher, playing both sides of the board, far too many draws, but it passed the time and kept his wits keen.

Very rarely, he'd pull a collection of bottle caps from the pocket of his pea coat and spread them out before him, pitting his improvised pieces against the ones supplied his adversary from his imagination. And he would stare at them with ferocious intensity, with all the still considerable will power he possessed, and try to make them move.

Today was such a day. And as with every such attempt since that fateful confrontation on the bridge, Magneto was disappointed.

A shadow fell over him and he glanced up from under lowered brow to see a woman of medium height, forty-something and quite handsome, dressed with careless style that told him she had the wealth to afford good clothes but little interest in appearing fashionable. What marked her most was an obvious intelligence.

He ignored her and hoped she'd go away. She didn't take the hint.

"May I join you?" she asked, with an evident Scots burr.

He said nothing.

"I can help you," she said.

Again, he said nothing, thinking that the fact that he was here should have made abundantly plain that he wanted no such help.

She set a business card on the table: MUIR ISLE RESEARCH CENTER; KINROSS, SCOTLAND. And beneath it: MOIRA KINROSS MACTAGGART, DIRECTOR.

"And I pray y'can help me." The slight hitch in her voice made plain that what she was asking was both intensely important and wholly personal.

"I'm at the Fairmont these next few days, for a conference. If y'wish, ring me on my mobile. If not, I'll not bother y'again."

She had a Highlander's directness, of speech and manner, and a brilliance to match that of the two men she'd teamed with fresh out of University. The work she and Charles had done with him was groundbreaking; by rights, it should have won them all the Nobel Prize. But both men insisted she was the one to go to Stockholm, to be the public face of their joint researches. Her second Prize she'd won on her own.

"The next move is yours, Erik."

He watched her all the way down the hill, until she turned the corner towards Market.

He tapped his fingers absently on the table in a random pattern. He thought about what she'd said, and how she'd acted and what they'd all once meant to one another. Lee was cooking cioppino tonight, from fish they'd caught with their own hands.

He couldn't go back. That path had brought nothing

but grief, to those he cared for, those who trusted him, to himself. This was better.

Magneto reached out to gather up his bottlecaps . . .

. . . and one of them trembled, ever so slightly, as if caught by a puff of breeze—except that the air had fallen completely still.

And then, just a little bit, it moved.